MW00717189

The Relationship

by

John H. Hyman

E.M. Press, Inc.
Manassas, VA

This is an original work of fiction.

Copyright © 1995 by John H. Hyman
All rights reserved
ISBN: 1-880664-14-3
Library of Congress Catalog Card Number: 95-38416
Illustrated by Wilma Fulkerson

E.M. Press, Inc.
P.O. Box 4057
Manassas, VA 22110

To my grandson, Andrew Patrick Perry

ACKNOWLEDGMENTS

To my daughter, Melanie L. Hyman, and my best friend, Sharon J. Mahoney, both of whom offered help, encouragement and enthusiasm far beyond the call of duty. Many thanks.

PREFACE

This story is part fiction and part autobiography. It focuses on a struggling Southern family in North Carolina in the 1940's, during the "Romantic War." But it is primarily about two young boys—one black and one white—and their various adventures and episodes and the intertwining of their lives that caused a life-long bond. Their respective colors aside, they could easily have been Tom Sawyer and Huck Finn. On occasion, it has strong racial overtones and is punctuated with traditional Southern dialect, including Southern black dialect as spoken in North Carolina in the 1940's. It is laced with religion and true American patriotism. Some of the recorded events really occurred, but have often been embellished. Others are pure fiction. Should this story find a reader, I take the privilege of quoting Mark Twain's preface to *The Adventures of Tom Sawyer*, written in the year 1876:

> Although this book is intended mainly for the entertainment of boys and girls, I hope it will not be shunned by men and women on that account, for part of my plan has been to try pleasantly to remind adults of what they once were themselves, and of how they felt and thought and talked, and what queer enterprises they sometimes engaged in.

There really is a Scotland Neck, North Carolina. And it survives to this day. Some of the characters in this story still exist. To them I say, "Thank you." To those persons who do not yet exist, when you do, I only hope you are fortunate enough to live a part of your lives in a town much like Scotland Neck.

John H. Hyman
Alexandria, Virginia, 1995

Chapter 1

*T*he relationship really began before 1944, but in retrospect it seems that it somehow crystallized during that long, hot summer. Of course, every summer was hot in Scotland Neck, North Carolina, which had a population of approximately 2,000, as recorded in the official census. This number included most of the surrounding farms, and the Negroes who worked those farms. Never quite able to get an accurate count of all the Negroes, they just settled for an approximation.

All indications were it would be a big year for Scotland Neck. The weather had been right, so the farmers expected a record harvest of their crops, which consisted mainly of cotton, tobacco and peanuts. The Scout Pond had enjoyed major improvements; and the Dixie, the town's only theater, had been newly renovated with the addition of air conditioning.

The origin of the name Scotland Neck is of considerable doubt. It lies in the northeast section of the state and is situated in a rich, fertile plateau fed by the rapids of the Roanoke River. The original settlement dates back to 1720, and was situated in the neck of the Roanoke River, just below the Burgywn-Rodgers Bridge on U.S. Route 258. Among the early settlers was a group of Scots who had migrated from Surry, Virginia. The settlers soon moved away from the banks of the flood-prone Roanoke and nestled themselves in the villages of Greenwood and Clarksville. These villages soon became the southern and northern portions of Scotland Neck, which was ultimately incorporated in 1867. The earliest form of transportation was provided by a stage coach line, which operated between Charleston and Norfolk.

But the greatest benefit to the town's growth was provided by the railroad. The town fathers gave liberally of their money, land and time to bring the line to town.

Gradually, Scotland Neck became a very charming community. Church Street was graced with beautiful homes and two of the town's four churches. Main Street was broad and sweeping and had the unique feature of perpendicular parking, right out in the middle of the street. In fact, what most impressed those passing through was the unique parking and the lovely array of lush crepe myrtle bushes which filled the yards of many of the homes and artfully dotted a good portion of Main Street. This visual effect of beauty suggested a friendly, carefree town, filled with homey cordiality.

You knew everybody and everybody knew you if you lived there. Children freely fished in ponds and at the river and safely played in the woods, or down by the canal.

The really big event for Scotland Neck in the summer of 1944 was the arrival of German prisoners-of-war. They had been carefully and secretly transported from some unknown point of origin. The prisoners were being delivered to many Southern towns to help work on the farms. Nobody in town ever dreamed that some of Hitler's "Supermen" would be in America, much less right there in Scotland Neck, North Carolina!

I remember well the day they arrived in a large, covered U.S. Army truck that was painted that dreary, camouflage mustard-green. The whole town turned out as the prisoners were unloaded at the farmer's market area on Main Street. They were to be distributed to the farms on a proportionate basis. They looked so big and mean in their gray, cotton work shirts with the letters "P.O.W." inscribed in a bold white on their backs. It struck fear in the hearts of most every citizen in Scotland Neck. Most of us had only seen Nazis in war movies and newsreels. But to have them there in our town brought the war much closer than we liked.

Wormy and I crawled in the dust, around pants legs and dresses to get through the crowd to gain a better view. As we cautiously peered up, we were greatly relieved to see our U.S. Army men standing by, guns raised and ready to shoot each and every P.O.W. if they dared get out of line.

"I hate 'um! I really hate 'um!" were the first words Wormy muttered, certain we were far enough away so they couldn't hear his raspy whisper. "One of 'um prob'ly killed my cousin, Elisha. I shore wish I had a gun right now," he whispered. "I'd shore git rid of one or two of 'um. Johnnie, if you think I shoot possums good, I bet I could bang off three or four of 'um befo' they knew what hit 'um."

Wormy, or Worthington Woodrow Wilson, and I met—well, we had met long ago, down by the old canal, where I had wandered aimlessly from our house on Sunset Avenue, which was about three blocks away. The canal snaked along the western portion of the town limits. I'd noticed a tall, wiry Negro boy about my age. He was down on his knees, digging in the silty banks of the canal. There was a rusty tin can sitting next to him.

"Hey, whatcha digging for?" I had asked.

"Whatcha think I'm diggin' fer, gold? I'm down here diggin' for worms. I catches 'um to sell 'um, or to keep 'um till they dies leastways. Diggin' worms and watchin' 'um squiggle all around is my favorite thing. Real name's Worthington Woodrow Wilson, but everybody calls me

:ause I spends so much time studyin' 'um.

fter a United States president, you know. Plan
_ ~~ ~ne myself one day. Then I could move myself
outta this town and live in that big white house in
Washington, D.C."

From that day on, Wormy and I were inseparable.

Staring back up at the Germans, we heard, "Hush
up, Wormy. You and Johnnie get to the back of the crowd
where all you children belong. S'pose there's shooting
up front here. What would you do then?"

It was big old Clive Dawson, the mayor of Scotland
Neck, who often managed to spoil our fun. Clive Dawson
had been mayor of Scotland Neck for at least the nine
years of my life. And maybe all my momma's life too. He
was a huge man with a mop of gray hair that looked like
a big windstorm had just blown through it. His belly
hung over his belt like a sack of potatoes and swung from
side to side when he walked. He always wore the same
white suit, summer or winter, with a chocolate-colored
necktie that hitched up about 10 inches above his belt.
Mostly he was known for his broad-brimmed straw hat
with all that hair bristling out the sides. My daddy said
anybody who was mayor of Scotland Neck ought to be
dressed up, so I just figured that was why the mayor
always wore his suit and tie. Course, he always took off
the hat when he went inside a building, and he was
certain to tip it to any lady who happened to pass by.
Mayor Dawson was in charge of the Scout Pond, too, and
I knew he must be important 'cause there was a crossroads named after him between Scotland Neck and
Weldon. Every time we drove towards Weldon, Daddy
would say, "Johnnie, we're passing through Dawson's
Crossroads. You know it's named after Clive Dawson."

Anyway, Wormy and I squiggled back through the
crowd and climbed up on Marmaduke Allsbrook's truck
bed so we wouldn't miss anything. From there, we could

see just about all the goings-on, including Harry Lee Smith walking around selling Coca-Colas for 8 cents each. Now, anybody would be a fool to pay Harry Lee 8 cents when you could walk right across Main Street to the Idle Hour Restaurant and buy one for a nickel. Cokes from the Idle Hour even had a little slushy ice around the top, which always made them worth every cent of that nickel. But, leave it to Harry Lee to figure out just how to make some extra money.

Pretty soon, Mayor Dawson told everybody to go on about their business so he and Sheriff Orton Calhoun could help the soldiers disburse the Germans to the various farms.

It was certain that Wormy and I hadn't had our last look at the Nazis. Knowing they were coming to town, the two of us had laid out big plans on how we were going to spy on them. We had even discussed writing a letter to President Roosevelt if everything didn't go just right. I felt like I knew the president real good 'cause Daddy always listened to every one of his speeches on the radio and we were always seeing him on the newsreels. He seemed like a mighty fine president to us.

Additionally, Wormy and I had always dreamed of having the power to become invisible at will. We wanted to get to Germany, go unnoticed right into Hitler's headquarters and steal all his secret plans and take them to Washington, D.C., to the President's office. We knew we were too young to fight, but we loved our country and wanted to be heroes.

I always felt that it would be easier for me than for Wormy to become invisible because I was white and he was colored. How in the world could anything colored become invisible? Sometimes we tried mixing Coca-Colas, Dr. Peppers, orange Truaid and water together, pretending it would become the magic potion that would cause us to vanish. As of July 12, 1944, none of our formulas had worked. But the war was still going on, and there were a lot of mixtures we hadn't had time to concoct.

As a matter of fact, we'd had a pretty busy summer so far. Wormy and I started each morning on some secret mission that never quite seemed to materialize but always filled our time.

And each morning it was the same thing from Momma: "Johnnie, you can play ball, go to the Scout Pond, or even go to the picture show this afternoon, but don't you be going over to East Scotland Neck."

"Momma, why can't I meet Wormy and play with him? You know he's my best friend in the whole world."

I always received the same reply. "East Scotland Neck is for Negras. They live there; they like it; and a lot of them don't like white folks nosing 'round their territory. Besides, you know plenty of white boys you can play with."

"I don't understand, Momma. Why is it all right for Mrs. Wilson to wash and iron white folks' clothes, cook pies and even barbecue chicken that we eat right here at our table, but it's not right for me to play with Wormy?"

"Johnnie, I got a switch right on top of the icebox, and you know I'll use it if you don't mind what I say."

"Yes, ma'am, Momma," I replied as I walked out the door and headed right for Allsbrook's Blacksmith shop where Wormy and I met each morning. My mother was really a fine person, but she was set in her Southern ways and no amount of pleading was about to change her mind. And I did remember what that switch felt like on my bare legs.

Mr. Allsbrook was usually at work when Wormy and I arrived. He'd have the red-hot coals smoldering, and those old, worn leather bellows puffing away as he forged the shoes for so many farmers' horses. Why, people from as far away as Raleigh came to Mr. Allsbrook because he was the best blacksmith in North Carolina, and maybe in the whole world. At least Daddy said he was. Mr. Allsbrook didn't particularly like Wormy, but tolerated him because he seemed to like me. His son, Hiram, was in my class at school, and Mr. Allsbrook was a good friend of my daddy's. Daddy owned the one and only taxicab in Scotland Neck. The two of them would get in Daddy's 1940 Hudson (with step down drive), and head down to the river where they would buy their bootleg whiskey from Tazwell Judson. Then, they would just waste away the long afternoons fishing and drinking and telling tales of Scotland Neck in the "good old days." According to Daddy, Marmaduke Allsbrook was tough as whitleather. "Anybody would have to be to work over hot coals all their life," Daddy would say.

Tazwell Judson's helper and partner was "Shoofly" Smith. Shoofly was Harry Lee Smith's daddy. They seemed to run a mighty profitable business and never seemed to want for customers or companions. Rarely was there taxi or blacksmith service available on those lost summer afternoons, but no one in town seemed to mind very much. Course, Momma minded when Daddy would come home with maybe two dollars from his days' work, reeking of the pungent aroma of Judson's fine moonshine. They often had heated discussions around the supper table about his drinking and its effect on his health. But things never seemed to change.

That day, Wormy and I had planned to visit one of the nearby farms and spy on the Nazis, and then maybe go to the Scout Pond.

The Scout Pond had been hand dug by the Boy Scouts sometime in the 1930's. It was much more than just the local swimming hole. It was a popular gathering spot as folks from all the surrounding towns would come for swimming, partying in the dance hall (which had recently added the town's only Juke box), and eating some of Mayor Dawson's famous Brunswick Stew. Brunswick Stew is a traditional Southern dish with more ingredients than I can count. I know it had lots of fresh, chunky chicken, stewed tomatoes, fresh corn, butter beans and several other secret ingredients that the mayor would never reveal. But it was not the fixings that made the mayor's stew so famous. It was, according to him, his magic cooking and the secret flavorings that he added. He always cooked the stew right there at the Scout Pond, in a large, black cast iron pot that hung over an open fire, casting tongues of flames that always caused your cheeks to flush, especially on hot days.

Negroes were not allowed at the Scout Pond, but Wormy always seemed to find a way to sneak around with me long enough to do or see whatever curious items of interest drew us there. And sure enough, somebody would always shout to the mayor that there was a nigger boy on the property. We then managed to vanish through the surrounding tobacco fields before Wormy was caught.

But that day, the Scout Pond would have to wait for us. We had bigger plans. The Moore's farm was just on the outskirts of the town's limits, and we knew the Moores would have at least a few of the Nazis working for them. They also had Negroes working the cotton fields, so Wormy could go pretty much unnoticed as we diligently sought out the enemy.

"Wormy," I said, "why did you bring your dern rubber gun? You know you won't use it; and if Mr. Moore or one of them U.S. guards sees it, we'll be in a heap of trouble with the Nazis here and everything."

Now, constructing rubber guns was our first chore each summer when school was out. We would find a piece of soft wood and, borrowing some of Mr. Allsbrook's tools, fashion the shape of a gun handle and barrel. Then, we'd tie a clothespin to the handle with string we'd been saving all winter. String, like most everything else, was scarce as a result of the war effort. Anyway, once the gun was assembled, we needed ammunition. We located an old, rubber inner tube from some long-ago abandoned automobile tire. We carefully cut the inner tube into round rubber strips, attached the strips to the end of the barrel and stretched them back to the open mouth of the clothespin. As we opened the clothespin by gently squeezing on it, the rubber band would fly off in some errant direction, never quite hitting any of our targets. Regardless of their ineffectiveness, we always felt naked without our rubber guns. Had I left home with my gun that morning, Momma would surely have suspected that I was going off to join Wormy in some playful pursuit.

"I brought it 'cause I might need it if'n any of 'um tries to git away. Besides, I might jist take a pot shot at a coupla 'um, jist fer my cousin Elisha."

"If we get anywhere near them Nazis, the guards, or Mr. Moore, you best hide that dern gun. We seem to git in enough trouble without lookin' for it," I argued.

Sure enough, as we shuffled barefooted down the dirt road leading from the highway to the cotton field, we spied the army guards standing watch as the Nazis worked. Each of the Germans had a burlap bag hung over his shoulder. As they worked their way down each precise row, they picked the fluffy white cotton bolls from the spindly branches and dropped them in their bags. We meandered around the guards and noticed the area where the Nazis would be resting when, and if, they were allowed to take a break.

There was a large, tin water cooler sitting at the end of an old, weathered wooden bench. It was marked "Moore's Farm." Wormy and I found a spot about 20 yards away in a stand of pine trees, quite concealed by a marshy area covered with tall, green mush stalks and brown cattails. As we hunched ourselves down in our hiding spot, the morning sun was at its boiling point, even in the obscured shade of the pines.

"It must be break time soon," I said, hoping to get a better look at the prisoners as they would approach the bench.

"You know, Johnnie, if this here was a real gun like them soldiers has, I think I'd shoot every blame Nazi in that field, and then stick 'um with a bayonet, 'cause I prob'ly hate 'um more'n the devil hisself."

"Wormy, just be quiet and watch, 'cause you know you ain't gonna shoot nobody, especially a Nazi."

"Well—I'd like to 'cause I hate 'um. You think if John Wayne was right here and he had a gun, that he'd be hidin' like we are? Garden peas! He'd blow 'um right away and then shine that ole grin of his and say somethin' like, 'Yep.'"

The morning seemed to stretch out forever, until finally we heard a loud whistle and saw the soldiers raise their guns and corral the prisoners over to the rest area. All of a sudden a bit of scare shot through me. My heart started pounding and I felt the intense heat more than ever. There, only 20 yards away, were some of the worst people in the world. *HITLER'S SOLDIERS!* I shrank back and mired myself as flat to the ground as possible. The heat that I felt quickly turned to a cold chill and I began to shiver. Every movie and newsreel I had ever seen of the war flashed through my mind. I envisioned Adolph Hitler standing before thousands of worshiping admirers chanting his wild rages of world conquest. I saw tanks rolling through European towns, systematically blowing them to smithereens. But most of all, I saw, in my mind's eye, American soldiers wounded or lying dead in some foreign field.

Even now, I vividly recall sensations never before experienced in my young life. It was certainly fear, mingled with hate, and yet—a definite awe. The war had been going on as long as I could remember, and the Germans had always been our most hated enemies. What childhood dreams I now recollect dealt with Germans and bombs and cruelty and the killing of our men. To be there, in their presence, at that time, was both exciting and a living nightmare.

As expected, the prisoners were led over to the bench under the careful scrutiny of the guards. As each Nazi passed the water cooler, he stopped and filled an aluminum cup with water. They all drank with a passion, and some poured a cupful over their heads. Whatever Germany was like, it must not have had the same sun that so fiercely beat down on them in North Carolina. Once watered down, they were allowed to sit on the bench and were handed towels to mop the hateful sweat off their brows.

One very large Nazi stood and started speaking to the chief of the guards. It soon became apparent that neither understood the other, until the German started making gestures that the guard seemed to understand. They immediately turned from the bench and started walking away, the guard in the rear with his rifle pointed at the back of the prisoner. To our alarm, they headed directly for the pine grove in which Wormy and I had found some slight feeling of security. I glanced at Wormy and a small wrinkle of concern marred his usually placid forehead.

"What they doin'? Where they goin'?" Wormy whispered to me.

"I don't know, but it's for sure we can't run outta here now, or everybody will see us."

We hastily slid backwards, right into the marshy part of the grove, allowing the greenery and cattails to provide more cover for us. As we peered through the casual openings of our sanctuary, it became more obvious they were heading toward our hiding spot. The earlier pounding that I had felt in my heart immediately encompassed my whole body, and I actually began to quiver.

Had they found us out? Were they after us? Just what should we do?

We were lying side by side, about a foot apart, in a quagmire of mud and mush. The nearer they got, the greater the fear I felt.

Finally, they stopped at the very edge of the pine grove, prisoner in front, and guard behind. When the German took a couple of more steps into the marsh and began to unbutton his pants, the purpose of their mission became apparent.

Suddenly, "Oh, my Gawd!" came from Wormy. "He's peein' on my foot!" Wormy leapt up, pulled out his rubber gun and let fly part of an old inner tube. We both began running for our lives. As afraid as we were, and as fast as we were running, we could hear the Nazi yelling in a loud, yet unintelligible language. It seemed that for the first time in either of our lives, one of us had actually hit the target we were seeking with our rubber gun!

Departing the dirt road and racing across the highway, we could hear, pitched above the outburst from the wounded prisoner, a great deal of laughter from the guards and even some of the other prisoners.

We didn't stop running until we felt safe enough to look around to see who, if anyone, was chasing us. To our complete surprise and utter relief, no one was on our trail. We still only slowed our pace enough to decide the safest direction to head in, and we ended up in Ed Jones' victory garden. Fortunately, it was filled with corn that was about breast high.

Finally, we stopped, knelt at first, and then fell gratefully to the ground in total exhaustion. We lay there panting a few moments. After regaining our breath, we ventured a peek above the corn stalks and felt comforted that our activities had gone unnoticed by anyone out-side the cotton field.

"Did you see that, Johnnie? Did you see it?" Wormy yelled between pants of breath. "I shot him! I shot him! I really shot him, and I think I shot his tallywhacker right off! I tole you I was a good shot and now you know I am, even wif my rubber gun! I jist hope my cousin Elisha was lookin' down and seen what I done fer him. Johnnie, there's only one thing in this world that I hate more'n Nazis. And that's Nazi pee, 'specially when it gits on me."

Still a little nervous, I said, "Wormy, if you ever, and I mean ever, do anything like that again, we'll just stop being friends for the rest of our lives."

But even as those words were coming out of my mouth, I felt a sense of pride in my heart for Wormy. It seemed, at that very moment, America had won at least one small battle in World War II, and that Wormy and I had some scant part in that great victory!

Chapter 2

The Scout Pond was probably my favorite place in the whole world. It was about the size of a football field and was fed by, what I imagined to be, the clearest spring water anywhere. It was located on the outer limits of town, just where the farm lands began, almost a mile off the main highway, at the end of a winding dirt road. The pond was nestled in the midst of a lush, green, wooded region of mostly tall, willowy pine trees. The lovely cluster of pines provided the perfect seclusion from the surrounding farming areas.

It was, as I recall, like an oasis, a small paradise filled with both God-given and manmade wonders. Certainly God had created the setting and provided all the natural beauty. When He planned this particular spot, in a very small part of North Carolina, He must have had the Scout Pond in mind. However, a much younger Clive Dawson did the rest. Years before, when a swimming and recreational area was needed to make Scotland Neck a complete community, Scout Master Clive Dawson took the initiative. Now, all this happened long before my time, but I had heard the story told over and again.

He assembled all the Boy Scouts and their parents from Scotland Neck and the surrounding towns. They worked almost two years in hand excavating the site. He then had his work force divert several small streams to fill the pond. The stories of the glory of the pond were only exceeded by its grand opening, which was held on a festive July 4th, 1932. Such doings had never taken place in Scotland Neck. There were fireworks and a minstrel show, and the high school band played patriotic music. There was even a reporter from Raleigh's *News and Observer* there to cover the story. Folks came from all the towns in Halifax County. They sang and danced in the newly-constructed dance hall. But most of all, they swam in the crystal clear waters and frolicked on the pond's sandy beach.

It was then that they were introduced to Clive Dawson's Brunswick Stew. The reporter even asked Mr. Dawson for the recipe, but Clive refused to give it out— mainly because his ingredients were secret.

The soil surrounding Scotland Neck consisted of very sandy pockets of earth beneath the dark, rich topsoil that was so well-suited for farming. The sand that had been dug from the pond was carefully placed around its entire perimeter, creating a manmade beach, perfect for sunbathing and picnicking.

There were two diving boards, neither of which I ever got the nerve to try, mounted on a floating platform. The platform was secured to the north end of the shore with heavy, woven ropes. Located in the very center of the pond was another wooden platform, sized to hold about 10 sunbathers.

At the south end was the most magnificent manmade structure I had ever seen. It consisted of several components. There was a large, rounded wooden pole, roughly the diameter of a telephone pole, that rose approximately 75 feet above the ground. Very near the top was a platform, just large enough to hold one daring person. Wooden step-rails ascended the pole. They were the only means of reaching the platform. They appeared safe, but were menacing obstacles to me. Often, when we were holding our secret inspections of the pond, Wormy would confidently assure me that they didn't scare him none. And, given the chance, he would go up that pole in a minute. I wasn't so sure of his courage.

Above the platform, and mounted to the very top of the pole, was a stranded steel cable about one inch in diameter. The cable sloped at a 45-degree angle from the pole to the water, spanning about three-quarters the length of the pond. A hand pulley glided the length of the cable and could be retrieved to the platform by an attached rope. All that paraphernalia allowed the courageous to mount the platform, pull the rope to retrieve the pulley, grasp it, and go gliding down the cable, dropping off anywhere along the way, or concluding with a resounding splash in the water. It was commonly referred to as The Glide Ride. It had become the custom to mark one's manhood by taking one's first glide ride. I had yet to venture up the pole. But someday—maybe!

Since the Scout Pond was Clive Dawson's idea, and his Scouts had completed the construction, the town made him its proud curator. He had established 10 cents as the admission price, and it remained unchanged all during my childhood.

The major improvements of the previous fall included painting the dance hall, enclosing its open walls with screen wire and replacing the leaky wooden roof with a shiny tin covering. The current Mayor Dawson had the town run electricity out to the dance hall and there he proudly installed Scotland Neck's first nickelodeon. New dressing rooms were added to the left end of the hall, and one outhouse had been neatly tucked back in the pines. The entire town was justly proud of those glorious improvements.

Often, as I both enjoyed and admired the Scout Pond, I thought to myself, "What more could I ask for?"

Scotland Neck was indeed the perfect place to live—for white folks.

As much as I loved Scotland Neck and the Scout Pond, I couldn't openly share all its pleasures with Wormy.

The injustice seemed to start at home in a very innocent way. "Remember, Johnnie," Momma would say, "you don't call a colored woman a 'lady,' you call her a 'Negra woman.'" I readily accepted this very early in life. But as I grew closer to Wormy and his family, I wondered just how one's skin color could make one female a woman and another a lady. Maybe, I thought, it's the way God meant it to be, for certainly in 1944, everyone, black and white, in Scotland Neck accepted it (outwardly, at least).

At any rate, anytime Wormy and I visited the Scout Pond together, it had to be on the sly. And we couldn't go into the Idle Hour and certainly not attend the picture show together. At the Dixie, whites were seated on the first floor and coloreds had to use the balcony. Often, I thought God did things in a very peculiar way.

This was the first summer with the Scout Pond's new facilities, and I had a greater desire than ever to share them with Wormy. All we could do together was to sneak around the perimeter and watch as all my white friends enjoyed themselves. The first time I watched Harry Lee Smith descend the glide ride, my heart was pierced with jealousy. I just knew that if Wormy was with me I would have the courage to climb those wooden steps.

The day Harry Lee came down the ride, Wormy and I were camped in the pines, listening to the resonant sounds from the juke box, winding their way through the screens.

"Johnnie, you go on in swimmin' and jist let me watch," Wormy unselfishly stated. But I couldn't find it in me to abandon him, even though the water looked wonderfully tempting.

"Naw," I said. "But we gotta figure out a plan, just like we always do. There must be some way for us to go in together. Besides, I ain't going down that glide ride 'til you do."

"Yeah," he replied, "if one of yo fool invisible mixtures ever worked, I could shore go in then. Might even be able to scare some of them white boys jist seein' some invisible splashin' round in the water," he chuckled, "'specially that show-off Harry Lee Smith. And that ole glide ride don't scare me none."

But as shrewd as we thought we were and as hard as we made our brains work, we hadn't been able to come up with any safe plan that wouldn't get Wormy in trouble. Although he never said so, I knew that the Scout Pond held the same fascination for Wormy as it did for me.

We had moved out of the shade of the pines and were squatting down in a field of sticky, green tobacco leaves, so we could get a better view of the ride. Sweat was dripping off my body and forming a small mud puddle next to my knees. The water looked absolutely inviting and I sure didn't like Harry Lee outdoing me. In deep concentration, I slowly began to conjure up a delicious expedition for us.

"Wormy," I asked, "do you think you could sneak out of your house at night? The pond closes at sunset. We could meet, slip away down here and have the whole area to ourselves."

"Johnnie, sometimes you sounds like a numskull. You know I help Momma with all her chores, plus gittin' all the chillun to bed at night. If my sometimes daddy caught me sneakin' anywhere, he'd beat my britches off. He don't usually need no excuse to beat me and his hound dogs anyway. But whatcha got in mind?"

Even at the possible expense of punishment, Wormy was rarely averse to some excitement.

"Well," I said, "it's for sure we can't go in during the day. And if you can figger a way of getting out at night, I gotta plan that just might work."

Wormy had a long, thin, handsome face. He had large, brown eyes, deep-set behind the high, sharp cheek bones that he had inherited from his mother. I always knew when he was doing some serious thinking, because he would roll his eyes up and down until he finally reached his conclusion. Then he would focus directly on me and give his answer.

After pondering for a moment, he quickly blurted out, "There might jist be some chance this Saddy night. Momma and all the fambly is goin' out to Tillery to some church social party. I'm s'pose to go but Momma knows I hate them things, less course, Mary Beth's gonna be there. But I know she ain't comin' over from Rich Square. And my daddy usually spends Saddys in Raleigh, doin' God knows what. But how 'bout you? You and yo momma usually spends Saddy nights studying the Bible and yo Sunday school lesson."

"You leave that part to me. If you can meet me at 8 o'clock Saturday night, we can have the best time of our lives, right out here."

Truth be known, I hadn't devised a total plan, but I had the seed of an idea. All I had to do was work out the details.

We parted that afternoon, both slightly puzzled about the secret plan to accomplish Saturday night's mission, but determined to study on it. It was very important to both of us since we had so often fantasized about enjoying the glide ride together.

The rest of the week was fairly uneventful as far as Wormy and I were concerned. My relatives from Washington, D.C., or right outside of Washington, in Virginia, had come down for their annual week's visit. And Momma wanted me available and on my best behavior.

My aunt and uncle, Sadie and Sam Moore, had moved from Scotland Neck years ago. Sam's brother, Josh, owned the large Moore farm where Wormy and I had our eventful encounter with the Nazi. Sadie was just one of Momma's three sisters. Aunt Sadie had three boys, all slightly older than I. One of my cousins was a part of my plan for Saturday night.

We had spent most of Friday at the farm, seeing and doing all the boring things I could see and do any day. Josh did drive us past the field where the prisoners were working. I sort of slunk down in my seat when he stopped long enough to ask the guards how everything was going.

When we returned home, I approached Bobby, Aunt Sadie's middle son. Now, Bobby was almost four years older than I, and certainly the most devilish of the three boys. On one of their previous visits, Bobby had taken my Red Ryder B.B. gun, killed a bird in our backyard, and even took a shot at Mary Elizabeth Whitehead, who lived just across the hall from us. He had blamed the whole incident on me and I had paid the price. I was still mad at him, but felt if anyone could and would help me with my plan, it would be Bobby.

During the week of my cousins' visit, our trip to the Scout Pond had been the highlight. I remembered that Bobby was particularly fascinated with the ride, but never mustered up the courage to give it a try.

When I called Bobby out on the front porch and briefed him on my plan, he was immediately in favor of it. There was a Johnny Mack Brown Western showing at the Dixie on Saturday night. Since the actor and I shared the same first name, he was my favorite cowboy of all time; and Momma and Daddy knew it.

I finally got up enough nerve to approach Momma. Bobby and I wanted to go to the 8 o'clock show, instead of attending the family picnic at the farm. At first, I received a definite "No" from her. But by then, Daddy and Sam had joined us all on the front porch. They were both feeling "pretty good," as Daddy tucked a brown paper bag in his pocket. Hearing my plea, Daddy and Sam set in on Momma and finally convinced her to let us go. "You know Bobby will look after Johnnie. He's a good boy and certainly old enough to go to a picture show, 'specially here in Scotland Neck," Sam insisted. "And after all, we've spent a good part of the week out at the farm, and both boys want to see the show."

So a settlement was finally reached. I would do my Sunday school work in the afternoon and we could attend the 8 o'clock show. But we had to be home no later than 10:30. Bobby and I joyfully agreed, hoping all the while we could carry out our plan in the allotted time.

When I said my prayers that night, I had a hard time. Blotting my scheme from my mind, I still wondered what God would think. I finally fell asleep, half-believing that since He was allowing it to happen, it must not be too bad.

∽ Chapter 3 ∽

I awoke Saturday morning with mixed feelings of guilt, anxiety and excitement. Rarely in my nine years had I lied to my parents, and I had never plotted and schemed like this. I dwelt only momentarily on the guilt; then, with a little rationalizing, I jumped out of bed. The sooner the day started, the sooner the evening would arrive.

My first step would be to introduce Bobby to Wormy, so we could all go over the plan. My daddy always said jokingly, "Three heads is gooder than two." Right after breakfast, I went by my Aunt Bessie's house where the Moore family was staying, because our apartment had only one bedroom, which was shared by Momma, Daddy and me. Bobby and I left my aunt's with the intent of my showing him a real working blacksmith shop.

Apparently Mr. Allsbrook had had a long Friday evening at the river, since there was no activity in the shop when we arrived. Wormy was sitting on a wooden nail keg in the shade of a large pecan tree. The tree rose high above the shop with its branches bowing towards the ground. They were filled with an abundance of nuts, almost ready to be plucked. The shop was constructed of weathered wood siding showing only a hint of white-wash that appeared to have been splashed on over 50 years ago. The left end of the building fronted on Main

Street and had one crooked window set in its middle. There were two sliding doors on the front that opened into Mr. Allsbrook's cluttered yard. There was a cupola on the roof with a rusty tin covering and a lightning rod perched on its peak. The sides were open to allow some of the searing heat to escape the inside of the shop. On the far side of the pecan tree, between the shop and the Allsbrook house, were four hitching posts. I had spent many hours watching Mr. Allsbrook remove old, worn horseshoes and replace them with his newly forged "sandals."

I never understood how horses could stand to have those spike nails driven right into their hooves. Mr. Allsbrook was not particularly religious, but he often told me that horses were a lot like Jesus; that is, a man could just drive nails right into them and, like Jesus, they never let out a whimper. And since Jesus wore sandals, he forged sandals for his customers. I think that's when I really started to have a lot of respect for Jesus.

"Wormy, this is my cousin, Bobby Moore, from Washington, D.C." Although Bobby lived in Northern Virginia, I always felt it more impressive to say Washington. Everybody in Scotland Neck had a notion that anybody from our nation's capital must be pretty important.

Bobby was uncommonly friendly in sticking out his hand and saying, "How you doing, man? Johnnie tells me we've got some exciting plans for tonight."

Wormy's eyes sparkled as he asked, "You know President Roosevelt? If you do, Johnnie and me got somethin' mighty important he should know 'bout a certain Nazi prisoner."

"Hush up, Wormy," I said. "We got plans to make."

After discussing our secret details, and while Bobby was looking around the shop, Wormy whispered to me, "Why does he talk so funny? He don't sound like no American to me."

It occurred to me that perhaps this was the first person Wormy had ever met from anywhere north of Richmond, Virginia.

"He's from up North. You know that people all over the country don't talk exactly the same. Don't you remember the tent revival your momma took you to, and you laughed at the way those Yankees spoke?"

"I sorta like the way he talks. Someday I'm gonna learn to talk like him," he added, with a serious note in his voice.

The three of us walked on down Main Street, generally discussing where we would meet and just what the evening held in store for us. We agreed to get away from our houses as soon after 7:30 as possible, and to meet near the ESSO station at the other end of town, since it was closer to the Scout Pond.

Every Saturday, all the Negroes from the surrounding farms arrived in town by truck, wagon or foot. Saturday was their day in Scotland Neck. Most of the white folks left Main Street to them, except for those who set up small stands for rummage sales of old clothing and generally useless household furnishings.

Many of the Negroes would go to one of the two general stores where the farmers for whom they worked had set up credit for them. After working the fields all week, they would go to the store on Saturday and charge up to the limit established by their employers. I often wondered how they had any real spending money since most of their purchases were made on that credit system.

They ate at the barbecue store that had a side entrance marked "Coloreds Only." The public drinking fountains were marked the same way. All of that was a real puzzle to me. But like so many other things I didn't understand, no one else seemed bothered by it.

They always lined up in front of the Dixie by noon,

as the balcony had a limited number of seats, and a picture show was another of Saturday's big events for them.

Back home, Daddy and Sam were sitting on the front porch reminiscing about the days when they (just the two of them) had led Scotland Neck to the state semifinal game in football. Their one real regret was that they hadn't won and made it to the final game, which was held in Raleigh. They were both laughing and blaming each other for the loss. Having already finished their morning coffee, they were passing the brown bag back and forth. This would carry on the rest of the day, culminating at the big picnic at the farm.

As Bobby and I approached the house, Poochie, our delightful little mixed-breed dog, ran out to greet me with his usual enthusiasm and tail wagging. Picking him up, he felt like a fluffy snowball, with his shaggy, white fur almost covering his eyes. Poochie was another important part of my life. I never thought of him as just a dog—he was a member of the family.

"Where you boys been?" Daddy asked.

"Just down to the blacksmith shop and walking along Main Street. Bobby said he had never seen so many colored folks at one time in his whole life. I told him it was mainly that way just on Saturdays."

The afternoon was a tormenting bore. But as evening approached and the families started getting ready for the picnic, I became increasingly nervous and excited. By 6 o'clock, both families were packed in the Moore's 1939 Chevrolet, ready to head out to the farm.

"Remember, Johnnie," Momma cautioned, "you two go right to the show and be back here by 10:30, just like we agreed."

"Yes, ma'am," I replied, feeling a slight foreboding.

Finally, they were gone and we were alone. Bobby and I sat in the swing awhile, impatiently waiting for 8 o'clock to arrive. Bobby asked if Daddy had left the keys to the Hudson at home.

"Why do you want to know? You can't drive; and even if you could, we could really get ourselves in a mess if we get caught."

He promptly withdrew his wallet and proudly displayed his learner's permit to drive. "I do know how to drive," he said. "My father lets me go around the block at home all the time. Of course, he's with me. But I can drive anything on the road."

"Bobby, we're already going where we're not suppose to go and doing what we're not suppose to do. We could even get put in jail if Sheriff Calhoun catches us. I remember Harry Lee Smith taking his daddy's car one time; his daddy made the sheriff put him in jail for one night, just to teach him a lesson. No, sirree, we can't take the Hudson."

"But just think of all the time we could save getting there and back. That would leave us more time for swimming and fun. And besides, if we don't take the car, I don't go."

Now that really posed a dilemma for me. Fear and discouragement shot through my body. I had waited a long time for this experience with Wormy, and I sure didn't want us to miss out on it. And it did sound rather appealing. Since Bobby was almost five years older than I, and really in charge of the evening, I figured if anything happened, he'd be blamed. So I finally gave him the keys and off we went.

Now Bobby could drive, but not very well. We sputtered and jumped out of the yard, crossing the log-covered ditch that fronted our large, two-story house. The house had originally been built for one family, but was later converted into three separate apartments. Ours was on the left side of the first floor. The house was set back off the road about 50 yards and had a wide, wraparound porch across the front and down the left side. There were several huge trees in the otherwise bare front yard. A 3-foot wide ditch separated our yard from Sunset Avenue. Wormy and I spent much time playing in the heavily-wooded backyard while Momma was at work and couldn't object. We had built forts and tree houses and even set up tents. We did a lot of target practicing out there with our rubber guns. My B.B. rifle had been taken away after Bobby had gotten me in trouble with it.

Entering the front door of the house, you walked into a long hallway with one apartment on each side. The upstairs was all one large apartment.

Our unit consisted of one bedroom on the front. A dining room was behind it and had a connecting kitchen, which led out to the back porch. A small bathroom had been added during the apartment conversion. The bathroom had been literally stuck on the rear of the house. One oil stove heated the bedroom and a large, potbellied coal stove was set in the dining room. The only way of heating the bathroom was to leave the door open into the dining room, forgetting all privacy. I remember many winter mornings when I could see my breath as a fog before my face, until the warmth from the coal stove slowly crept into the bathroom, which I called the ice house.

For baths during those cold times, Momma would usually haul hot water from the kitchen into a large tin tub in the dining room. My evening baths took place as near the stove as possible. I would dry off, jump into my pajamas and make a mad dash for the warmth of the bedroom.

Momma, Daddy and I shared the one bedroom. Their double bed was set against the front wall and I slept on a couch, which was converted into my bed each night. There, in the warmth and comfort of my own bed,

Momma read me evening Bible stories. I always seemed
to drift off to sleep, never quite hearing the end of any
story.

As Bobby and I anxiously bucked down Sunset
Avenue towards the ESSO station, little did I realize that
I was to regret that evening for the rest of my life.

About half a block from the station, I told Bobby to
pull over to the curb. I went to fetch Wormy. We planned
to follow Church Street towards the north end of town,
since it was more dimly lit and there was less chance of
being noticed than if we took Main Street.

Wormy was nowhere in sight. I was afraid to go to
the station in case Charlie Milford, its owner, asked
some awkward questions, and I was nervous enough as
it was. I moped back to the car and Bobby insisted we
didn't need any colored boy with us anyway. Just then,
I saw Wormy streaking across Main Street. I jumped out
of the car and ran to meet him.

Spying the car behind me, Wormy said, "Whatcha
doin' bringin' yo daddy? He shore ain't gonna take us to
no Scout Pond."

"Don't worry, it ain't Daddy; it's Bobby. He's gonna
drive and save us lots of time."

"I don't like this, Johnnie, ridin' in a car wif somebody who prob'ly can't drive and who all I can't hardly
understand anyway."

"Just get in the car and let's get outta here before
anybody recognizes us and sees it's not Daddy driving."

Reluctantly, Wormy climbed in the back seat and we
were off on our high adventure. We headed towards the
north end of town where we could exit Church Street
and enter Main at a less conspicuous place.

In spite of Bobby's driving, in just a few minutes we
were bouncing down the winding dirt road that led to
the Scout Pond. My mouth was as dry as cotton but my
heart was pounding with enthusiasm. As always, the

mayor had rolled an old pine log across the road to keep out evening intruders—like us. It took Wormy and me only a minute to roll it aside and allow the car to pass. We then replaced it in case the sheriff made one of his occasional evening checks of the area.

The setting sun shone sparingly through the tall pines on either side of us. We slowed as we approached the crest of a small knoll. Just over the knoll lay the Scout Pond. We decided to turn the car around facing back towards the dirt road, in case we had to make a fast getaway.

The three of us jumped out of the car without noticing the small incline on which we had parked. Instead, we were all caught up in the beauty of the moment. The last golden rays of the sun found their way through the thick pine needles, reflecting their muted slivers of gold on the surface of the pond. Even Bobby was impressed with the setting and its serenity.

"Man," he sighed, "we don't have anything like this at home. Just regular old concrete swimming pools."

"Aw, shoot, we didn't bring our bathing suits," I stammered, somewhat embarrassed.

"Don't make no never mind," Wormy said. "Whenever we git to go to the canal fer a dip, we don't wear nothin'."

We instantly raced each other to get undressed, tossing our clothes in the car. We charged off towards the pond. I realized that we were finally there, *Wormy and I, together!* The fact that we had a visitor went almost unnoticed.

I had been able to swim for as long as I could remember. I had no fear of the water. But suddenly, the thought of climbing to the very top of the glide ride gave me pause to wonder why I decided to test my manhood that particular evening.

We decided to splash around awhile, and maybe

gain the nerve to start up the pole which, at that moment, seemed almost dreadful—but also imperative to me.

While Wormy and I swam out to the platform in the center of the pond, Bobby headed for the diving boards.

"Show off," Wormy said as we lay, side by side, on the platform, enjoying the cool evening breeze drifting across our damp bodies. Wormy just looked around and said, "Garden peas! Johnnie, this is jist fantastic."

And then, unexpectedly, he turned rather serious. "You know, Johnnie, someday in the future, they is gonna let colored folks in the Scout Pond. And even if I move away and becomes a big shot, I'ma comin' back here, jist to swim in the Scout Pond. It jist ain't fair, you know, the way we is treated and all. We's people too. And we got rights. And someday, I'ma gonna do somethin' to help all us coloreds do everythin' all the white folks can do."

In the waning light, I could barely see his eyes. He was gazing into the distance, seeing a future that only he could imagine.

The moment was broken as Bobby joined us on the platform. We all three lay there, face down, occasionally turning our heads up at the intimidating tower, casting its long shadow across the entire length of the pond.

"I think I'm getting stomach cramps," I said, trying to steal more time to work up my courage.

"Yeah," Bobby said, "sure is cool out here tonight."

"Chickens! Chickens! Chickens!" Wormy squealed. "I ain't scared a nothin'. Did you tell Bobby what I done to that dern Nazi?"

"Yeah, Wormy, you want a medal or something? I think what you did was great, but I also think you were as scared as I was. Anyway, what you done was in self-defense and don't have nothing whatsoever to do with this situation facing us now."

The Scout Pond

By then, the sun had set and we could barely see the pole. So we lay there, worrying what the climb would be like, worrying if the steps would hold and worrying if the cable would break and—just plain worrying!

Pretty soon, the moon appeared and cast a slight glow that seemed to brighten the area. Without saying a word, Wormy stood up, dove off the platform and headed for the shore. I followed with Bobby right behind.

We ambled around in the sand for awhile until the moon lit up the whole area, casting its silver splinters all the way over to the tower.

"Les draw straws to see who goes first," Wormy suggested.

"Listen, Mr. Big Shot," I replied. "We've waited a long time for this and you always said you would go up first, so lead the way, you brave Nazi-slayer."

"Shazam!" he shouted. "Here I goes. You jist better be right behind me, Johnnie." He gradually started up the ladder, testing each step with his hands as he climbed.

A knot slowly swelled up in my throat and I briefly wondered if anyone as young as I could have a heart attack. Reaching as deep inside me as possible, for every ounce of courage I possessed, I finally placed my nervous hands on the first rung and started up after him. I took one step at a time, not daring to look down but staring up at a shiny, black bottom dripping water in my face.

What had always appeared as about 75-feet instantly seemed like the Washington Monument. About halfway up, Wormy must have regained some of his courage as he started laughing out loud.

"What's going on up there?" I asked, afraid to stop or use any muscle except my mouth.

"I jist wish every nigger in Scotland Neck and in all North Carolina could see me now: Wormy Wilson goin' up on the tower at the Scout Pond."

A sudden grin jumped on my face and I felt a little more relaxed. But I said, "Git on up. I bet if your momma could see you now, that bottom would be red and not so shiny black."

Reaching the top was everything I had ever imagined it would be. I felt like Jesus, standing on the top of a high mountain, viewing all the kingdoms of the world. I imagined myself Tarzan, Superman and Captain Marvel all rolled into one. I felt a thrill I'd never experienced in my life—and I was scared to death! I knew I could never climb back down those steps. But, troubled at the thought, I also knew I would have difficulty grasping that pulley and gliding down the cable as I had envisioned for so very long. I suddenly became chilled and wondered if it was from fear or from the breeze still cooling my naked body at that moonstruck moment.

We were both standing on the platform, Wormy tightly holding onto the cable above his head and to me. My arms were securely plastered around the pole. Ever so slowly, he released me and took the rope, pulling the handle from the water to the platform. Soon enough, he held the pulley in his hands. He glanced at me with enormous eyes, and then he was gone. All I heard was, "Shazam!" until, a moment later, there was a big splash at the far end of the pond. He emerged shouting and yelling, "I done it! I done it, Johnnie! It's jist beautiful. You grab that rope and come on down here right now befo' you gits scared and fall off that fool platform."

His words seemed to give me the courage I needed to let go of the security of the pole and start pulling the rope. Soon I had grasped the handle, wanting to make the move, yet still frozen in place. In the next instant, I summoned up all my nerve, gave a gentle shove with my feet, and started down.

Immediately, I was in heaven. I knew I was Orville Wright because I was flying. All fears left me and an

overwhelming sense of excitement, joy and pride engulfed me; before I knew it, I hit the water!

Now I could die happy. If I never accomplished
anything else in life, I was a success. My only regret,
much like Wormy's, was that everyone in Scotland Neck
was not standing by, cheering the two of us on our
victory. I swam to the shore. Wormy and I, black and
white, naked and cold, grasped hands and danced around
in the soft sand. We had forgotten about Bobby, who, by
that time, had made his splash and was headed towards
us.

The next five trips were almost as exciting as the
first. So far, that evening was every bit as wonderful as I
had imagined. If we got caught now, it would be worth
it; even if it meant a switching.

We lay there in the sand for awhile, staring at the
moon and basking in the glory of our daring feat. Bobby
then suggested that we explore the dance hall and check
out the juke box. But first, he wanted to go back to the
car, put on his clothes and get a flashlight out of the
glove box. A flashlight was a necessity for any taxicab.

In a few minutes, Wormy and I could see the small
spot of light leading from the car back to us. We all
entered the large, empty dance hall and Bobby shined
the flashlight on himself. Reaching down in his damp
pocket, he brought out a crumpled pack of Lucky Strikes
and a half-used pack of matches.

Looking rather smug, he said, "Either of you kids
want a smoke?"

"Not me," Wormy replied. "Them things make you
little."

We had been taught that smoking stunted your
growth.

"I might have to pick the dern stuff sometimes, but
I shore don't have to smoke it," he continued.

Bobby responded, "Smoking puts hair on your chest

and makes you feel like a real man. Tastes pretty good too."

"I don't think I want one either," I said. "I tried chewing some Red Man one time and got sick as a dog."

After Bobby lit up, I took the flashlight, and Wormy and I walked over to the nickelodeon. "Wish we had a nickel so we could play the fool thing," I said.

"You is the fool yo'self, Johnnie. Ole Harry Dawson's farm is jist the other side of them pines. He's chased me away from here more'n once. Why, he'd be over here in a minute if he heard this here machine. You know the mayor has him keep a watch on this place."

The cigarette smoke drifted through the hall, followed by an occasional cough. Bobby kept puffing away so Wormy and I walked back out in the moonlight, savoring every moment of the night. We perched on a picnic table and tossed pebbles at the mayor's cooking pot.

Bobby rejoined us and we discussed the time. We decided it must be getting on towards 10 o'clock, and thought we'd best be heading home. We took one more walk down to the water's edge, reluctant to end the evening.

In a moment or two, I thought Bobby was smoking again as the smell of smoke was more pronounced than when we were in the hall. Suddenly, we observed a pitiable sight. Red flames were shooting out of the screen wire of the dance hall.

I shouted, "Bobby, did you put your cigarette out when you finished?"

Before he could answer, we were racing around to the side where the entrance was located. It took only one glance to realize we had started a tragedy. By then, the flames were so severe, the new paint was peeling off the outside walls.

"Let's get out of here!" Bobby exclaimed.

"But we gotta do something," Wormy and I said at the same time, not having the faintest idea of just what to do.

Bobby was already running away from the hall and back towards the car. In our moment of panic, Wormy and I followed. We had to get around the end of the pond where the tower was, climb the small hill, get the car and get out of there, quickly!

But the sight that we beheld paled all the other fears we had experienced during the entire evening. While we had been in the dance hall, the car had rolled backwards down the knoll and directly into the other side of the pond. All we could see was a small part of the bumper with the black and white license plate standing almost straight up in the water.

"Oh, my Gawd!" Wormy yelled. Both Bobby and I were so shocked we couldn't even speak.

I felt as if all the blood had drained right out of my body and I briefly wondered, "How could this happen to us? How could something so wonderful turn into a nightmare?" But, sadly enough, it was no nightmare; it was very real!

We briefly glanced back at the dance hall and saw the brilliant flames lapping under the edges of the new tin roof, which would surely melt and cave in. From a distance, we saw Harry Dawson running, in just his underwear, carrying a pail of water. We ran down the dirt road.

We didn't know what else to do but run. So we ran and we ran, and somewhere along the moonlit road, Bobby tripped, flipped over, hit the ground and let out a wailful moan. He had stumbled over the log that Wormy and I had so carefully replaced to its original position.

In obvious pain, he said, "I think I broke my leg." All the while he was grabbing at me to help him up. At that very moment, I remembered that Wormy and I were stark naked.

"Be careful what you're grabbing," I said as I pulled him up. He stood, putting pressure on his leg. Unsteady as he was, at least he could hobble. That was a relief.

What were we to do? Our clothes were floating somewhere inside the 1940 Hudson which was on, or very near the bottom of the Scout Pond.

"Oh, my Gawd!" escaped Wormy's lips again. "We shore can't go out on the main highway with all our privates showin'; and we shore can't go home like this! What we gonna do?"

By that time, my mind was so boggled with worry and confusion I didn't know what to say, but I knew we had to get away from the Scout Pond area. With Bobby hanging onto me, we continued our trek down the road at a much slower pace.

Approaching the main highway, I spied Mrs. Thigpen's big garden just across the road. It seemed to me that I'd noticed her usual scarecrow keeping watch over her crops. Each year Mrs. Thigpen decorated her scarecrow and gave him a name. This year she had called him Jumbo.

"You guys wait here a minute," I whispered, "and let me check something out." I tiptoed to the very edge of the highway and peered both ways. All was clear, so I made a mad dash across the road and into her garden. Fortunately for us, Jumbo was still standing, mostly concealed by cornstalks. Jumbo was wearing some worn-out dungarees and a red and white checkered flannel shirt. I crawled to the fringe of the garden, pushed aside the cornstalks and motioned for them to come on over. Wormy took Bobby's arm and almost dragged him across the road and into the privacy of the garden. I gave Wormy the dungarees. They were so large they wrapped around his body twice. I put on the shirt, which was just long

enough to cover me. Hot and sweaty from all the running, the remnants of straw in the shirt added to my
overall discomfort.

We had finally stopped running, mainly because
Bobby was so feeble, and we were all completely tuck-
ered out. We headed back towards town, walking through
people's yards and staying away from the street lights.
Approaching the Episcopal Church, we sought momen-
tary seclusion at the rear of the building. I attended this
church every Sunday.

Falling down, we lay there resting and thinking, but
mostly just worrying. I wondered why God had let all
this happen to us. I ventured my thoughts with, "Mr.
Jacobs, my Sunday school teacher, said just last Sunday
that we would all be punished for our sins. Do y'all think
that's what's happening to us for what we done tonight?"

"I don't know that I believes that," Wormy answered. "I think I does some sins 'bout every day, and I
ain't ever had nothin' like this happen to me befo'.
Course, they's little sins and what we done tonight was
pretty big sins."

"Yeah," I sighed, "tonight was a whopper. I just
know this. If we get outta this mess, I'm never going to
miss Sunday school again; I'll say my prayers every night,
and maybe again in the morning, and *never* lie to my
parents again."

Bobby, still in pain, muttered, "Look at my leg and
see if you think it's broken."

We slid around the side of the building where there
was a little more light. I could see that the skin was
broken, and he had a long, blood-red scrape on his left
shin.

"I don't think it's broken, but you really skinned it
up."

We all went silent for a few minutes until I finally
said, "Regardless of the mess we're in, we gotta go

home. They'll have the sheriff out looking for us pretty soon. And I'd just as soon not face him tonight."

Thoughtfully, Wormy asked, "Do y'all think we outta have a prayer first? I ain't much for prayin', but I ain't much fer goin' to no jail neither."

"To hell with a prayer," Bobby replied. "Just give me a hand and let's get it over with."

We left Main and slowly plodded down Church Street, ducking behind trees and bushes whenever a car passed or we heard any noise. At the corner of Church and Sunset Avenue, Bobby and I parted company with Wormy.

I frowned and said, "We better not see each other tomorrow. And if I'm still alive on Monday, I'll meet you at Allsbrook's in the morning."

As Bobby and I approached my house, we knew we were dead. There, sitting in my front yard, was Sheriff Calhoun's big, black Ford police car with the spotlight shining on the front porch.

"Oh, no!" I whimpered. "How do you think they found out about us so fast?"

"I don't know, but my leg's killing me. Let's go on in and fess up."

Walking up on the front porch, we heard several voices. But above everything, I heard Momma crying.

"She knows! I know she knows and she's so mad with me she's crying."

Unfortunately, it wasn't as simple as that. As we entered the bedroom, the sheriff was standing over the bed and Daddy was laying there with only his pants on. Momma was looking down at him and crying.

As Bobby and I walked in the room, Momma looked up and said, "Johnnie, where in the world have you been, and where are your clothes?" The appearance of Bobby and me caused her to momentarily lose sight of whatever was wrong with Daddy.

"We had some problems, Momma, but what's wrong with Daddy?"

"We don't really know yet. He passed out at the picnic and we had to call the sheriff to help us get him home."

Scotland Neck didn't have a rescue squad in those days. Everything that ever happened resulted in calling the sheriff.

Orton Calhoun was maybe the most respected man in Scotland Neck. He was well over 6 feet in height and possessed the strong, firm body of a well-trained athlete. He had a stern face with a ruddy complexion and reddish-blond hair that was always trimmed to perfection, in crew-cut style. The most distinguishing feature about the sheriff was the black patch worn over his right eye.

In high school he had been all-state in football and basketball and had turned down a scholarship to the University of North Carolina to become deputy sheriff of the town. When the war broke out, he was the first man in town to volunteer for military service. On December 8, 1941, he joined the marines. He served, with honor, in the Pacific, receiving several citations, including the Purple Heart. He had lost his eye after only a year of service and was honorably discharged, returning home as a war hero. It was just at that time that old Sheriff Jamision was retiring, so Orton Calhoun became the new sheriff. Only a couple of people in town were opposed to a one-eyed sheriff, but the town council overwhelmingly appointed him. He and the mayor ruled the town comfortably and I knew of no one who didn't like and respect him. His word was law. He and Daddy were good friends and frequently hunted together.

I knew that Daddy suffered from several different ailments. Momma said most of them stemmed mainly from his drinking. He had diabetes and kidney disease and had previously spent some time in the veteran's hospital in Fayetteville. I just knew he was sick a lot and spent many days in bed. He was always having to use a needle to inject some medicine called insulin into his leg.

"You two go in the dining room with Sadie and Sam. We're waiting for Dr. Thigpen to get here."

Upset as I was, it dawned on me that no one had mentioned the missing Hudson yet.

Sadie, Sam and the other boys were sitting around the dining room table. Looking more at Bobby than me, Sam said, "Mr. Moore [he always called his boys 'Mr.' when he was mad], I don't know where you've been or what you've done, but you're in trouble. I'll deal with you when we get home. We've got to get on the road now, 'cause we've got a 5-hour drive ahead."

Almost angrily, Sadie said, "Sam, you know we can't go off and leave Bug alone here in this condition."

My momma's real name was Ethel, but when she was born, her father had said she was as tiny as a doodlebug, and the nickname Bug had stuck with her.

Sam replied, "Sadie, I feel the same way, but I want to keep my job. I've got to be in Charlottesville for a meeting first thing Monday morning. And there's a whole day's work waiting for me tomorrow."

I do remember in those days jobs were hard to come by. Sam had a good job as an insurance salesman. It was for that job that they had moved from Scotland Neck.

"Well," Sadie said reluctantly, "let's go in and see if there's anything we can do before we leave."

Bobby and I went in the kitchen and tried to agree on what we would say when the fatal moment of exposure arrived and we had to tell our whereabouts during the evening. We finally determined that since the Hudson was where it was, along with the devastated dance hall, there would be nothing to do but tell the truth. Bobby wanted to put the whole blame on Wormy, car and all.

I was determined that just Bobby and I share the blame, not mentioning Wormy.

We left the kitchen agreeing we would tell exactly what happened, except maybe we wouldn't know how the fire started. Neither of us was sure we wouldn't crack under pressure, but at that point one little lie may not have hurt—too much.

Sam returned to the dining room and said Daddy was now conscious and there was nothing more they could do. Momma followed and we all said our good-byes. I walked them out to the car. While Sam had apparently sobered up, he said it would be better if Pete, the oldest son, drove. The Moore family pulled out of the yard, bounced across the log bridge and headed north to Virginia.

Still no one had mentioned the car. I thought of suggesting it had been stolen. But I already knew I was doomed to hell and I had better set about to mend my ways. I knew Momma was already worried to death.

Daddy was 51 years old, and, if I ever thought about it, I assumed anyone that old could die anytime. Anyone but *my* daddy! My sorrows seemed to be multiplying from the night's events and Daddy's condition.

I could hear Daddy's voice when I walked back in the hall. I heard him ask, "Where's Johnnie?" I was almost afraid to go in the bedroom, especially with the sheriff right there. I quietly slipped in and said, "Here I am, Daddy." I had never before seen him look exactly as he did then. He was a rather short man with a full head of thick, white hair. His cheeks were always rosy, and he laughed a lot, and had a rather carefree spirit about him. His appearance had totally changed since I had seen him earlier in the evening. His breathing was slow and heavy, and his complexion had changed to a sallow, yellowish color. Momma had the electric fan blowing on him, but he was sweating a lot and his voice had an unusual raspy tone to it.

"Johnnie, get up here on the bed with me."

I obediently walked around past the couch and climbed up beside him. He took me in his arms and held me to him a moment before he said anything. One thing I had always been sure of was that my daddy loved me very much. I could feel the sticky sweat and the smell of alcohol was very noticeable.

"Johnnie, Orton went across the hall to Mr. Whitehead's and used his phone. They're bringing an ambulance in the morning. They're just going to run me to the hospital for a few days. I'll be back soon. We'll go hunting just like I promised you 'cause you been a good boy this summer. While I'm gone, your momma is gonna need your help with the house and Poochie. You'll need to look out for yourself as much as possible. Whatever you do, don't you and Wormy get in any trouble so you don't add any worries to your momma."

Hearing that, all the night's events began whirling through my mind, and huge tears spilled out down my face and I began crying uncontrollably. I managed to get out, "Yes, sir, Daddy. I'll do everything you say and more. Just don't you worry about us. Please hurry and get well and come back home. I'm going to miss you, Daddy."

We lay there a few minutes and his breathing became more even as he fell asleep. I gently slipped out of bed and walked in the dining room where Momma had fixed coffee for the sheriff.

Momma wiped her eyes and said, "Johnnie, the ambulance won't be here until early in the morning. They'll take Daddy and you and I'll follow in the car. In case they need to keep him a couple of days, we can come back home. Mrs. Whitehead will take care of everything, including Poochie."

By then I was praying that Sheriff Calhoun would leave because I had to tell Momma about the Hudson, especially now that she was planning to drive it tomorrow.

When he finished his coffee, the sheriff told Momma that as soon as the doctor arrived, he would go home, get some rest and be here in the morning.

About that time, we heard the door open (no one seemed to knock in Scotland Neck in those days), and Dr. Thigpen walked in with his little black bag. Dr. Thigpen was, I believed, about a hundred years old and had taken care of everyone in Scotland Neck for as long as I could remember. I thought that he could cure anybody. I just knew that his black bag contained some of the missing ingredients that I needed to complete my invisible formula. But I had never gotten around to discussing it with him and that night was certainly not a good time. I also wondered if he recognized the shirt taken from his garden.

He, Momma and the sheriff went back in the bedroom and I heard Momma begin to cry again. They closed the door and left me in the dining room.

The sheriff finally came in and assured me that Dr. Thigpen had everything under control and I should get ready for bed since we had a long trip in the morning.

Suddenly, everything came apart for me and I began crying again.

Putting his hand on my shoulder, he said, "Johnnie, don't you worry about your daddy. Once they get him to the hospital, they'll fix him up good as new."

"It's not just Daddy, Sheriff Calhoun. I have to tell you something, and I just hope you don't put me in jail, with my daddy sick and all." I decided to tell him everything, but to leave Wormy out of it altogether. I would let Bobby and me take the blame. Bobby would be in Virginia, and with my daddy in the hospital, maybe the sheriff wouldn't go so hard on me. I also knew if Wormy's daddy found out that he had anything to do with the Scout Pond disaster (as it was to become known), he might just come home drunk one night and beat him to death. Wormy was the oldest of a young family, and they always seemed to hold him responsible, since his daddy was away so much.

My mouth quivered with fear as I stammered for the right words. I finally unloaded the whole story on him, starting with Bobby driving the Hudson and bringing him right up to why I had the straw-strewn shirt hanging loosely around my body.

He took it better than I'd anticipated. I had fully expected to see those big, silver handcuffs come off his belt. Or maybe worse, to see the belt itself come off.

The sheriff was known for his temper, but usually only showed it with those people who had broken the law. And we had certainly done that. I remembered a night when the Ku Klux Klan held a big rally on the high school grounds. The whole town had turned out to witness the sheriff handle the entire matter by himself. He didn't swear in a single deputy. He had made all the Klansmen disband immediately, take down the cross and clean up the mess they had created. There was even a write-up in *The Standard*, Scotland Neck's bi-weekly newspaper. The paper referred to itself as "The Standard Against Which All Other Literature In the World is Measured." But generally, everybody just call it *The Standard*.

All those thoughts crossed my mind as I completed my story, telling him *almost* everything. I was staring blankly at the floor, too scared to look him in the face. Again, I felt his hand on my shoulder and I thought, "This is it. I'm a goner."

In a very stern tone, he said, "Johnnie, you know you done wrong. You and your cousin done a big wrong tonight and you gotta be punished for it. I don't rightly know what I'll do because of your daddy's situation.

Tomorrow, after you and your momma have gone to Fayetteville, I'll take care of getting the car outta the Scout Pond and back here to your yard. It's a good thing the town had Dawson get insurance on all the buildings at the pond. Otherwise, there would be hell to pay. I'm gonna have to think about this whole mess, and when you and your momma get back, we'll talk again. Right now, I reckon you got enough problems for one night, having to explain to your momma where the car is and figuring out how you two are gonna get to the hospital.

"I will say this, Johnnie.W hile everything you done was completely wrong, you were right to tell me. I'm leaving now, and I hope your daddy has a good night."

I knew I was still in big trouble, but felt that the burden of the world had been slightly shifted, maybe just from one shoulder to the other. Now I just had to deal with Momma—and try to help her, too.

I walked to the bedroom door, quietly pulled it open and peeped in. Dr. Thigpen was seated by the bed with Momma standing at his side. I could hear the doctor speaking to Daddy in hushed tones. I strained my ears to hear what was being said.

Dr. Thigpen had what appeared to be radio earphones on his head with a long tube running down to Daddy's chest. His bag was open and I had never seen so many gadgets in my life. He whispered something to Momma and she went to the kitchen and brought him a small bottle, which I knew contained insulin. He proceeded to inject some of it into Daddy's left thigh.

I could see Daddy talking to him and I felt some better. Then the large doctor struggled to get out of the chair, and he and Momma walked into the dining room.

"Bug, I think he's stable for now and will probably sleep the night. I'll be here in the morning when the ambulance arrives and see that he's in traveling condition. I know Oscar Thomas, the driver. If you want, I can arrange for you and Johnnie to ride along in the back with Gavin."

For one brief moment, I felt I may not have to explain the missing car. And maybe, if the sheriff got it back to our yard, it just might be running fine when we returned.

"Thank you anyway, Claude, but I think Johnnie and I will take our car in case Gavin has to stay over a few days. I want to be with Gavin as long as possible, but I can't miss any more work than necessary. These last few months, with Gavin being laid up so much, plus the last trip to the hospital, I've missed a lot of time from work. And you know the old story—no work, no pay."

Momma worked at the Boston Store located on Main Street. Course, every store in town, except the funeral home, was located on Main Street. And I never quite figured that to be a store. The Boston Store sold second-hand clothing, mainly to the coloreds. But most of the clothes I wore came from there. Momma always had first pick of everything so most of mine were almost like new.

"As a matter of fact, Doctor, I know I'm behind on your bill right now. But you know I always manage to catch up."

"Bug, how many times has Gavin driven me out into the country on a call and never charged me a cent? Don't you worry about that bill none."

Dr. Thigpen would drive around town, but being as old as he was, whenever he had to make a house-call out in the country, he always had Daddy drive him, day or night.

W alking out in the hall, Momma asked, "Claude, do you really think this is just his diabetes acting up again, or something more serious? You know, he's been drinking mighty heavy lately, and nothing I say or do will stop him."

"His diabetes certainly doesn't help matters, and he's never reacted like this before. Try not to worry 'cause they have good doctors and the most modern equipment at the hospital. If Gavin can be fixed, they can do it there."

Walking behind them, that "if" really worried me. Right then I had a hard time spreading my worries between Daddy and me. That may have been the worst night of my life. And it still wasn't over.

"Night, Ethel, night, Johnnie," he said as he drove out of the yard. "See you early in the morning."

It was then that she noticed the missing car. "Johnnie, where's the Hudson? Did your daddy move it around the side before we went to the farm?"

"No, ma'am. Momma, I've got something to tell you but I don't want Daddy to hear, so let's go back in the kitchen and talk."

By then, with all the experiences of the evening, I was about cried out. I knew I was going to have a hard time telling her. But most of all, I hated to hurt and upset her more.

"First," she said, "tell me where all your clothes are. You know I just bought that outfit for you to start school. I wouldn't have let you wear it if Sadie and Sam hadn't been here, or you hadn't been going to the show at night."

"Yes, ma'am, I know. The clothes are just part of my problem. The Hudson is the big problem." It was getting harder and harder to unfold my story to her, knowing how worried she already was about Daddy. I didn't know how to start. Under normal circumstances, I would be in for some real punishment, just for messing up my good clothes. Now what would happen to me?

Finally, with a slow precision in my voice, the words started. As soon as I mentioned Bobby driving the car, she interrupted and nervously asked, "Did you two have a wreck in the car? I noticed Bobby limping right bad."

"No, ma'am, it wasn't a wreck. But maybe it was

worse than a wreck." Having just told the entire story to the sheriff helped me a little, and I managed to get most all of it out, skipping the dance hall and never mentioning Wormy. Mainly I just told her where the Hudson ended up.

Whether from worry or the evening's fatigue, she seemed more lost in my story than in showing anger towards me.

"Johnnie, are you telling me that our car is *at* the Scout Pond, or *in* the Scout Pond?"

"Momma, it's in the Scout Pond. When we left, all I could see was the front bumper sticking out, and we never looked back again." I hastened to tell her that Sheriff Calhoun already knew and was going to see about getting it out of the pond in the morning.

I now realize that story was so outlandish that she had a hard time accepting it. She didn't fuss or cry, but just sat there, staring off into space.

"Momma, we'll get the car back, and maybe when it dries out, it'll be just as good as new. Anyway, Dr. Thigpen said we could ride to the hospital in the ambulance, so we can be there with Daddy the whole time."

Wearily, she said, "You know we need to get back as soon as possible so I can get to work. We need the money, Johnnie."

That faraway look returned to her face; and not really addressing me, she whispered, "What in God's name am I going to do?"

That moment of guilt became deeply etched in my mind forever.

"I promise, Momma, when all this is over and Daddy is home again, I won't do anything else bad, not ever again. I won't fuss about my bath at night. I'll shine my shoes every day and take off my school clothes as soon as I get home and even hang them in the closet. I'll come down to the store and sweep up every night so you won't have to do it. Please don't be mad with me, Momma!"

For the first time since I had gotten home, a haggard smile spread evenly across her lovely face, and she told me to come around and sit on her lap. She just hugged me and in a very forgiving tone said, "I love you, Johnnie."

Chapter 4

The ambulance arrived at 8 o'clock the next morning. Momma had been up early and helped Daddy with his bath. He looked slightly better than the night before, but something told me he was really sick this time. I heard him ask Momma to fix him a little "toddy" to help him get started.

Irritably, she said, "Gavin, are you completely crazy? That's half the reason you're in this condition now." She refused and prepared him some milk-toast and coffee instead.

She didn't mention the car. She had decided to ride to Fayetteville in the ambulance with Daddy and take the Carolina Trailways bus back home, if need be. She used the Whiteheads' phone to call her sister, my Aunt Bessie, and arrange for me to stay with her. I had stayed with Aunt Bessie Brundige before. Aside from all my worries, I was looking forward to staying at my aunt's house. She trusted me to do most anything I wanted and was always lots of fun to be around.

Dr. Thigpen, the sheriff and Mrs. Whitehead were all there to help in getting Daddy settled in the ambulance. We all exchanged embraces. Momma had been crying again, and I suspected some of her feelings had to do with the mess I had created.

The sheriff didn't mention anything about our conversation.

Daddy told me to be a good boy and to mind Aunt Bessie. As the ambulance pulled out of the yard, I experienced a sinking feeling. Somehow, I knew things were never going to be the same at home again.

Aunt Bessie was one of my very favorite people. She had three children, all girls, but always treated me like one of her own. Possessing a keen intelligence for someone who had only gone through the fourth grade, she had a wonderful personality and an excellent sense of humor. She was always able to make me laugh. Aunt Bessie had thick, red hair, tied back in a bun with some colorful ribbon attached. She wore reading spectacles that always seemed to slide down her long, rather pointed nose; and her face was dotted with freckles that matched her red hair. She usually wore cotton dresses that were covered by lovely aprons, all of which she had made herself. Outside of her family, her two loves in life were cooking and costume jewelry. She wore dangling earrings and flaring bracelets and some glowing necklace hanging down to the bib of her apron. She was usually dressed up like an overly-decorated Christmas tree. But on her, none of it looked garish; it looked charming. Anytime she went shopping in Rocky Mount or Tarboro, she returned with a new selection of valuables.

She had even named her two youngest daughters Jewel Star and Ruby, in keeping with her love for jewelry. Sometimes she called Ruby "Bright" because Ruby had the same freckles as Aunt Bessie. Aunt Bessie said her face looked like a bright red ruby. But I knew my cousin preferred to be called just Ruby.

I felt nothing but anticipation as I strolled down Main Street towards her yellow frame house, just one block from the shopping area.

She was sitting on the front porch with a large pail of snap beans from her garden, snapping and cracking them in just the right places in preparation for the evening meal. Most all our vegetables came from home gardens or one of the local farms.

In Scotland Neck, food preparation was an art, passed on from one generation to the next. All the foods were carefully prepared from homegrown ingredients. They were flavored with fatback and ham bones, and all sorts of delicious seasonings. Every meal was meticulously prepared and served with pride and Southern hospitality. And each one was a feast. This was just one other reason why I loved Scotland Neck and felt quite content to spend the rest of my life in that small town.

"Sugar Pie," she said, as she put her pail down, "come here and sit on my lap and tell me all about your daddy. Your momma called all upset. I assured her not to worry. You know you can stay here as long as you want to."

I told her everything I knew about Daddy and she hugged me and said what a good time I was going to have with Jewel and Ruby, who had just joined us on the porch.

After chatting with the girls, I asked if I could go and play.

"Sure you can, but be here for dinner time 'cause I've made something special, just for you."

In Scotland Neck, the first meal was breakfast. The noon meal was dinner and the evening meal was supper. It was only in later years that I learned the rest of the world was wrong in naming dinner and supper.

"Yes, ma'am," I replied, jumping from her lap and leaving my little satchel laying there beside her.

The blacksmith shop was only a half-block away. I was anxious to get there, knowingW ormy would be waiting. I was even in a rather good mood since our recent tragedy seemed to be tucked away, at least for awhile. My mood abruptly changed as Sheriff Calhoun's Ford pulled up beside me.

"Oh, no!" I thought, all my worst fears returning. I remembered only too well what he had said about being punished. I just knew this was lockup time and I wanted to cry again. But I remembered what I had told Daddy and was determined to get through things like a man.

"Johnnie," he called as he beckoned me over to the car.

I thought maybe he would just take me to the station without my having to suffer the humiliation of being handcuffed right there on Main Street.

"Yes, sir," I answered as I hesitantly wandered over to the car door. At least the cuffs weren't out and the gun certainly was not drawn. I breathed a sigh of relief.

"I just want you to know that last night, after I left your house, I went to Columbus Jones' house and got him out of bed.W e got his towing truck and went down to the Scout Pond. After a heap of work, we were able to hitch up the Hudson, pull it out and tow it to his station."

Columbus Jones owned the other filling station in Scotland Neck. It was a Sinclair Station located right across Main Street from the sheriff's office. Columbus had more modern equipment than the ESSO and owned the only towing vehicle in town. Mr. Jones always swore he was a direct descendant from Christopher Columbus, and that he had the papers to prove it. But nobody in town ever saw those papers and nobody really believed him. But he had a good filling station.

"Right now," the sheriff said, "the car is sitting behind his station drying out. Columbus thinks, with a lot of work, he might even get it running again. Since it was 3:30 in the morning when we finished, I don't think anybody else in town, except Slim [Columbus' brother who helped him run the station], knows where the car has been. You just hush up about this and I'll see if I can get it all straightened out before your daddy comes home.

"I also think I got something here that belongs to you," he said as he tossed me a bag of still wet clothes.

"One other thing, Johnnie, I guess you heard about the big fire at the dance hall. I made a private investigation and talked to the town's inspector this morning. Me and him concluded that darn fire must have been started by some kind of short circuit in that newfangled juke box. I told old Clive Dawson not to run no electricity out to the Scout Pond in the first place."

A small smile creased his face. He winked at me and left. I stood there astonished and relieved, watching the rear of his Ford take off down Main Street.

His smile had been like a ripple of silver to me. If Daddy's problems hadn't been cluttering my brain, I think I would have started singing praises to God, right then and there.

But as it was, I just took off as fast as I could for Allsbrook's Blacksmith Shop and Wormy. I had so much to tell him. But mainly, I had to tell him Scotland Neck had some mighty fine folks, and that there really was a God. And even in spite of what we'd done last night, He'd still look out for us.

$\mathcal{M}$omma was always warning me not to count on everything in life happening just because I wanted it to. "Especially where other folks are concerned," she warned. "You always be dependable, Johnnie. Just don't count on everybody else being that way. Remember, your word is important to your reputation. And a good reputation is mighty important in life."

So far, I had found that one person I could always count on was Wormy. He never promised anything he didn't do, if it was within his power to do it. Sometimes his daddy or family responsibilities would change our plans. But he always let me know. I tried to be much the same way and I know that concern for each other was one of the common bonds in our relationship.

He was sitting under the pecan tree, chewing on a straw.

"Where you been, Johnnie? You think I ain't got nothin' better to do than sittin' 'round waitin' fer you? I was 'bout to go on down to the barber shop by myself."

"Wormy, ain't you worried none about last night?"

"Lawd, I done all my worryin' last night when I got home befo' my fambly and didn't get caught. Won't do no good no how. That ole sun's gonna be floatin' up there, hot as ever, with or without that car; and who cares about the dern dance hall, anyway? Alls I know is

I had myself a bodacious time at the Scout Pond."

"Did you ever think we would be put in jail for what we did?"

"What *we* did? Whole thing won't nobody's fault but that know-it-all Yankee cousin of yos. He caused all the trouble. Now, I s'pose he's all safe back in Washington, and you's walkin' 'round sweatin' like a turkey the day befo' Thanksgivin'. Anyway, don't make no matter to me. Sometimes I think jail would be better'n home, least where my daddy is concerned. If it won't fer my momma and the other chillun, I think I'd hi-tail it right outta this town. Let's go to work and git paid so we can git a Coca-Cola and a Moon Pie. I'm starvin' myself to death. My momma gives everythin' to the young chillun first, and if there's anythin' left I git it. This mornin' won't nothin' left but some cold grits and one half-bottle of beer my daddy left on the table last night. So let's git goin'."

Wormy and I had a once-a-week job at Smith's Barber Shop. We cleaned, swept up and emptied the trash cans, for which each of us received 25 cents.

On the way to the barber shop, I told him everything that had just happened since last night, including my most recent meeting with the sheriff.

"I shore am sorry 'bout yo daddy, Johnnie. Don't you worry none. That God you jist told me 'bout will take care of him, and yo momma, too. We jist gotta worry 'bout Wormy and Johnnie, and course, gittin' somethin' to eat."

To my dismay, he didn't seem the least bit relieved that I had kept his name out of the entire incident.

Melvin Smith was a distant cousin of Shoofly Smith. It seemed that everybody in Scotland Neck was somehow related to everybody else. Melvin owned the barber shop/pool hall, which was the town hangout for most of the men when they weren't working, and for some even when they were supposed to be working. His shop held a certain enchantment for me, and it was the one place in town that I would have liked to own. The red and white barber's pole was mounted above the entrance to the long, narrow brick building on Main Street, right in the middle of town. The pole looked like a giant candy cane that had been revolving as long as I could remember. Melvin liked two things: to see that pole turning and to have clean, neat pool tables.

The front room had two barber chairs. I had received my first real hair cut in one of them. Back in the corner, next to the door that led to the pool hall, was a fat, potbellied stove with six or seven wooden chairs neatly encircling it. Around that stove, many a tale was spun about what had been and what would be in Scotland Neck and, for that matter, in the whole world. Daddy always said you could get a better education sitting around that stove than at any school. He said we would already have won the war if Congress had just met at Melvin Smith's Barber Shop.

In the other back corner of the room, opposite the stove, was a large, wooden checker board. Years before, it had been mounted atop an old nail keg that was still held together by rusty, metal flanges. The board had been worn smooth from years of sliding gray and red slate checkers across its surface.

Each of the checkers was like a gem to me because each had been handled, at one time or another, by almost every man in Scotland Neck (except maybe our preacher). The ritual had started before my birth. After the yearly checker tournament, the winner's name was inscribed on an old parchment, which was framed and hung above the board. There must have been over 50 names on that old paper. I was always proud to see that down towards the bottom of the list was my daddy's name.

Tales had it that the checkers had been made from

old, slate stones stolen from the sacred Indian burial grounds out beyond the Scout Pond. Some even said they possessed magical powers, and that whoever owned the barber shop also possessed those powers. Half of them had originally been painted red, and the others were left their natural, dark gray slate color. By then, most of the red had been worn off, and they were all as smooth as finely-polished marble.

I often imagined buying the shop when I grew up, just to gain the magical powers and to handle the checkers as often as I liked. Even though Melvin was one of Daddy's best friends, Wormy and I were never allowed to play with the checkers and could only touch them when we were dusting everything, and then, only under the watchful eye of Melvin Smith. I even remember Daddy telling me that Melvin threatened to shoot some fella from Winston-Salem who was just passing through town and got into a checker game. He dropped one of the red ones on the floor and chipped off the edge. That fella never did stop in for checkers again.

The rear part of the building was my favorite. Walking through the door that led from the barber shop, you entered a large, dimly-lit room. There were several wall shelves housing various barbering supplies. Next to the shelves was an old file cabinet whose top was covered with ashtrays and an empty beer bottle or two. There were no windows or other doors, but situated precisely in the middle of the room were two beautiful, well-kept, Champion slate-bed pool tables. There were at least a dozen chairs and benches set well back from the tables. Cigarette butt containers separated most of them. Mounted on the wall were four separate wall racks that housed the straightest, most precise cue sticks imaginable. Hanging above each table was a row of three light bulbs, with silver shades directing the light down to every nook and cranny on each table.

Melvin was more particular about those tables than about his checker board. I dreamed of the day when I would be tall enough to take one of those pool cues and challenge Wormy to a championship match.

But right then, our job was to clean up the place so we could get paid. Melvin didn't like us to be there as the day wore on, 'cause some of the men would get drunk. Then the language got rough and he knew Momma would have a fit if he allowed me to hear that kind of talk.

"Shucks," I would say to her, "you know I've heard every word they say there, Momma. Besides, I don't talk like that because I know it's a sin."

I said that 'cause she liked to hear it and it made her proud of me. Course, when Wormy and I were alone, we would have cussing contests. It always astounded me just how many bad words he knew.

"Okay, Johnnie, you and Wormy get your work done and get outta here. I don't want you hanging 'round no more than you have to, 'specially with your momma and daddy outta town," Mr. Smith said.

Wormy and I took turns cleaning the back area. That day it was my turn to clean the pool room. We both enjoyed brushing down the pool tables and emptying and cleaning ashtrays more than we did sweeping up old dead hair and dusting down the barber shop section. I felt a great sense of responsibility when I took the long bristle brush and carefully stroked down the tables. I treated them with a great deal of care and respect, because someday, I would be the best pool shooter in Scotland Neck, and I wanted those tables in good shape when that time finally arrived.

The floors in the back room had never been covered and consisted of very hard, smooth earth, firmly packed down from years of use. While the tables were precisely level, there were certain spots in the floor, just a tad lower or higher than others. Those slight imperfections were undetectable, except to the regular users. That meant that not only did you have to play position on the tables, you also had to situate your feet just right to accomplish a good shot.

The four mahogany legs of each table had been expertly set on cement blocks, insuring perfectly level tables. Melvin kept a 6-foot carpenter's level available. Anytime there was an important game, everyone would gather around while he placed the level diagonally across the table. He would let them check the level bubble to prove that the playing conditions were, apparently, perfect.

Whenever out-of-towners played, the local men would have Melvin check the level of the tables, without mentioning the floor. Many a dollar had been won by Scotland Neck men who not only knew how to play, but also knew exactly where to stand. If anyone did suspect, Melvin would swear that one of the stranger's legs was shorter than the other, because neither the floor nor the table affected the game of the Scotland Neck men. As the out-of-towners left with empty pockets, the local men would sit down around the stove and laugh and talk about what had become known as "Melvin's Jinx."

We finished our work in a little over an hour and Melvin paid us each our quarter. We immediately headed for the North End Drug Store for our snacks.

Just outside the barber shop, we ran into Harry Lee Smith, who had a stack of comic books under his arm. Now, comic books were an important part of our entertainment, and we got in a conversation about trading a few with Harry Lee. I suspected he knew we had our big pay in our pockets as he invited Wormy and me to go by his house and review his entire collection.

Captain Marvel was one of my favorite heroes. Wormy liked to read about the comic character Billy Batson who was transformed into Captain Marvel when he spoke the magic word "Shazam." Billy was a very slight little fellow who would be transformed into a muscular superhuman hero. He would then proceed to save the world from the forces of evil. Wormy would just stare at the page and repeat "Shazam!" hoping it would work for him. We both believed that, second only to becoming invisible, the ability to fly would be the next greatest feat. Often, we took large towels, pinned them around our necks, and charged off as fast as possible, hoping our capes would help us defy gravity. But, much like our invisible experiments, we hadn't yet gotten off the ground.

At any rate, we agreed to take a quick detour and go by Harry Lee's house. His daddy was down at the river and he had no mother that we had ever seen.

Momma often said she could understand why no one ever married his father. "Who in their right mind," she would say, "would marry anyone with a name like Shoofly Smith?" She always added that Shoofly wasn't "all there," whatever that meant. He surely looked like a full-grown man to me.

Whenever she and Daddy talked about Shoofly, they talked of the big flood some years back. Daddy had driven down to the high-water level at the river to check on Tazwell and Shoofly. When Shoofly sloshed out of the wood shack where they operated their business, Daddy noticed that Shoofly had cut off the bottom of his pants to just above his knees. When Daddy asked what had happened to his pants, Shoofly said he had cut them off so they wouldn't get wet. It made sense to me, but Momma and Daddy always laughed when the story was told.

I really didn't understand that family anyway. Shoofly was Melvin Smith's cousin and Harry Lee's daddy. Harry Lee had two sisters, Reba and Betts, but no mother (as far as I knew). I only knew that Reba was the first girl that

I ever deeply loved. She was about five years older than me and was always nice to me. But I never felt she loved me. I thought she was beautiful and Wormy was always teasing me about my "sweetheart." Even Harry Lee knew how I felt. Sometimes I would go to his house with a stack of comic books that I knew he already had, just in hopes of seeing Reba.

They lived in a large, old house, much like ours. Shoofly was hardly ever there and the girls took care of everything, including Harry Lee, as much as anyone could take care of him.

Climbing the stairs to Harry Lee's room, we saw Reba walking down the hall towards the bathroom, which was next to Harry Lee's room.

"Hey, Johnnie and Wormy," she said, with a smile on her lovely face. "Gonna trade some comic books?" she casually asked, as she entered the bathroom, closing the door behind her. I felt my heart flutter and I'm sure I blushed.

We went into Harry Lee's room and pulled out three large cardboard boxes from under his bed. They were filled with comic books I had already gone through a dozen times. He gently pushed the door closed and asked, "Didn't you two just get paid for working down at the barber shop?"

"Yeah, and soon as we leaves here, we gonna git somethin' to eat," Wormy answered.

In almost a whisper, Harry Lee said, "I'll make a deal with you. How would you like to watch Reba take a bath?"

"Garden peas!" said Wormy. "How we gonna do that? Jist walk right in the bathroom?"

"Naw," Harry Lee said. "I have a secret peephole and I'll let you watch. But it'll cost you 25 cents each."

Suddenly, experiencing feelings that were new to me, I asked, "Where is it?"

"First," Harry Lee asked, "do we have a deal or not? You each give me a quarter and I'll let you watch Reba take a bath."

When he said that, I felt something inside me that had nothing whatsoever to do with comic books. I said, "First, tell us exactly how we're gonna get to see her."

In his usual clever manner, Harry Lee said, "No. First the 25 cents, then I'll guarantee it."

All thoughts of Coca-Colas, Moon Pies and everything else quickly slipped from my mind and I instantly produced my quarter. Wormy just stood there, watching and listening.

Holding out his hand, Harry Lee said, "Just gimme that money, Johnnie. Then watch me and do exactly what I tell you."

By then, I could hear the water running in the tub and I think I started sweating a little. I handed over my shiny, hard-earned coin with, as I remember, wild anticipation.

"Now, Johnnie, you gotta be careful 'cause when the water stops running, she can hear us if we make any noise. 'Specially if you step on the hall floor 'cause it squeaks something awful."

The door to the bathroom was just outside his bedroom and immediately to the left. Very carefully, Harry Lee placed his left hand on his door frame and stretched his body across part of the hall, leaving his feet glued to the floor in his room. Using his right hand, he reached up on the bathroom door and removed a small piece of white toilet paper that had been used to fill a hole he had previously drilled in the door. Holding to his door frame with his left hand and balancing against the door frame of the bathroom with his right, he could peep right through the revealing hole, getting a good view of the bathtub.

He pulled himself back in his bedroom and said

again, "Whatever you do, don't step on the hall floor."

We were whispering in tones as low as possible. By then, Wormy seemed a little excited and was busy digging his money out of his pocket.

Impatiently, I said, "Lemme go first. I paid first." I really didn't know what to expect, but I was drawn to that door frame.

Very carefully, I grasped the frame on his door and extended myself across the doorway of the bathroom. But my arm wouldn't quite reach the bathroom door frame. Stretching with all my might, I couldn't get my eye over the secret peephole. I was breathing hard, not knowing whether it was from anticipation or frustration. I didn't dare step out in the hall, as the water had stopped running, and it was relatively quiet. I certainly didn't want to be discovered encroaching on the privacy of someone who I loved so much. I hung on for a long minute, using every muscle in my body—but to no avail.

Just above the beating of my heart, I heard Wormy whisper, "I seen my sisters plenty of times, but I ain't never seen no white girl befo'. Are they diff'rent, Harry Lee?"

"Let's just say you'll get your quarter's worth," Harry Lee replied.

"Hey, you guys," I whispered, "pull me back in the room. My hand's sweating and I'm starting to slip."

Wormy reached around and took my free arm and Harry Lee grabbed my belt loop, and together they pulled me back into the bedroom. I felt utter frustration. I didn't know what I'd missed. But that little voice kept whispering that I wanted to see it.

"Lemme there," Wormy said. "It's my turn and I already paid, too."

He was several inches taller than I and was able to maneuver himself into position with ease. He silently moved his head up against the door, closed one eye and peered in the hole. For a couple of seconds he didn't say a word and then, "My Gawd," quietly escaped his lips. He hung on for what seemed an eternity, pressing even tighter against the door.

All of a sudden his fingers slipped and all I heard was "Shazam!" as he hit the floor with a loud thud.

Reba shouted from the bathroom, "Harry Lee, what y'all doing out there. Get away from that door. I'm gonna be outta here in a minute and I'm bringing the hair brush with me."

Wormy jumped up and the three of us scrambled down the stairs as fast as possible, with Harry Lee wildly laughing. We scooted out the front door and ran around to the side of the house.

As soon as we stopped, I told Harry Lee I wanted my 25 cents back.

"Deal's a deal," he said. "You had your chance. Is it my fault you're such a runt?" He had a smirk on his face.

Wormy pushed him up against the house and angrily said, "You better give Johnnie his money back or I'm gonna kick yer butt. You promised he'd see somethin' and he didn't, so pay him back."

Harry Lee, looking slightly uncomfortable, pulled out my quarter and handed it to me.

"Don't you two ever come around here to trade comics with me again. 'Specially you, Johnnie. Everybody knows you'd rather be with this nigger than your own kind."

Those were the last words Harry Lee was able to speak as Wormy balled up his fist and whumped him right in the stomach, causing him to start crying as he ran back in the house.

"Thanks, Wormy. I don't like Harry Lee anyway. And he's always after somebody's money. Anyway, I've seen all his stinking comic books. I just hope Reba ain't mad with me after this."

I had always planned to marry her right after I bought the pool hall, and I thought the three of us could play pool anytime we wanted—and checkers, too.

Chapter 6

It was almost dinner time, and I knew Aunt Bessie would be expecting me. I suggested that Wormy and I meet at 2 p.m. at the Sinclair station. I wanted to take a look at the Hudson and ask Columbus Jones if he was going to be able to fix it.

Remembering Wormy's earlier hunger pangs, I said, "I'm gonna eat dinner at my aunt's house. You walk down to the drug store and I'll go in and get you something to eat. I shore don't want you starving to death on me."

Wormy generally didn't like to take anything for free. But I knew he was hungry, and if it weren't for him, I wouldn't have my quarter anyway.

He waited outside while I went in and made the purchase. I still had 15 cents left, which wasn't bad for the excitement that I'd almost enjoyed.

"Thanks, Johnnie. I'll pay you back next payday."

I arrived at Aunt Bessie's around noon. Walking up on the porch, I enjoyed the delicious smell of her dinner wafting through the screen door.

Dinner in Scotland Neck was the premier meal. Everything and everybody stopped at 12 noon, regardless of what was going on. Dinner at Aunt Bessie's was like a banquet. She always had more than one meat from which to choose. There could be fried chicken and ham, or barbecue and Brunswick Stew, or some of my other favorites. The meats were always accompanied by a host of fresh garden vegetables, seasoned to perfection. She also offered a choice of desserts, and everything was still warm from the oven.

Greeting me with her usual warm smile, she said, "You're just in time, Johnnie. Run and wash up and give a yell to the girls in the backyard that dinner's ready."

Uncle Jimmie came in and we all feasted and retired to the front porch for the usual after-dinner conversation. Life was not at all hectic in Scotland Neck, and the mid-day break was a ritual for everyone in town. Most of the husbands came home from work for dinner.

Aunt Bessie's jewelry was particularly sparkling as she seated herself in the big rocking chair with a cold glass of iced tea in her hand. As she rocked, her long turquoise-colored earrings swung back and forth. She said, "Your momma called from the hospital. Gavin has been admitted and they'll start the tests tomorrow morning. She said to give you her love and tell you your daddy is being taken care of, real good. She also said to remind you to go by and check on Poochie this afternoon. And the last thing she said was to be sure you say your prayers tonight, and remember your daddy when you do."

"Yes, ma'am," I answered. Remembering how Daddy had looked the night before, I experienced that same uncomfortable feeling in the pit of my stomach.

"Aunt Bessie, what do they do at hospitals? Will they do an operation on him? Do you think they'll make him well?"

"Honey, sometimes hospitals are almost like magic. A body can go in there real sick, and before you can say Jack Sprat, you're healthy and well and back home with your family. Why, they have a lot of machines and all the best medicines and lots of good doctors and nurses. You can bet they'll fix your daddy up before you know it."

After a little more idle chatter, I asked if I could go down and maybe see if they needed help at the Sinclair station. Occasionally, Columbus would let me clean up and put new oil cans out front. And once he had even let me pump gas. Course, it was into Daddy's car and Daddy was right there with me. I was never paid any money but he would always give me a Coca-Cola and maybe a pack of Cheese Nabs. That day, I really wanted to check out the Hudson.

"Okay," Bessie said, "just stay outta trouble and remember to go by your house. I know Poochie misses you already."

"Yes, ma'am," I said as I gave her a hug. "And thank you for the dinner. It was really good. Bye, see y'all this afternoon."

"By supper time for sure, Johnnie. You know your Uncle Jimmie don't like to be kept waiting. Besides, it's your turn to say blessin' tonight."

I secretly knew that Ruby, Bessie's youngest daughter, wanted to go to the Sinclair station, too. But Daddy always said two places no girls belonged were filling stations and the pool hall.

When I got to the station, they had the Hudson up on the grease lift and Slim was walking around under the car with the air hose, blowing it dry. He said something to me, but I couldn't hear his words above the noise of the air compressor. Now, an air compressor somehow made blowing air out of still air. I didn't understand how that machine worked, and neither did most of the townfolks. When Columbus had it shipped in from Raleigh, almost half of the town turned out just to see it in action. Some of the folks wouldn't get too close to it because it made so much noise, they thought it just might blow right up. But by now, it was pretty commonplace, and Columbus was right proud of the big sign that said "Free Air." It still amazed me.

When the blowing stopped, I asked, "What'd you say, Mr. Slim?"

"Boy, you really done it this time, Johnnie. Good thing this car went into the shallow part of the Scout Pond. If it'd been the other end, it would be 'good-bye, Hudson' and 'good-bye, Scotland Neck Taxi Service.'"

"Mr. Slim, I'd just as soon not talk about it, if you don't mind. I been worried 'bout this mess all night. Do you think it'll start once you get it dried out?"

"Gonna take a lot more'n drying her out. Most everything in the engine will be partly rusted. And you can forgit that radio. I know it's ruined for good."

Pangs of anxiety rushed through my body again, and my stomach began churning around all that good food I'd just eaten. Since there weren't too many calls for taxi service in Scotland Neck, Daddy spent a lot of time sitting in the car listening to the radio when he wasn't at the pool hall or down at the river. Whenever President Roosevelt made his important speeches, Daddy would sit in the car and listen to every word. He thought an awful lot of President Roosevelt.

To the best of my knowledge, there was only one other car in town with a radio. That belonged to Zed Kitchen who owned the town's only new car company. Zeb had a lot of money and Daddy seemed to think his radio made him every bit as important as Mr. Kitchen. I made a mental note to ask God in my prayers that night to please let the radio work.

I walked all around under the car, looking with fascination at all the mechanical wizardry that made it go—or at least used to make it go. "Maybe," I thought, "I better pray for the whole car and not just the radio."

Lost in those thoughts, I hadn't noticed Wormy walk up behind me.

"Gotcha!" he said as he punched me in my ribs, knowing how ticklish I was.

"Mr. Slim, do you or Mr. Columbus have any work for us this afternoon?"

"Naw, Johnnie. If it wasn't for this here car of your daddy's, I'd just be sittin' inside waitin' for business. You two skedaddle so I can lower the car and see what I can do about gittin' it to run again."

"We'll be glad to help," I anxiously volunteered. "Just let me know if there's anything we can do. I'll drop by later and check on it. 'Bye, Mr. Slim, and thanks for working on the car."

"Whatcha wanna do, Johnnie?" Wormy asked in his usual restless manner.

"Well, first we gotta go by my house and check on Poochie and see if I can do anything to help Mrs. Whitehead. Then maybe we'll take a walk down to the cemetery."

"You know I hate that place. Why you always wanna go there?"

Before I could answer, we had turned the corner from Church Street onto Sunset Avenue, and I could see Poochie wagging his tail and hear his little woofs of excitement. I always knew Poochie loved me as much as I loved him, and he always showed it.

Thinking out loud, I said, "I wonder why dogs are always in a good mood?"

"'Cause they ain't got nothin' to worry 'bout, and prob'ly ain't got no brain to tell 'um to worry."

"I know Poochie has a brain. How else would he recognize me and act so excited every time I come around?"

"If dogs had brains, I know ours would of left home a long time ago. Daddy beats them two coon dogs and they still stay there and even act like they like him. They don't hardly git anythin' to eat. And every time he comes home drunk, which is every time he comes home, he kicks at 'um and cusses 'um and they still act like they like him. The only time he treats 'um decent is when he wants to use 'um to flush out rabbits and coons or whatever it is he wants to kill that day. Now you tell me how anything with a brain at all could act like they likes somebody like my daddy. I don't even like him myself, and Momma hates fer him to come home."

"I can't explain it, but my Sunday school teacher says God works in mysterious ways, probably even regarding animals. I just know Poochie has a brain and does most everything I tell him. And he loves Momma and Daddy, too; but I know he loves me the most special."

"Look at him now," I said as he charged towards me, prancing and pawing and wanting me to pick him up. I gathered him in my arms and he excitedly licked my neck and face.

"Hey, Mrs. Whitehead," I said as we walked on the porch. "Is everything all right? Can I do anything to help you? Has Poochie been fed yet?"

"Land sakes, Johnnie, you ask so many questions I don't know what to answer first. Everything is fine. Poochie's been fed, and I checked your apartment this morning and pulled down the shades to keep out the afternoon sun. I don't think there's a thing you can do for me. Has Bessie heard anything from your momma?"

"Yes, ma'am. She called this morning and there's nothing to report yet. He's all checked in, but they haven't started working on him. Momma's gonna call Aunt Bessie as soon as she knows anything. And we still don't know when Momma's coming home."

"Johnnie, where's your daddy's car?" she asked.

"Oh, uh, well," I said, giving me some time to think. "It needed some work and Momma didn't think she should drive it to Fayetteville with it needing work and all. As a matter of fact, we just came from checking on it, and Mr. Slim thinks he might be able to get it fixed. Gotta go, Mrs. Whitehead. Would you please hold Poochie while we're leaving? He's sure to follow me, and I don't want him to get in any traffic down on Main Street."

"Sure, hand him over. You boys be good and stay outta trouble."

"Yes, ma'am," I said, wanting to get away as fast as I could before she asked any more questions about the car.

"Johnnie," she yelled as we were just about out of the yard, "did y'all hear about the big fire down at the Scout Pond last night? Seems like the dance hall and the new dressing rooms all burned down. Something about the new juke box catching on fire and starting it all."

"Yes'um, we heard all about it. See you tomorrow, Mrs. Whitehead.

"Let's get outta here, Wormy."

He mockingly laughed and said, "Boy, Johnnie, you shore done some fast thinkin' 'bout that car."

"Well, I didn't tell a lie. The car did need some work; and it is at the Sinclair station; and Momma couldn't drive it—so there. Let's don't talk about it anymore."

We walked back to Church Street and turned in the direction of the Scout Pond. The cemetery was about a quarter-mile past the road that led to the Scout Pond, on the same side of the highway.

"Johnnie, the only reason I go to the dern cemetery wif you so much is to watch the trains passin' by. That place spooks me. What you like 'bout it so much?"

"I love going to the cemetery. I like to look at all the graves where my ancestors are buried. Besides, I brought some bread scraps from Aunt Bessie's, and we can go down to the pond and feed the ducks."

"Well, I jist hope some trains go by 'cause I don't care a whit 'bout them ducks. I wanna do somethin' excitin'."

I always felt a certain peacefulness at the cemetery.

It was quiet and beautiful. It had a lovely pond, filled with lily pads and surrounded by cattails and tall, green water stalks. We usually found several hungry ducks there who would waddle right up to us and take food from our hands.

The cemetery was divided into four main sections, one each for Episcopalians, Baptists, Methodists and Catholics, which were all the denominations in Scotland Neck. There were a few Jewish people in town, but I never knew where they would be buried. All I knew about them was that they didn't believe Jesus was Jesus, so I reckoned they couldn't go to heaven. Maybe they just died and went right to hell, without being buried at all.

As we passed the entrance road to the Scout Pond, neither of us said a word, but just knowingly looked at each other and quickened our pace.

Approaching the cemetery, I could see the small, brick Episcopal meeting house. It was surrounded by graves and stood amid bushy pines, large magnolia trees with lovely white blooms and several green holly trees dotted with colorful red berries. Its architecture was early American with old-fashioned attractiveness. As I admired the structure and its picturesque setting, I thought to myself, "This is one of the reasons I like to come to the cemetery."

Each Christmas, my Sunday school class would collect huge pine cones that had fallen from these trees. We would paint some of them red and green, leaving a few their natural brown, and decorate the meeting house.

When Scotland Neck was settled by the Scottish people, most of them were of the Episcopal faith. They built the meeting house as their original parish, and it served them many years, until the larger church had been built closer in town. For as long as I could remember, it was used only on special occasions, like weddings and at Christmastime. It was well maintained by the ladies' auxiliary of the new church.

Daddy often took me through the entire cemetery. We would spend most of our time in the Episcopal section, looking at the graves and tombstones. Many of them bore the same last name as ours. We would pause at one or another, and he would tell me a story about our ancestors.

My very favorite grave was the one which had my exact name on it. Daddy said that my forefather had been one of the founders of Scotland Neck. He was the town surveyor and did the planning for the main part of town when the several small communities were united. I knew George Washington had also been a surveyor, and I always felt very proud when Daddy told me that story.

On occasion, I would go to the cemetery by myself. I would imagine that someday I might do something special for the town, so that years later, when people looked at my tombstone, they would think that I had been an important person. Somehow, owning the pool hall didn't quite fit this idea.

If the war went on long enough, Wormy and I planned to join the service together and go overseas and kill lots of Nazis and return home as heroes. If that happened, I could be important and still buy the pool hall. Then they could put on my tombstone that I was a war hero and not mention the pool hall.

We left the highway and walked down to the pond. Wormy made a couple of quacking sounds and the ducks paddled themselves over to our side. I gave him half the bread and the happy little ducks waddled over and took the small chunks right out of our hands.

"I s'pose you gonna say these dern ducks got brains too, Johnnie. Sometimes you really say dumb things."

"If they didn't have brains, how would they know to swim over here? They knew they had a chance to get

The Cemetery

some food. Something inside them told them that, and since they shore don't have no radio in their heads, it must be brains."

"Shucks," he said, "les go up in the yard. I see they done dug a grave hole for somebody. Les go look down in it."

We walked on up the hill, past the meeting house and over to the freshly-dug grave. Off in the distance we could see Charlie Diggins packing his tools on the back of his horse-drawn wagon. Charlie was a tall, burly colored man who dug all the graves and generally took care of the cemetery. He never had much to say to anybody, just went about his work.

Daddy said he was shiftless and no account, and the only reason they hired him was his name. I think he felt that way because Charlie had Daddy drive him over to Palmyra one time; when they got there, Charlie didn't have the money to pay him. He just promised Daddy he would dig Daddy's grave for free, anytime he wanted him to.

Generally, Daddy didn't say many bad things about anybody in town, and I knew most everybody liked him. I remembered just how good the townfolks had been to Momma and me the last time Daddy was in the hospital. Many of them visited and brought us food. Even a lot of Daddy's colored friends came by to see if they could do anything for us.

We wandered on over to the grave and climbed up on the pile of dirt that Charlie had neatly placed beside the hole. We sat there, just looking down in the hole and, every now and again, tossing in a pebble or a small clod of dirt.

"Johnnie, what you s'pose happens to a body when it's put in that box and down in this here hole?"

"I don't rightly know what happens to the body itself, but I do know that the spirit leaves the body and goes to heaven or hell, depending on whether you've been good or bad."

As we spoke, the sun moved slightly westward, casting long cooling shadows across us, offering some relief from the afternoon heat.

"I don't like talkin' 'bout no spirits. My granmomma use to say if you was in the cemetery at night, you jist might see some spirits flyin' all 'round, and they jist might put you right in a grave in their place. Then they could be free to fly all over the whole world."

"There ain't no truth in that," I replied. "I been here the last coupla Christmas Eves, and I ain't never seen one spirit. Anyway, the Bible says we will only see spirits when Jesus comes back, and we're suppose to look forward to that."

"I shore would like to meet that Jesus. But I ain't so shore 'bout meetin' no spirits. You shore do believe in that Bible stuff, don't you?"

"Sure I do. I want to be a good person and when I die, I want to go to heaven and be with Jesus forever and ever. That's what it teaches. And we just might get to see God, if we're good enough."

"How 'bout that devil? Does it say we'll see him?"

"Course not, 'less you're real bad. And if you're bad and steal and tell lies and everything, you might just see him and then you won't like it one bit. Why do you think I told Momma and the sheriff almost the whole truth 'bout the Scout Pond?"

"Yeah, but I heard you tell lies befo'. You think yer gonna go to hell fer 'um?"

"Well, I think everybody tells little lies sometimes. Everybody but Jesus, anyway. He never did tell one lie in His whole life."

"If what you say is fer real, I shore am in a lotta trouble," he said with a look of trepidation on his face.

"How 'bout them brains you is always talkin' 'bout? Does the Bible say what happens to them?"

"I don't know for sure. But I think the brains and the spirit are somehow tied together. So when the spirit leaves a body, the brain just naturally goes along with it."

"Now how can that be?" Wormy asked with a puzzled expression on his face. "Yo brains s'pose to be in yo head—and I s'pose you don't know just where that dern spirit hangs out. Shoot, Johnnie, I ain't never gonna talk 'bout brains with you again."

We just sat there awhile, tossing stones and pondering the reality of our discussion.

In a few minutes, we heard the high pitch of the train whistle from the station in Scotland Neck. That was to let everybody in town know the train was leaving for Rich Square, filled with peanuts, cotton or whatever.

Rich Square was about 10 miles north of Scotland Neck. It was the central shipping point for produce grown in all the farming communities nearby. The produce was taken to Rich Square and from there, shipped to its ultimate destination, depending on the crop. Much of it was sent to larger cities in North Carolina, and some went on up north.

Excitedly, Wormy jumped up and said, "Les jump the train and ride to Rich Square. Then we can catch the fertilizer train that comes back this afternoon."

Even though we had taken that round trip excursion several times before, with Momma and Daddy out of town I was a little reluctant to do it that day.

"Whatcha scared of, Johnnie? We done it befo' and always got back all right."

It did sound appealing and would help break the monotony of the afternoon.

"Okay, but we gotta get the first train back from Rich Square 'cause I promised Aunt Bessie I'd be home at supper time. Uncle Jimmie gets real mad if he's kept waiting."

"Ain't no need to worry. Besides, I might jist git to see Mary Beth over in Rich Square."

Mary Beth was Wormy's sort-of girlfriend. Actually, she was some relative, but since she lived in Rich Square, and he didn't see her often, he called her his girlfriend.

All the fertilizer for Scotland Neck's farmers came from Rich Square, and trains continually ran back and forth. So it seemed like a safe and exciting way to fill the rest of the afternoon.

The railroad tracks ran smack dab through the middle of the cemetery. The Episcopalians and Catholics were on one side of the tracks; the Baptists and Methodists were on the other side.

I followed Wormy from the dirt pile, as we headed over to the tracks. We would generally hide behind a large tombstone until the engine had passed, then run out and pull ourselves up on one of the rear cars. The cemetery was so close to town that the train wouldn't have gained much speed by the time it reached our location. Daddy always said trains shouldn't go fast through our cemetery anyway, since it was sacred ground.

We tucked ourselves down behind a large stone with the name Staton on it, feeling sure we wouldn't be seen by the engineers. We heard the second toot of the whistle and knew it meant the train was rounding the bend that took it beyond the town limits. It would be arriving in our area in just a few minutes.

Staring at the tombstone, Wormy said, "Who you s'pose is buried in this here grave?"

"Somebody named Harvey Staton," I answered. "Why?"

"I jist don't like standin' on top of a grave. S'pose Harvey's spirit is leaving the grave and goin' to heaven and we git in the way? What you s'pose would happen to us?"

"Wormy, this Staton was buried in 1842. I'm sure his

spirit has gone wherever it's going by now. Just stay crouched down till the engine gets past us."

That day, we were in luck. The train was filled with cotton, which meant a soft, comfortable ride to Rich Square.

We peered around the stone and caught a quick glimpse of two men in the cab of the engine. They were busy with their work and never noticed us. There were eight open-top cars being pulled by the engine. The sides of the cars consisted of heavy wire with gates, so the cargo could be unloaded.

We waited until the last car had gotten about even with us and then hurried around behind it. By grabbing the back rail slat, mounting was no problem. We climbed over the top rail and allowed our bodies to fall down into the large, white cushion of soft, fluffy cotton.

It was early afternoon so we figured we'd have plenty of time to catch one of the returning trains. After our trip back, we would have to take a quick dip in the duck pond. A ride on a fertilizer train always left telltale smells on a body. I sure didn't want to sit down at the supper table smelling like manure.

One final glance back at the tranquility of the cemetery gave me pause to remember what Daddy had said about it.

"Johnnie," he had said, "everybody who ever passed through Scotland Neck and saw this place always wanted to die here, just so they could be buried in our cemetery."

Wormy had a broad smile on his face as he said, "Ain't this better'n sittin' 'round all them dead folks?"

Gradually, the train picked up a little speed and we just lay on our backs looking up at the cloudless blue sky. There even seemed to be a delicious crispness in the air.

Train Ride

e~ Chapter 7 e~

*T*he cooling breeze and the rhythmic clickity clack
on the rails were almost enough to make us nod off.
There was no need to do that as we would be in Rich
Square shortly, and we'd start seeking our return pas-
sage. Of course, we figured we might have to make a
slight detour to Mary Beth's house so Wormy could
make a complete fool of himself, as he usually did when
he saw her.

As the train approached the large bridge high above
the violent rapids of the Roanoke River, we crawled over
to the side of the car to try and catch a glimpse of Tazwell
Judson and Shoofly down by their ramshackle work-
place. Sure enough, they were sitting on wooden benches
outside the shack, probably spinning some far-fetched
stories to each other. From our viewpoint, we saw a
maze of contraptions, secretly located out behind the
shack. We knew that was where they blended the special
ingredients for their famous bootleg whiskey. They were
well concealed from the road, but everybody in town,
and maybe the whole state, knew they were there—and
really didn't seem to mind at all. However, our preacher
often referred to the shop as a "den of iniquity." I wasn't
exactly sure what that meant, but suspected he didn't
care for it too much.

Taz had served in World War I with my daddy. Other

than moonshine, all he ever talked about was his exploits in France and how he had "almost" been cited for bravery. Daddy had been an ambulance driver. While he observed a lot of fighting, it had been from behind the steering wheel of the ambulance. He always felt he had been cheated out of his chance to be a war hero. He said he wanted a gun, not an ambulance. But he had come home safe and healthy, and that was all that mattered to me. Anyway, I planned to be a hero for our family.

After crossing the bridge, we had only about a 15-minute ride before we reached Rich Square.

But at that moment, something unusual happened. Instead of maintaining its normal speed, the train accelerated. And rather than following its usual route to Rich Square, it was diverted over to another set of tracks, which would take us north of Rich Square.

That had never happened before, and we didn't know what to think. Headed in its new direction, the train picked up so much speed, we couldn't safely jump off. I judged that we were traveling about 40 miles an hour. I knew if only we could get off, we could walk back down the tracks and make it home in plenty of time.

But no! The train continued on towards some new and unknown destination. I could tell we were still gaining speed.

"What's goin' on?" Wormy shouted above the noise. The gentle breeze had gradually become a noisy wind and the wheels were clacking louder than ever.

"Derned if I know. But I sure know we ain't headed towards Rich Square," I ruefully replied.

"Yeah, and if we jump off this train we'll be killed and end up back in that cemetery as spirits ourselves. I'm gonna start using my brain right now and figer out what to do," he added with a breezy frankness.

We were beginning to feel very uncomfortable. After a good 30 minutes on the new route, I said, "Wormy, you and your dern 'excitin'' ideas. Here we are, headed to God-knows-where, when everything was fine right back there in the cemetery."

"Ain't my fault, I didn't exactly pull you up on the train. Anyway, all we gotta do is ride this baby out and then find some train that takes us back to Rich Square. That's what I call usin' yo brain, Johnnie."

That sounded fine but the miles and the time kept taking us further and further away from both Rich Square and home.

Once, when rounding a sharp bend, we slowed to around 20 miles-an-hour and we both gave some consideration to jumping off.

"I ain't jumpin' off here, not knowin' where we is," Wormy firmly stated. "Besides, you know there's hoboes livin' all along the train tracks. I heard tales of 'um killin' little boys and eatin' 'um cause they ain't got no real food. Course, I always heard they only eat white boys 'cause they don't like no dark meat. So maybe we better git off here," he said, with that broad grin creasing his face again. He was real pleased with his remarks.

"Wormy, that ain't funny. Sometimes you're 'bout as subtle as a pig squealing for supper."

I pondered his idea and knew it couldn't be true. But I'd also heard tales of hoboes. We both decided our best chance was to ride on into some town where there would be other trains.

We'd been traveling over an hour before I really began to worry. "Suppose," I thought, "this train is headed for New York City. Suppose it don't stop all night. How am I going to let Aunt Bessie know I'm safe?" I knew what would happen if I didn't show up for supper. She would immediately call the sheriff and have him look for me. I sure didn't want another encounter with him. I felt it was only good luck, and his liking Daddy so much, that had kept me from being behind bars right then.

I guessed it must have been something past 3 p.m. If only the train stopped pretty soon, we could still get home on time. That was only wishful thinking as the train kept chugging along in its northward direction.

"Clickity clack! Clickity clack! Won't this fool thing ever stop movin'?" Wormy said, breaking our worrisome silence.

Just about that time, after what I considered about two hours of traveling, the engineer tooted the whistle and the train began slowing down.

"Thank Gawd, we is finally here," Wormy said.

"Yeah," I said, "but where is *here?*"

We crawled to the front of the car and searched around, looking for something familiar. Up ahead was a much larger train yard than Rich Square's. The closer we got, the larger it became. All we could see were trains and tracks and more trains, all going and coming in different directions. We had never seen so many trains in our lives.

Nervously, I said, "Where in the world are we?"

The answer came abruptly as we neared a large underpass with the words "WELCOME TO NORFOLK, THE GATEWAY TO VIRGINIA" boldly painted across its side.

"Wormy!" I yelled. "We ain't even in North Carolina; we're in Norfolk, Virginia!"

"I kin read and I know where we are. What I don't know is, how we gonna git home. But garden peas, Johnnie, I ain't never been to Virginia! Wait till I tell my fambly 'bout this."

"Just so my family don't find out. If they do, I think I'd rather be with the hoboes."

By then, the train had slowed enough for us to consider jumping off; but we couldn't decide what to do. There must have been a thousand trains around. We didn't know which one was going where. I began to tremble from fear and confusion.

Wormy said, "We'd better git off befo' it stops, 'cause we're shore to be seen if we git off right near the station."

I agreed. So we climbed over the railing, down the side of the car, and jumped off between another set of vacant tracks. With all those trains whizzing by, we didn't feel very safe. We decided to get out of the track area as quickly as possible.

It appeared we were still on the outskirts of the yard. We headed toward a wooded area to the left of the tracks. As we jumped and ran, helter-skelter, across the tracks dodging trains, we heard several engineers shouting at us. Our hearts were going as fast as our legs. We were greatly relieved to get off the tracks and over to the woods.

"Now," I thought, "we can get out of the yard without being caught."

But as soon as we started through the woods, we found the entire yard was enclosed by a tall chain-link fence with spiked barbed-wire at the top. We reasoned the barbed-wire had been placed there to keep out any Nazi spies who may try to get in the yard and blow up the trains.

We followed the fence, hoping it would lead us to a gate and freedom. "But to go where?" I wondered.

Up ahead was a clearing with a wooden shed situated right in the middle. When we got to within 50 yards of the shed, two of the most ferocious-looking dogs I had ever seen, spied us. They instantly started barking and relentlessly running towards us.

"Holy Moly!" (which was what Billy Batson often said), I shouted, and we both grabbed hold of the fence and pulled ourselves up to avoid the on-rushing dogs.

Right behind the dogs were two soldiers with their rifles leveled at us. They were shouting for us to get down off the fence

My pulse quickened and we were scared stiff by the

savage barks and snarls of the dogs. We clung to our positions of temporary safety until the soldiers were right down behind us.

"What are you two boys doing in this yard?" one of them angrily yelled. "How the hell did you get in here anyway? Don't you know this is U.S. government property, and you are trespassing?"

"No, sir," I replied breathlessly, still riveted to the fence, with my fingers and toes yelling to me in pain. I hurriedly added, "We didn't know we were trespassing. We were just riding a train to Rich Square and going to ride another one back to Scotland Neck so's we could be home for supper. The train didn't stop in Rich Square and here we are in Norfolk. Please, sir, call them dogs back so we can get off this fence. My hands and feet are hurting an awful lot."

The second soldier spoke sharply to the dogs and they turned away. We both dropped mercifully to the ground, panting and sweating and hurting, all at the same time. We felt relieved, but still scared. It dawned on me that lately we'd been scared a lot.

The first soldier demanded, "Where the hell are Rich Square and Scotland Neck? I've never heard of either of them."

It was apparent he was a Northerner. His speech indicated it, and I couldn't imagine anyone not knowing where Rich Square and Scotland Neck were.

"Them's towns in North Carolina, General," Wormy replied, apparently attempting to impress the soldiers with his military knowledge.

The Northerner's face flashed with anger as he said, "We are not generals, and you are not supposed to be here. We are going to have to take you to the sergeant and find out what to do with you."

"You could jist put us back on a train headin' fer Rich Square," Wormy fantasized.

My real fear was they'd mistake us for Nazi spies and put us in a military prison. I'd seen that very thing happen in a recent war movie.

The soldiers had lowered their guns, but the Yankee, still with rancor in his voice, announced that we should come with them. We marched past the shed where the two dogs obediently stood and headed towards what appeared to be the central part of the yard.

Looming ahead was a dreary, two-story brick building, much of it blackened by all the smoke from the trains. It, also, was enclosed with barbed-wire. There was another guard at the gate. He allowed us to pass, remarking to our captors, "Caught you a couple of spies, I see," followed by a chuckle. We didn't feel like laughing.

There we were, in another state, miles from home and supper time only a couple of hours away. Even Aunt Bessie was going to have trouble being nice to me when, and if, we got back home. I feared that the army might even treat us like prisoners-of-war, and put us to work on a farm, especially if the Yankee had anything to say about it.

We walked through a main office filled with soldiers and civilians. They all seemed to be doing their jobs, running the train yard and keeping all the trains from bumping into each other. We went to the back of the office and up one flight of steps and entered a small room.

At the back of the room was a tan, wooden desk with a huge, angry-looking soldier sitting behind a gigantic stack of papers. He looked like an overweight football player, with the buttons bulging open on the front of his coffee-stained, brown army shirt. The shirt was open at the collar, exposing a massive amount of black hair on his chest. He had rough-hewn features and weathered skin. His sea-green eyes looked impassively up from his papers and he barked at the Yankee, "What y'all got here, Private Vincent P. Smythe?"

I felt immediate relief as he spoke. He sounded just like we did. I figured he certainly must know where Rich Square and Scotland Neck were. Surely he would believe our story.

"Sergeant, we found these two trying to climb the fence to get out of the yard. What do we do with them?" Vincent P. Smythe asked.

Looking at us, the sergeant's face softened, and in a gravelly voice, he said, "Well, boys, tell me your story. It's for sure you ain't no spies trying to steal none of our trains." With that, he let out a thunderous laugh that rattled his desk, causing a few of the papers to flutter to the floor. Vincent P. Smythe politely retrieved the papers and placed them neatly back on the desk.

Before we had a chance to reply, Private Smythe said, in his sneering way, "They claim to be from somewhere called Scotland Neck, and just hitched a ride on a train headed for some place called Rich Square. They, somehow, mysteriously ended up here. You certainly don't believe a cock-and-bull story like that, do you, Sergeant? Just from my observation, I believe they are troublemakers."

The sergeant's bullet-like eyes strafed the room and landed on Smythe. He said, "Private Smythe, that comment was absolutely profound, for a Yankee."

Then, facing us, his loud voice spewed out, "Scotland Neck! You two squirts from North Carolina? You know Shoofly Smith? Is he still peddling that God-awful stuff he calls whiskey?"

"Yes, sir," I replied. "We're both from Scotland Neck and Mr. Shoofly is one of my daddy's best friends, and my daddy was in the army, too, and he is sick right now and in the veteran's hospital and we both need to get back to Scotland Neck real soon or we'll be in a heap of trouble." Perhaps plying his sympathy, all that gushed out before I had time to think.

"Well, listen to me, boys. I just happen to be born in Hobgood. Every time I pass through your town, I make a little stop down by the river to replenish my supply. Know what I mean?" He raised his eyebrows and let out another guffaw, causing a few more papers to flutter.

He looked up at the two soldiers and bellowed, "You two git back to your post and I'll call you if I need you again. And another thing, who's watching your post? Anytime in the future you capture such dangerous criminals, I believe just one of you needs to bring them in. You understand that, Private Vincent P. Smythe?"

To our satisfaction, Private Smythe showed utter embarrassment, as they both turned and promptly left the room.

"Damn Yankee," the sergeant muttered to himself.

"Now, boys, you slow down a bit and tell me just how you got here and what your problem is. Ole Sarge Sanders would never let a coupla fellow Tarheels down who was in any trouble."

That time, much more slowly, I began to narrate every event, from the cemetery departure until that very moment. Wormy interrupted occasionally, adding his certain comments.

"And the problem is, Sergeant, if my Aunt Bessie hasn't heard from me by 6 o'clock, she'll be worried and me and Wormy will surely be in trouble."

"Look here, boys, I been in just such messes most of my life, so I'm gonna do everything I can to help you."

He picked up his phone and dialed one digit. And in that same magnificent, authoritative voice, he yelled in the phone, "Corporal, git in here, right now!"

No sooner was the phone back on the hook than a door to his left opened, and a tall, neat-appearing soldier very curtly made his entrance.

"Corporal, I got two ole friends here who is in a little trouble, and you're gonna help 'um out."

Swinging his stomach to the side, he pulled open his top desk drawer and took out a road map, flattening it out on his desk.

"Now look at this, Corporal. You are here, right in Norfolk," he said as he jabbed a large finger down on the map. "You do know that, don't you, Corporal?" he stated, not waiting for a reply. "Now you see here," as he pointed to another spot, "this here is Scotland Neck, in the great state of North Carolina. I figure it's maybe two, two and a half hours away. I want you to secure a jeep, one of them with a flashing light on the hood. And I want you to have these boys in Scotland Neck by no later than 6 p.m., sharp!"

"Aw, Sarge," the corporal moaned, "you know I've got a pass tonight. You signed it yourself. I've got a date."

The sergeant raised his eyes from the map, casting a scowl towards the soldier, but didn't utter a word.

The corporal, almost inaudibly said, "Yes, sir, I'll get them there. But what about some paper work in case I'm questioned?"

"Anybody bothers you, you just tell 'um you're on a secret war mission for Sarge Sanders, and that these boys are part of your cover. Any questions, you tell 'um to call me."

Instantly, I felt that I wanted to hug this giant man. But for reasons beyond my control, I reached out, shook his hand, took one step back and saluted him, as best I knew how.

Wormy immediately threw his hand up to his forehead and said, "Now I know how we is winnin' the war, wif men like you in charge."

"Boys, you just tell Shoofly he owes me a big one the next time I come by. Hope your daddy's okay, son. Now, you two git."

As we walked out the door, the thought occurred to me that with him being from Hobgood and being the important soldier that he was, he was more purely American than anyone I had ever met.

The ride from Norfolk to Scotland Neck was an experience I have never forgotten. The corporal had the big yellow light flashing during the whole trip. Anytime he anticipated trouble, he turned the siren on, too.

Amazingly enough, we arrived at the corner of Main Street and Eighth about four minutes past six. I knew that because the town clock was just sounding 6 o'clock, and everybody knew it was always four minutes slow.

"Just let us out here, sir; we can walk the rest of the way. And we certainly do appreciate it, sir, and are really sorry about messing up your date."

He didn't bother to reply. He just made a U-turn and headed back towards Norfolk.

Chapter 8

As I walked in the kitchen, Aunt Bessie said, "Johnnie, I was getting a mite worried about you. You know it's almost 6:15? Where you been so long?"

The entire afternoon was almost a blur to me, but I explained. "Yes, ma'am, I just lost track of time. First I went to the Sinclair Station and they didn't need no help. Then I did like you said, Aunt Bessie. I went by my house and played with Poochie and asked Mrs. Whitehead if I could help with anything. After that, Wormy and I walked down to the cemetery and fed the ducks and started watching the trains. That's when I lost track of time. You know, Aunt Bessie, you can really get caught up with them trains and all." I knew there was a smattering of truth in what I had said.

Then I made a hasty retreat, saying I was sorry about being late and would wash up, as I rushed away to the bathroom.

When I said the blessing at supper, I added a secret thank you to God for Sarge Sanders.

Aunt Bessie said Momma had called and they were going to keep Daddy for a few days. Momma was taking the 2 p.m. Trailways the next day, arriving back in town in the early evening.

"Did she say if they found out what was wrong with Daddy?"

Aunt Bessie paused a moment before answering, and then said, "No, she only talked long enough to tell me her plans, and say you should meet her at the bus station tomorrow evening."

I felt she was withholding something from me, because I couldn't imagine Momma not mentioning Daddy's condition. But I figured if she was supposed to tell me something, she would, so I didn't ask any more questions.

After supper, Aunt Bessie and Uncle Jimmie went to sit on the front porch, while the girls and I cleaned up the kitchen.

Ruby asked, "What kinda trouble you and Wormy been in?"

Crossing my fingers behind me, I said, "None at all. I promised Momma and Daddy I'd behave myself while they were gone."

"Yeah, you may stay outta trouble when you ain't with that Wormy. But whenever you two get together, there's some kinda tomfoolery going on. I'd bet a penny on that."

"That's not so, Ruby. Wormy and I play together a lot, but we try and stay outta trouble. You notice I ain't saying nothing to your momma 'bout you and Harry Lee Smith."

"You just hush up," she said, sashaying out of the kitchen. She had a liking for Harry Lee, which I couldn't understand for the life of me. It always got her goat when I mentioned him.

The rest of the evening looked to be rather quiet. The girls and I sat on the front porch, wishing a new picture show was playing at the Dixie.

In no time, I was painfully bored. I finally asked Aunt Bessie if it was all right to walk down to the Sinclair and check on the Hudson. They had worked on it that day, and I knew Momma would want to know when she got back if it was fixed.

"Just so you're back by dark. You know you gotta take a bath tonight."

I told her I'd enjoyed my supper and then headed down Main Street, praying all the while that the car would be running good as new.

Just as I reached Hamilton's Drug Store, out walked Tilly Hancock. His real name was Tillford, but he hated it with his whole heart. Since he also hated Tilly, he asked to be called just plain 'T.H.'. He was my age, tall, skinny and redheaded, with hair as straight as a stick. He used pomade to keep it in place, because without it, his cowlick stuck straight out like a bantam rooster's tail. That night it was all shiny and slicked down.

Tilly had the misfortune of having his right eye shot out when he was only seven years old. It seems he had gotten a brand new gun for Christmas. He was proud as a possum of that gun, always cleaning and polishing it. He wouldn't let anybody else even touch it. But his momma made him let his brother, James, try it out. That angered Tilly to no end. So the first time James went to shoot the gun, Tilly, in a mad rage, grabbed it out of his brother's hand. The rifle accidentally went off at close-range and a B.B. hit Tilly directly in the right eye. Everybody in Scotland Neck knew about the tragedy. Tilly had to wear a patch over that eye and became quite self-conscious about it, until Orton Calhoun returned as a war hero, wearing a patch over his eye, too. That made Tilly feel somewhat more comfortable. In a strange sort of way, Tilly had made that accident pay off for him.

After Tilly wore the patch over that eye for a couple of years, his parents took him to Raleigh and had a glass eye made for him. When he got that glass eye, everybody said it gave him a lot more self-confidence, and even helped his personality.

Anyway, everybody was fascinated with the glass eye and wanted to get a good look at it whenever they could. That really made Tilly feel important.

And if that weren't enough, after getting used to wearing it, Tilly got so he could take his finger and just pop the glass eye out, right in his hand. That feat astonished everybody even more. Pretty soon, anybody who really wanted to see him pop it out started calling him T.H. That pleased him to no end, so he would usually accommodate them.

Tilly and his glass eye became such an attraction in town, he started charging a nickel just to watch him in action. He'd also let you look right into the bald socket, if you were a friend. But most folks didn't want to do that.

"Hey, T.H.," I said, "do you mind taking out your eye for me?"

"Cost ya a nickel," he replied.

I dug down in my pocket and pulled out one of the two coins remaining from last payday.

"Here you go, T.H.," I said, handing him the nickel.

He quickly pocketed the money, took his right index finger, and in a flash, popped the eye out and into his left hand.

As always, I was amazed. He even let me look right in the socket and all I could see were red veins and stuff. It didn't look too scary to me. But then, I'd seen it before.

It reminded me of a picture show called *The Return of The Invisible Man*. Daddy always said the first show, which was just called *The Invisible Man* was much better. But I hadn't seen that one, yet.

In the show, as the man was becoming invisible (which is where I got my idea), his skin gradually disappeared, until you started to see his veins—and then—you didn't see anything at all!

Well, anyway, looking into Tilly's eye socket made me think of those veins in that invisible man.

"T.H.," I asked, "would you please let me hold your glass eye, or just touch it?"

"Cost ya another nickel, Johnnie. You know, if I ever break this thing, my momma and daddy would execute me to death. Or even worse, I'd have to start wearing that ugly patch again."

I gave the matter some serious consideration and decided the 10 cents I had left over had to last me almost a week.

"Naw. Guess I'll have to wait till next payday," I said.

"Okay," he replied. And in just a moment, he spit on the eye, rubbed it between his fingers, popped it back in the socket and said, "See you later, Johnnie."

In some ways, I sort of envied Tilly. But I was glad I had both my eyes.

I wandered on down Main Street. Since most of the cars were parked out in the middle, the road was divided with a lane for traffic on each side. That unusual feature was often remembered by strangers who passed through our town. Years later, whenever I told people I was from Scotland Neck, those who had passed through would say, "Oh, yes, that's the town with the beautiful crepe myrtles and the cars parked in the middle of the street." I was always proud of that. Both of those unique landmarks gave our town its own distinctive flavor.

At that time of year, the crepe myrtles were breathtaking. Their rosy-pink buds peeked out of a background of dark green foliage. Crossing the street, I passed between the cars in the middle. It was twilight, and I glimpsed the setting sun scattering its waning light on the lovely bushes further on down the street. It gave me a warm, comfortable feeling.

Even with all my current problems, I realized how fortunate I was to live in a town that was both beautiful and fun. I knew if I ever left, it would only be to join the service.

Columbus Jones was just turning on the outdoor lights as I walked in the station. Slim was tucked under the hood of the Hudson, busily working on the engine.

"How's it goin', Mr. Columbus? Y'all been able to get the car running yet?"

"Well, Johnnie, we been tinkering with that ornery engine all gosh-darn day. But we can't get the electrical system dried out enough to get the engine to turn over."

Looking at all the complicated parts, I wondered just how an engine could turn over. Seemed to me it should work right-side-up. But I didn't want to ask any dumb questions.

"Can I help?" I asked.

"No, thanks, Johnnie. I think we're gonna lock her up in the stall tonight, leaving the hood and doors open so as to let it dry out some more. We'll give her another shot tomorrow. Heard anything about your daddy?"

"Only that they started some tests. Momma's coming home tomorrow evening on the Trailways. Then she'll tell me everything. I'm trying not to worry too much 'cause Aunt Bessie says it never helps to worry anyway. But I do wish I could help you fix the Hudson. I feel sorta useless, and I caused a big part of this mess."

"Johnnie, in my years, I done a lot worse things than this, and I don't worry 'bout nothin'. Bessie is right. You run along back to her house now, 'cause it's almost dark."

"Night, Mr. Columbus and Mr. Slim. Wormy and I'll stop by in the morning and see if you need us. I sure would like to have the car fixed by the time Momma gets home."

"Night, Johnnie. Tell Bessie and Jimmie and the girls 'hey' for us."

I started skipping on back down Main Street. When I passed the barber shop, I felt a need to take a peek in the back. I knew there was some big-time pool-shooting going on inside. There were a couple of out-of-town cars parked in front. It seemed that people would come to Scotland Neck just to play pool and go to the Scout Pond. I also remembered some others wanted to be buried there.

I thought back over the day, with our train and jeep rides, and I felt quite exhausted. I dreaded the bath I had to take and was ready to go right to bed.

My ever-caring aunt was standing on the front porch with her hands on her hips. "Lordy, honey, I was just about to send Jewel Star out to fetch you. Your momma would have a fit if you weren't here by dark. Come on in, I already got your bath water run."

Jewel Star was the older of my two cousins, who still lived at home. She was my favorite. Ruby was always nagging at me for something. It was Jewel who would tuck me in at night when I stayed with them. She'd tell me a ghost story or read from the Bible. She knew all my favorite stories from the Old Testament, mostly about Moses and David or Sampson, always picking one filled with adventures. After the story, she'd tell me how it related to my life.

After a quick bath, I headed for the back room where she'd prepared a pallet on the floor for me. Jewel brought me a small bowl of banana pudding and we sat on her bed, talking about Momma and Daddy and wondering what would happen.

Pretty soon, I crawled into my makeshift bed and lay there, staring at a naked light bulb and listening to how David had killed the terrible giant warrior with only a stone and a slingshot. The last thing I remembered was Goliath being hit squarely in the forehead and falling over dead.

Chapter 9

I must not have moved all night since I woke up in the exact position in which I'd gone to sleep. Parts of the room were bathed in the bright morning sunlight which was peeping around the edges of the tattered window shades, casting its warm glow across my face. I flinched slightly, still experiencing visions of David facing his menacing foe.

The girls were up and out of the room. The pleasing smells of breakfast gave me cause to jump up and stow my pallet. I hoped they had finished in the bathroom. On occasion, when I had waited so long for the bathroom, I sneaked out the back window and relieved myself behind one of the large trees in the backyard. Fortunately, it was free that morning. As I washed and brushed, I thought of Momma and how she was probably getting ready to leave Fayetteville. I had generally narrowed my worries down to Daddy's condition and getting the Hudson running.

Even though Momma had been gone only two days and I enjoyed spending time at Aunt Bessie's with Jewel and the pallet and all, I yearned to be back home with Momma and Poochie. I wondered if Mrs. Whitehead had remembered to feed him that morning, since she had two cats of her own to take care of. Right after breakfast, I thought, Wormy and I had better take a run around there and check on him.

After a meal of pancakes, eggs, ham and biscuits, I asked my aunt if I could go around and see Poochie.

"That'ad be a good idea, honey. You and Wormy have a good time today and be back here by dinner. You gotta get dressed up real pretty so's you'll look fittin' when you meet your momma."

Aunt Bessie never told me not to play with Wormy. She knew he was my best friend, and so long as we didn't get into any mischief, she even seemed to approve of our relationship.

"Funny," I thought, "how some white folks feel one way about Negroes and some feel another."

That morning I arrived at the shop before Wormy, so I went in to chat with Mr. Allsbrook.

The heat from the coals hung heavy and sweat poured off his forehead. It caused one sizzle after another as it dripped down on the edge of the large, round metal pit over which he labored. He wore a long-sleeve shirt, and a heavy, brown leather vest that covered the front of his body, hanging almost to his knees. He said the vest had belonged to his daddy, who had been the first blacksmith ever in Scotland Neck. It looked like it could be a hundred or a thousand years old, and was specked and etched from the small hot cinders that bounced off the sandals as he pounded them into shape. I always marveled at just how he could wear all that clothing, work over hot coals and still endure the stifling summer heat.

"Morning, Mr. Allsbrook, how's it going today?"

He slid the goggles off his eyes, set down his tools and said, "Hey, Johnnie. Right glad you're here. I need a little break. Set fer a minute and let me git a drink of water, and you can tell me about your daddy."

He walked over to a large water can, filled a cup with fresh water and momentarily turned his back on me. I knew he was adding something extra to the water, because I saw him slip a brown bag out from under his vest. I guessed that was how he endured the heat. He pulled an old sawhorse over next to me and said, "Okay, what've you heard from your momma?"

Before I had time to answer, we heard the jarring sound of Clint Hilyard's wagon rolling up in the yard. Clint was the iceman in Scotland Neck. Not everyone in town had electric refrigerators. Many still used heavy, thick wooden iceboxes. Mr. Hilyard made daily deliveries of large chucks of ice to all his customers. Mr. Allsbrook sat his drink down and we walked out to meet Mr. Hilyard. The horse-drawn wagon was filled with blocks of ice which were covered with a thick canvas mat to keep the ice cold as long as possible. He made his deliveries early in the morning, before it got too hot. Whenever Wormy and I were around, Mr. Hilyard gave us the small chips that were splintered off as he picked up the ice blocks with his metal tongs. When watermelons were in season, Mr. Hilyard also carried fresh melons, tucked between the ice. After he finished his regular deliveries, he would ride through town, ringing a bell and yelling, "Ice cold watermelons, yes, siree! Ice cold watermelons—but they ain't fer free." Everybody liked Mr. Hilyard a lot and was usually able to talk him down to a nickel or a dime, at the most, for his ice cold watermelons.

"Morning, Marmaduke and Johnnie. Gonna be a scorcher today," he said. He proceeded to put half a chunk of ice in the can in Mr. Allsbrook's shop and then took two full blocks up to the house where Mrs. Allsbrook opened the door for him.

Climbing back up on his wagon, he said, "Johnnie, how's your daddy doin'?"

"Pretty good, Mr. Hilyard. Momma's coming home today, and we'll know something more."

He flicked the reins and said, "Giddy-up, boys, we

got a lotta travelin' to do. Johnnie, tell Gavin I'm savin' my biggest melon fer him when he gits home. Won't cost him a cent," he proudly said as he pulled out of the yard.

Walking back in the shop, it made me feel good that everybody in town asked about how daddy was getting along. Not only was he so special to me, but it seemed that everybody else cared for him too.

We sat back down and I said to Mr. Allsbrook, "Momma's coming in on the Trailways this evening, and I hope she brings some good news."

"Yeah, me too. Me and the rest of the men miss ole Gavin. Jist ain't the same 'round here without him and that taxi."

"Why," I wondered, "did he have to remind me of that?"

"You know, Johnnie, yo daddy and me go back a long way."

He then proceeded to tell me a story he must have told me 50 times before. It was how he and Daddy had gone to school together; and how he, Taz Judson and Daddy had all joined the army together. But Taz and Daddy got sent off to France, and he had to stay right there in Ft. Bragg, North Carolina, making horse shoes for the whole army. During the first world war, many of the troops traveled by horse.

"Seein' Gavin leavin' to go over there and fight them damn Germans, and leavin' me right here in the state— well, it almost killed me. Now, don't misunderstand me none, Johnnie. I was mighty proud to serve my country any way I could. But I always wanted to cross the ocean on one of them big transport ships and see some of the rest of this here big world."

Just then, I heard Wormy's whistle and was saved from the balance of the oft-told story. Wormy wouldn't come in the shop while Mr. Allsbrook was there. I quickly stood up and told him I had to run home and check on Poochie.

He was still talking as I walked out the door.

"Anyway, I know you'll be glad for yo momma to git home. And you tell Rebecca Mae Whitehead to take care of your dog real good. And tell her 'hey' fer me."

I looked back, smiled and thanked him for his concern, as the last drops from his cup dripped off his chin and rolled down his vest.

"What we gonna do today?" was my greeting from Wormy. "It's too golldang hot to do anythin' hard. You wanna go fishin'? I heard the bluefish is bitin' down at the river. Or, we could jist go sit in the shade by the canal and dig us some worms. My supply is gittin' sorta low at home."

"You know Momma is coming home this afternoon. I gotta be back to my aunt's for dinner. Then I gotta get cleaned up so I can meet Momma at the bus station. That leaves only this morning to keep busy."

"Thas you; what I'ma do all afternoon?"

Smiling, I said, "Well, you could hop a train and take a run over to Rich Square and visit your sweetheart."

"That ain't even funny, Johnnie."

"We can talk about our afternoon on the way 'round to my house. I gotta check on Poochie and pick up my school shoes. Aunt Bessie says I outta be dressed up good to meet Momma."

I had almost forgotten what shoes felt like. Except for Sundays and other special occasions, we ran around barefoot, wearing only short pants and hardly ever a shirt. That late in the summer, the bottoms of our feet were as tough as nails. And nothing ever bothered them—except shoes.

"Has your daddy been home much lately?" I asked.

"One day a week is too much fer me. All he does is talk ugly to Momma and beat up on me and them coon dogs, and drink and sleep. Most times, I wish I wouldn't never see him again. The only times he's nice to Momma is when she's done some cookin' or washin' and has some money so's he can take it from her. If there really is a hell, he's gonna slide right down there, head first. And the sooner the better."

I never knew what to say when Wormy talked like that. So, I just kept quiet and heard him out. I knew he had a difficult life and at times was filled with anger.

Sometimes Daddy would let me and Wormy take a ride out in the country in the taxi when he was taking somebody out to a farm. Once, we had gone as far as Rocky Mount and Daddy bought us some frozen custard. Wormy must have talked about that trip and that custard for a month. He had never been on a car trip that far before; he rarely left Scotland Neck. He had no other family in town and his nearest relatives were in Rich Square. We often talked about saving our money and taking the Trailways to Raleigh. We thought that going to our state's capital would be the next best thing to going to Washington, D.C., together.

As we turned the corner at Sunset Avenue, I noticed Sheriff Calhoun's car across the street from our house, parked behind another car. He and some man and Mrs. Whitehead were standing by the cars talking.

As soon as Mrs. Whitehead saw us coming down the street, she quickly started walking in our direction.

"Hey, Mrs. Whitehead. Did the sheriff give that man a ticket for going too fast?"

"No, Johnnie." As she continued, her eyes were noticeably filled with tears. "I'm afraid I have some bad news for you."

"It's not about Daddy, is it?" I asked in alarm.

"No, Johnnie, it's about Poochie. I'm afraid he's been run over by a car. He was chasin' one of our cats, in a playful way, and ran right out into the street...."

I didn't hear another word she said, but started to run towards the cars.

Mrs. Whitehead grabbed me by my arm and said, "Don't go over there, Johnnie. Sheriff Calhoun's gonna take care of everything."

A pitiable fear clutched me as I asked, "Is he dead?"

"Yes, I'm afraid he is," she said with obvious anguish in her voice.

I was stunned. I felt such an enormous pain I couldn't even cry. I'd never lost anything or anyone that I loved before. I felt that my heart had opened and closed in an instant, leaving a gaping hole of sadness that I didn't know how to fill. I also felt a new anger that I'd never before experienced. As I turned away towards the house, a million memories rapidly shot through my mind.

I remembered the first day Daddy had brought him home as a puppy. Daddy had on his long overcoat when he walked in the house and said, "I brought you something, son." I hadn't seen anything in his hands, so I'd wondered if he had left it in the car. About that time, I'd noticed the left pocket of his coat begin to move. A small, shiny black nose peeked out. It was attached to a ball of fur with two tiny specks for eyes and an elfin pink tongue chewing on the edge of the coat pocket. Working his head free, his fleecy ears had popped out and his whole face seemed to smile at me. He'd looked like a wee, white snowball.

Filled with new-found excitement, I'd joyfully shouted, "Daddy! A dog!"

Daddy had lifted the small fur-ball from his pocket and carefully placed it in my excited, shaking hands. I'd felt a rush of happiness as I nuzzled his warm, wiggling body to my face, feeling his little tongue playfully licking my cheek. And I'd thanked and thanked Daddy.

"He ain't no special kind'a dog, Johnnie, just a pooch."

"Well, he's special to me, Daddy. But if he's just a pooch, I think I'll call him Poochie."

I remember he was so tiny that I had to feed him with a baby's bottle the first few weeks. I pictured him during one of the infrequent snows in Scotland Neck, running and chasing and barking, as I tossed small snowballs at him. I could still smell his damp fur as I had gathered him up and taken him in by the stove to dry. I could feel his warm body, nestled up to me in my bed, where he slept for his first year with us.

But most of all, I could see him running down the porch steps to greet my every arrival, tail wagging, and him yipping with the same joy I shared in greeting him.

All those things spun through my mind simultaneously. Suddenly, I couldn't see or feel anything but hurt. For an instant, I thought I might throw up or pass out.

I would never see Poochie again! I wanted to die right along with him. All my other problems seemed insignificant at that moment. The feeling of anger returned.

"Why, God? Why did Poochie have to die? He didn't deserve to die! He shouldn't have been hit by that car! Where were you, God? He never did anything but bring happiness and joy into everyone's life."

Gradually realizing I would never see, touch or play with Poochie again, I began to wonder how long "never" was. I knew it meant for as long as I lived here on earth. But did it also mean in heaven? I had been taught that we would see our loved ones in the hereafter. But I had to die to get there.

"Are dogs in the same heaven as humans? Or is there another heaven for animals?" I wondered.

I felt I wanted to hurt someone. "Maybe," I thought, "I should run across the street and hit the man or his car that killed Poochie."

I was gradually brought back to reality as I felt an arm drape around my shoulders.

"Come on, Johnnie, les go sit on the porch," Wormy said.

I didn't want to stay at that house. I didn't even want to be in Scotland Neck. "I just want Poochie back, Wormy; don't you understand that?"

"Yes, but les git away from here, right now."

Still not crying, but not able to see very well, I sensed the sheriff walking across the street towards the house. As he approached, I felt a desperate need to run and have him hold me while I cried. But whenever I was in his presence I tried to act like a man. So instead, I stood straight and tall and tried to listen to what he had to say.

"Johnnie, I shore am sorry 'bout this. And so is the man driving that car. It wasn't his fault; and I can see from his tire tracks that he tried to stop and avoid hitting the animals. I'll tell you what, Johnnie," he said, reaching in his pocket, "you take this here 50 cents and you and Wormy go on downtown and git a cold drink or something. I'll take your dog to my office. I've got a nice box that I can put him in. If you want, I'll pick you two up downtown. You can come back here and find some suitable place to bury him. You and Wormy can even have a little funeral if you want. Now take this, and I'll pick you up at Hamilton's in an hour."

I knew I needed to get away, so I reluctantly took the money and somehow looked him straight in the eyes and said, "Yes, sir, that'll be a good idea. Poochie surely deserves a funeral. And thank you, Sheriff Calhoun. Thank you for everything.

"Come on, Wormy, let's get outta here. I think I better go tell Aunt Bessie first and then meet the sheriff."

"Whatever you say, Johnnie."

When we got to Bessie's house, I was thankful the girls weren't around. I didn't feel like facing anybody. I really missed Momma and Daddy right then, although Wormy had offered all the comfort he could.

He waited on the front porch while I walked through the house looking for my aunt. I heard her out on the back porch. As I pushed the screen door open and looked at her, all my pent-up emotions were instantly released, and I began crying like I had never cried before, and I rushed to her open arms.

"What is it, honey? What's the matter? You ain't hurt yourself, have you?"

Wormy had heard me crying and walked around the side of the house. He said, "Miz Brundige, Poochie is dead. Some car done run over him, by accident, and he is dead. Me and Johnnie walked right up on it when we went 'round to his house. Sheriff Calhoun's fixin' a box so's we can rightfully bury him."

I was aware of most of what he said, but my sobs hadn't slowed down.

Aunt Bessie just held me and said, "Go on and cry, honey. I know just how much it hurts. Losin' a pet, 'specially one as good as Poochie, is almost like losing a member of your family."

For the first time, I felt someone else understood. Several years ago, she had lost one of her children in a household accident. As I focused on that, she became my source of strength. My crying gradually slowed down.

"Aunt Bessie, when does the hurting stop?"

"I wish I could say it would go away real soon, Johnnie. But with anyone that you loved that much, well—the hurt will be with you forever. You just learn to live with it and endure it. And it does, finally, get a little easier. You also have to know that Poochie is in heaven now. And you can be sure he's being well cared for. God put animals here for us. So you know He must be taking care of them. Poochie's probably making somebody happy up there right now."

"Wormy, run in the bathroom and fetch me a wet washcloth," she calmly instructed.

The next moment she was washing away the tears and hugging me and rocking away in her chair.

"Just hold on, Johnnie, just hold on. It'll get better."

Not until years later, in my adult life, when I had come to know real love, did I feel heartache akin to that. Back then I knew I had to deal with it and get myself straightened out before Momma got home. She had enough problems to face, and a crying child wouldn't help her.

"Thank you, Aunt Bessie. I'm feeling some better now. Wormy and I gotta get ourselves ready for the funeral. Do you think I should bury him at the cemetery? Even though I never took him there, I know he'd love it as much as I do."

"I don't think they allow pets there, Johnnie. In some big cities they got cemeteries just for pets, but not here. Why don't you just bury him in the woods out behind your house. Then you can visit his grave anytime you want."

I thought it might hurt too much to have him buried so near me, yet I didn't want to just take him out into the country.

"I guess I'll give it some thought and Wormy and I'll figure out what to do. We gotta meet the sheriff downtown in a little while. He's gonna have Poochie in a coffin."

I finished washing off and handed the cloth to Aunt Bessie.

"I might be a little late for dinner, but I'll be back in plenty of time to get myself ready to meet Momma."

"You take your time, Johnnie. I'll feed you and Wormy, too, whenever you get here. I already got your clothes laid out. You try and remember to bring them shoes."

When we got to Hamilton's, I had no desire to eat or drink anything. "You wait here, Wormy, and I'll be right out." I went in and bought him a Coca-Cola, a pack of Nabs and a Moon Pie. We sat down on the curb and patiently waited for the sheriff to arrive.

His mouth full, Wormy mumbled, "Johnnie, I know how hard this is fer you, but we gonna give Poochie a nice funeral. And from then on, jist like yo aunt said, God's gonna take good care of him. Jist do yo best not to worry no more than you already has. I'm gonna be with you the whole time."

Just then, the sheriff drove up and told us to get in the back seat. I was afraid to look up front for fear of what I might see. He drove off and in a few minutes we pulled in our front yard. All three of us got out and walked around to the passenger's front door.

"Johnnie, I done the best I could for you and Poochie," Sheriff Calhoun said as he opened the door and picked up a brown wooden box about the size of two shoe boxes. As he handed it to me, I fought to hold back the tears and thanked him for what he had done, and for the money. He drove off, leaving me and Wormy standing there, not rightly knowing what to do next.

As we walked around the side of the house, I said, "I guess we better go find some good burial grounds." I gently placed the box on the side porch and we started walking back through the woods behind the house. We passed one of our old tree forts and a trash pile that was filled with scrap wood, an old rubber tire and an abandoned set of box springs. I had a particular place in mind as we passed through a stand of large old oak trees. Just beyond them was a clearing where Daddy had planted a victory garden a couple of years before. The garden had failed miserably, but it was a pretty good spot.

There were two giant oaks towards the rear of the clearing, with a nice mossy spot just behind the trees. The late morning sun was dimmed by the large, green oak leaves that would soon be turning brown and going their way for another year. It dawned on me that, sooner or later, everything died.

"Right here, Wormy, this is the spot."

It was indeed a lovely area, carpeted with soft green moss and surrounded by the oaks and several dog-woods. The clearing allowed the sun to brighten the area. We stood there a few moments, hearing only the sounds of the rustling leaves and a woodpecker busily hammering away atop one of the trees. I heard the whistle of the train leaving town and knew, in just a few minutes, it would be passing through the cemetery.

"Johnnie, don't you think we should build some sorta cross? Seems like every grave or tombstone I ever seen had one on it. You know Jesus died on a cross. I think it would make Him and Poochie happy if we put one here."

"That's a good idea, Wormy. Let's see what we can find to build a cross."

We walked back to the trash pile and started digging around. Wormy found an old tomato basket made of thin wooden slats that were loose and easy to disassemble. We carefully picked the two best slats, which we re-moved with our hands. We took them to the back porch, and I went in to get some tools.

I returned with a hammer and a few small nails. We used the longer slat as the upright part. With the claw end of the hammer, he fashioned out the cross member and nailed the two pieces together.

"Don'cha think it should have some words on it?" he asked.

"Yeah, I s'pose so, but what're we gonna say?"

While we were mulling over the wording, Mrs. Whitehead walked out, carrying two glasses of lemonade.

"Thank you, Mrs. Whitehead. We're getting ready to have a funeral for Poochie and have built this cross, but don't know exactly what to write on it."

"Why don't you just put, 'Here Lies Poochie'? Lemme go get something for you."

I could tell she was a little upset and probably felt somewhat responsible. She came back with a small paint brush and a bottle of doll paint her daughters had used. She also had a big red bow that she must have saved from some old Christmas present.

"These should do the trick," she said with a thin smile on her face.

I shook up the paint; then very carefully, in bright pink lettering, printed, "Here Lies Poochie." Wormy tacked the ribbon right where the two parts of the cross came together.

I got a shovel off the back porch and asked Wormy if he would bring the box around. I really didn't want to touch that box.

We went back to the grave site and took turns digging until we had a hole large enough to accommodate the coffin.

"Wormy, would you please put the coffin in?"

Without saying anything, he carefully placed the box in the grave and I proceeded to fill it up. I worked as fast and as hard as I could, because I really wanted to get it over with. I patted the large shovel of dirt on the small mound. Wormy held the cross while I used the blade of the shovel to drive it into the soft earth. As we both stood staring down at the grave, he asked, "Ain't you gonna have no prayer?"

"Yeah, you're right. We sure gotta have a prayer," I said, giving some thought to the wording of my first real, out-loud prayer.

We both bowed our heads.

"Dear God, thank you for Poochie and all the fun we had together. And please, take good care of him and let him be as happy as he made me. Amen."

❧ Chapter 10 ❧

The Trailways bus was usually very prompt, but that evening it seemed it would never arrive. Aunt Bessie had walked down to the station with me. We were sitting on the bench outside, awaiting its arrival. The anticipation of seeing Momma was diminished by my thoughts of Poochie. How was I going to greet her with any enthusiasm? On the other hand, I felt I would burst into tears when I saw her. But I knew it would be important to her that I appear as happy and cheerful as possible. I wanted to be able to listen and help her with our problems. I had definitely decided not to mention Poochie until we both got home and were alone together.

Finally, I saw the long, red and tan bus slowing down for its stop in front of us. When the door opened, the driver stepped out and there was Momma looking down at us. Aunt Bessie stood in the rear as I ran up to greet her.

"Welcome home, Momma. I really missed you," I said as we embraced. I thought how pretty she looked, all dressed up in her Sunday clothes.

"It's so good to see you, Johnnie. Your daddy and I missed you, too. You haven't given Bessie any trouble have you?"

"He's been as good as gold, Bug," my aunt answered. "Get your bag and we'll walk down to my house.

I've got supper all prepared. You can catch us up on everything and Jimmie'll drive you home later."

I was determined to carry her one piece of luggage. Occasionally having to drag it, I used both hands.

Since it was still early, Uncle Jimmie wasn't home, so Aunt Bessie fixed us something to drink. We sat on the front porch and I said, "Momma, tell us everything about Daddy. How's he doing?"

"They still don't have any answers, Johnnie," Momma said. Her voice had a hesitancy that suggested that all was not well. "The hospital won't have all the results 'til the end of the week, but he's right sick. The first day he seemed a little better. But when I left today, he wasn't looking any too well. The doctors did say his kidney problems are flaring up again. They started him on some new medicine and have a few more tests to run. I'll get the results on Friday. I gave them your phone number, Bess. I'll be here around 4 o'clock to take the call."

Jimmie and the girls came in shortly and we all ate, after which Jimmie drove us home.

I didn't know how I would react on returning home without Poochie there to greet us, but I was determined not to cry. Momma surely didn't need that.

As we pulled in the front yard, Momma said, "Rebecca Mae must be feeding Poochie, or else he'd be out here dancing around."

Neither Jimmie nor I said anything in reply. I just swallowed hard. Jimmie took our luggage in and said to let him know if we needed anything. Then he was gone and the two of us were alone in the apartment.

"You better run over and fetch Poochie, Johnnie."

And then I just blurted it out. "Momma, Poochie is dead. He was hit by a car today, right in front of the house."

Her casual expression changed, and all the frustrations of the past week were released. I had seen her cry before, but never like that. I tried to comfort her, but was having difficulty myself.

"What else can happen to us, Johnnie? What in God's name else?" she sobbed.

Putting my arm around her shoulder, I said, "I don't know, Momma; but Aunt Bessie said we were gonna have to be strong the next few days, and everything would work out. And then, maybe Daddy'll be home."

We had a long and difficult evening as we unpacked and dressed for bed without much conversation.

"I took a bath at Aunt Bessie's, Momma, so I don't need another one."

She didn't even reply, but just disappeared in the bathroom for ever so long. When she came out, her eyes were damp and red. I wished at that moment that I had been an adult and knew what to say. I wanted to be her source of strength, as Aunt Bessie had been for me that afternoon. I was afraid if I said anything more, I would just stir her emotions and make her feel even worse.

"Johnnie, I have to iron a dress for work. You go ahead and get in bed. I'll come tuck you in shortly."

It was really too early for my bedtime, but I wasn't going to offer any arguments that night. I lay in bed, hearing her prop up the ironing board. The next thing I knew, it was morning.

Momma was stirring around in the kitchen. After breakfast, I asked if she would like to see Poochie's grave.

We walked out in the quiet of the peaceful morning. I led a path for her back to the two big oaks. We stood there looking at the tiny grave. She pulled me to her and said, "That's a beautiful cross, Johnnie. I'm real proud of the way you handled it without me or your daddy here. We just gotta get on with our lives and hope for better days."

Walking back to the house, she said, "I know you're

going to meet Wormy, as usual, regardless of what I say."

"Momma," I said, biting my tongue and crossing my fingers behind me, "I don't meet him *every* day. But he was so much help with Poochie. I still have some of the money the sheriff gave me. I thought I might just take him down to the Idle Hour and buy him a real good breakfast—just for helping me and everything."

"Well, that's a mighty sweet idea, honey. You can do that, but promise me you won't go over to East Scotland Neck."

"Yes, ma'am," I said joyfully; that being one of the few times Momma ever condoned my meeting with Wormy.

"Just how much money do you have, Johnnie?"

"Well, I still got 10 cents from payday, plus 35 cents from what the sheriff gave me. So I got almost a half-dollar."

"That's not enough to buy him much of a breakfast," she said as she reached in her pocketbook and handed me another quarter.

"Momma, I know you can't spare this with all the bills we got facing us."

"We always manage somehow, Johnnie. I may have to go to the bank and get Carlisle Tuttle to co-sign another loan for me, what with your daddy not working and me missing so much time. You let me worry about that. You just do your good deed for Wormy. But you know they won't let him eat in the Idle Hour."

The Idle Hour was the one and only real restaurant in Scotland Neck. Of course, there was the barbecue stand and Hamiltons. But at the Idle Hour, you could go in and sit at a table and actually have somebody serve your food to you.

"I know that, Momma. I can go in and buy the breakfast. We can take it down by the old academy and sit there and eat. I know he hardly ever gets any break-fast."

"Okay. Why don't you walk down to the store with me? And you can go on to the restaurant from there."

We enjoyed our casual walk down Church Street, admiring the stately houses with their lovely yards. We turned left at the Baptist Church and came out on Main Street.

Just as we were in front of the store, Columbus Jones came walking across the street. "Morning, Ethel and Johnnie. How's Gavin doing?"

"Just fair, Columbus. We hope to know more this Friday."

"Ethel, I need to talk to you about your car."

In all the anguish of the day before, I had completely forgotten to check on the Hudson. My stomach knotted up as I waited to hear it.

Columbus said, "She's really not in such bad shape, considering the bath she took." He sort of chuckled. "The only real problem is the electrical system. The distributor and all the wiring were pretty much ruined. I'd say she needs a whole new electrical system, and I believe we may get her running again. But the problem is, we ain't got the parts here. They got to come from Raleigh and I already checked out the cost. I ain't gonna charge you nothing for mine and Slim's time, but the parts are gonna cost 83 dollars. That's the best I could do, Ethel."

Momma just stood there in dreary silence for a moment. We both knew if we didn't get the car running, when Daddy did come home, he wouldn't have any way to earn a living. There just weren't any other jobs in Scotland Neck. A couple of years ago, Daddy had worked part-time on a W.P.A. project, helping build the town's library. But that government job was all finished.

"Look, Columbus, I got so many problems to deal with, and money is just one of them. Right now, that 83 dollars might just as well be 830 dollars, because we just don't have it."

"I shore understand that, Ethel," Columbus replied. "Whatcha want me to do with the car?"

"Could you park it over behind the station 'til I can work something out?"

"I can shore do that with no problem. You let me know when you figure out what to do. I just wish we could fix it, but all them parts are totally ruined."

"I know that, Columbus. Gavin and I really appreciate everything you've done for us already. Someday, I hope to pay you for everything. But right now, I can't. I'll talk to you real soon."

I knew she was thinking about that bank loan.

"One other thing, Ethel. I could probably get a coupla hundred or so dollars for it, if you decide to sell it."

That was a horrible thought. We couldn't sell Daddy's car. Not the Hudson. Not the only taxicab in town.

"Well," Momma sighed, "if I don't come up with the money, I might have to do that. Let me do some thinking on it."

"You take your time, and give Gavin my regards." He walked back across the street, leaving Momma with a dejected look on her face.

"Johnnie, you run on now. I've got to get to work."

I felt terrible about the car, but what could I do? My 70 cents sure wouldn't help much. I wished I had the whole 83 dollars. But I had never seen that much money in my entire life.

I stuck my hands in my pockets, lowered my head and started on down Main Street. When I reached the Firestone store, I paused a moment to look in the window. They seemed to have most everything in the world in that store—and I wanted most of it. While they mainly stocked tires and parts for cars, there were also toys, radios, hunting equipment and some farming tools. Some days, I spent hours just browsing around, wishing for most everything I saw.

One special item that I had previously admired caught my eye that morning. It was a radio, about the size of a shoe box. Most of the radios I had seen were large consoles that took up a good part of the corner of a room. Picture shows and radios were about our only contact with the rest of the world. *The Standard* printed mostly local events.

Daddy never missed the evening radio news. Every night after supper he would remove his shoes, take his after-dinner coffee and settle in his easy-chair next to the radio in the dining room. Then, we all had to be quiet while he listened to his favorite newscaster, a man named Gabriel Heater. I often wondered if Mr. Heater was also a preacher, being such a good talker and having the name Gabriel.

I, too, spent many winter afternoons huddled up against the radio listening to The Lone Ranger, Jack Armstrong—The All American Boy, The Shadow, and lots of other daily serials.

I was completely mystified by radios. Whenever I looked in the back at all those little lighted tubes, I just knew there must be people in them—very tiny little people. When the radio was turned on and lit up the tubes, it must have awakened those people. Then they started talking and singing and saying all sorts of interesting things. Whenever music came on, I couldn't imagine how they got all the musical instruments inside those small tubes. Daddy always laughed when I said that. But I sure did wonder how they worked.

About a month before, the Firestone had gotten in the smallest radio anyone in town had ever seen. When the store manager, Mr. Alvin Arnold, first displayed it in the window, practically everybody in town went to see and admire that little radio. It was the talk of the town for a week or more and everybody wanted it. But it cost 25 dollars! And who would pay that much for such a little radio? As of that morning, it was still on display.

I walked in and asked Mr. Arnold if he could turn it on, for just a second, so I could hear it. Of course, I had heard it before, but never right by myself.

"Sorry, Johnnie, you know I turn it on every day from four to four-thirty. If you want to hear it, you can come in with all the rest of the folks. I know I could talk your daddy into buying that thing if he wasn't sick. Incidentally, Johnnie, how's he doing?"

"Pretty good, Mr. Arnold. Thanks anyway. Maybe I'll come back this afternoon."

I peeked around behind it to see if I could see any of those tubes that lit up. I imagined that the people in those tubes must be super midgets to fit in anything that small.

I roamed around the store, wanting more and more things until I remembered Wormy, and hustled on my way. I walked past Aunt Bessie's and didn't see anybody. I didn't feel like talking anyway. All I could think about was that 83 dollars, wishing I could somehow raise it.

Wormy and I walked up to the shop about the same time.

"Yo momma git home all right, Johnnie? How's yo daddy doin'?"

"Yes, she did. Still don't know anything, but some doctor is supposed to call Friday and give us a report. Anyway, I have a surprise for you today."

"You does? What is it?" he excitedly asked.

A surprise to Wormy usually meant I had brought some dessert from home or a portion of something special Aunt Bessie had baked.

"Well, come on with me and I'll show you."

"Shucks," he moaned, "you ain't got it with you? Whatta I gotta do, work fer it?"

"Just follow me."

"Yes, suh, you leads the way."

All the way down Main Street he was nagging at me

about what his surprise was. When we stopped in front of the Idle Hour, he looked more puzzled than ever.

"What we doin' here? You know I can't go in that place."

I had often told him how good their food was, especially the desserts.

"I know that, but I'm going in and buy you whatever you want for breakfast. Have you had anything to eat?"

"Had one chicken gizzard and a piece of bread. Momma was cookin' a cake fer Dr. Thigpen's birthday, but you know none of us chillun can ever have any of what she's fixin' fer white folks. Where you git any money anyway?"

"I've got most of what the sheriff gave us yesterday, and I got a little more. Besides, half of what the sheriff gave us was yours, 'cause you were with me when he gave it to us."

As I have said, when it came to taking something for nothing, Wormy was right proud and I expected some argument from him. But instead, he squinted up his eyes and rubbed his stomach. I could tell he was thinking about all the food in the restaurant.

"Well, I'll let you do it, but I'm paying you back next payday."

"Don't worry none 'bout that. Just tell me what it is you want to eat."

He stood there a minute, rubbing his chin and thinking. He finally said, "I want me somma that banana puddin' you is always talkin' 'bout. And I want a piece of pecan pie and one glass of cold milk."

"You want that stuff for breakfast?"

"You ask me what I want, and that's it."

"Okay, but that sure is a funny breakfast. You wait here and I'll get them to put it in a bag for me. We'll go over by the old academy and sit in the shade, and you can eat it there."

Entering the Idle Hour, I was greeted by Betty Lou Wommack, who was an enormous woman. She was short and must have weighed over 300 pounds. Daddy always said never to trust a skinny cook, so I figured Mrs. Wommack must have been the best cook in the whole world.

She and her husband owned and operated the Idle Hour. They used to own a small farm outside town. Mr. Wommack's grandmother died and left him five hundred dollars. Now he was one of the best pool players in the entire state of North Carolina. He took that whole five hundred dollars and started hustling at the pool hall. Every time some out-of-towner came to play pool, Mr. Wommack would take him on for cash money. Within a month or two, he had won himself enough to buy the Idle Hour. He gave the farm to his son, Ned, and he and Mrs. Wommack opened the restaurant and moved into an apartment right upstairs. From that time on, he mainly spent his time eating at the restaurant and hanging around the pool hall—bragging and all. Daddy said Mr. Wommack was the one who had become idle, so maybe that's where they got the name for the restaurant.

"Sakes alive, Johnnie! What're you doing in here so early in the morning, and how's your daddy doing?"

"He's doing pretty good," I impatiently answered. "Mrs. Wommack, if I want to buy some food, can you put it in a bag for me so I can take it out to eat?"

"Sure I can; but why don't you jist sit down here and let me serve you? It's not often I have a young man in here for breakfast."

"Well, I sorta had my mind set on a picnic breakfast. Thought I'd take the food and go down by the old academy and sit under the trees. I gotta little problem I'm trying to figure out, and I can think better over there."

When I gave her my order, she spied me sorta

suspiciously and said, "That's a mighty peculiar breakfast, Johnnie. Does Bug know you're eating all these sweets so early in the day?"

"Well, sort of. She gave me some money and I told her I was coming in here."

"You're in luck on the pie. I just took two of them outta the oven and they're steaming hot. The pudding is in the icebox from yesterday, but jist as fresh as ever. You want me to put the milk in a paper cup for you?"

"Yes, ma'am, that would be nice. Mrs. Wommack, I've got 70 cents. Will that be enough to pay for my order?"

"You jist leave that to me, Johnnie."

Pretty soon, she came back with a good-size brown paper bag. I could tell the bag had been used before, but that didn't make any difference. I supposed that not too many people took food out from the Idle Hour. I took the bag and handed her my 70 cents.

"Here, Johnnie, you get some change," she said as she handed me 50 cents back.

"You mean I get all this food and still have two quarters left?"

"You take the bag and the money and git. I got to start readying this place for dinner."

I knew that was true. Everybody who didn't go home for dinner came to the Idle Hour. Daddy said it was not only for the good food, but for all the small-town gossip that was passed around there.

"Thanks, Mrs. Wommack. I sure do appreciate it."

"You're welcome, Johnnie. You tell your momma I want the two of you to have supper here one evening while your daddy is in the hospital. And tell her it'll be on the house."

"On the house, Mrs. Wommack?"

"You tell your momma what I said."

"Yes, ma'am, and thank you again."

I walked out front and Wormy was pacing back and forth. He said, "What you been doin' in there, cookin' the dern food? A hungry man could starve to death waitin' fer you. Les git goin'."

We headed down the street towards the academy. It was a large wooden building which had been abandoned years before. At some point in its history, it had been a private military school for boys. But as time passed, and less and less students enrolled, the school was closed, never to be used again. It had lots of rooms which were vacant, except for a few broken and worn-out desks and chairs scattered here and there throughout its musty interior. Situated two blocks west of Church Street, it was the only structure at the end of a winding dirt road. The shallow part of the canal was off the east side, about 20 yards away.

It was our private retreat, used by the two of us when there were any secrets to discuss or important plans to map out. We often played there, too.

That day I had some important thinking to do about how to raise that 83 dollars. If only I could do that, I'd not only help Momma and Daddy, but maybe redeem myself in God's eyes, for all the problems I'd caused lately.

I wasn't sure there was that much money in all of Scotland Neck. I'd never seen a bill larger than a twenty. Daddy'd let me hold it on the way to the bank one day. I remember thinking you could buy anything in the world for 20 dollars. Now I was trying to raise 83 dollars!

We waded through the canal, went around to the wooded side of the building and plopped down. As I handed the bag to Wormy, his eyes shown with excitement and anticipation. Mrs. Wommack had put a spoon and a couple of paper napkins in the bag. I made a mental note to return the spoon.

I always enjoyed sharing with Wormy, but I'd never seen him so excited about a "surprise" before. Mrs.

Wilson's only source of income was cooking and washing and ironing for whites. She did the best she could to care for a large family. Mr. Wilson never contributed anything—except trouble.

"Don't you want some of this, Johnnie?" he somehow managed to get out of a mouth crammed with pecan pie.

"Naw, you enjoy all of it. I already had breakfast."

As I sat there watching him savor every morsel, a money-making plan began to materialize in my brain.

As I explained the need for the 83 dollars, I said, "Wipe off your mouth. You got puddin' all over your chin."

He just laughed and said, "You gotta 'bout as much chance of makin' that money as we got of gittin' invisible. Course, maybe you could go to Washington, D.C., and see President Roosevelt, like you is always talkin', and he'd jist give it right to you. You know the president of these United States is right rich. Why, I'll bet he's got more money than old Zeb Kitchen."

Ignoring his sarcasm, I said, "You remember last Christmas when the Volunteer Fire Department wanted to raise some money to help the poor families in town? They raffled off a real live pig and some other things, and I know they raised a lot of money. They even brought us a food basket on Christmas Eve since Daddy had just come home from the hospital."

"What you thinkin'? You ain't got no pigs or nothin' like that to have no raffle with. How's a raffle work anyway?"

"Well," I said, "everybody who wants to pays something like 25 cents to get a ticket with a number on it. As the tickets are sold, they're put in a box. At the end of the raffle, somebody reaches in and pulls out the winning ticket. Whoever has the matching ticket number is the winner of the raffle."

"That's a mighty fine idea, Johnnie, but what you got to raffle? All's you got is that ole bicycle, and it don't run right half the time."

"Think about it, Wormy. What does everybody in Scotland Neck want right now, more than anything else?"

"To be rich."

"Yeah, that, too. But I mean, what's for sale that everybody's been looking at and wanting to own?"

"You mean that little biddy radio at the Firestone store?"

"Exactly! Most everybody would pay 25 cents to take a chance on winning that radio."

"What we gonna do, steal it, show it all over town and then raffle it off?"

"No, but maybe I could make a deal with Mr. Arnold to let us raffle it off, make money enough to pay for it, and still end up with 83 dollars."

"You ain't got a chance in hell a doin' that, Johnnie. This here's jist another one of yo knucklehead ideas that ain't gonna work out."

By then, the excitement was building inside of me, and I said, "You might be right. But with your help, we could shore give it a try."

"You think anybody in East Scotland Neck's got a quarter they wants to bet on that fool gadget? It's so little, you prob'ly can't even hear no words come outta it anyway."

"I wasn't thinking too much about East Scotland Neck. But I was mainly thinking of you helping me. There'd be a lotta work getting everything ready. You know Mr. Arnold wants to sell that radio so's he can get another one and sell it, too. Every time he gets anything new, everybody goes in his store to see it. And some of them buy other things while they're there. And Mr. Arnold will do anything to make a sale."

"Well, crazy as it is, you know you can count on me. I shore would like to see yo daddy's car runnin' again."

My head was spinning with plans and ideas. Of course, the key to making the whole plan work was getting Mr. Arnold to go along with the idea. Like most everybody else in town, he was a good friend of my daddy's. Maybe if I explained the idea to him, we could work out a deal that could benefit both of us. I hadn't felt such enthusiasm since I came down the glide ride.

The more I thought about it, I realized we'd have to sell over one hundred dollars worth of tickets to pay for the radio and still have enough to fix the car. Then I optimistically thought, "Heck, maybe we could even sell two hundred dollars worth and I could give Momma some money to help her. Who knows just how much money we can make on this deal?"

Alvin Arnold was a little peculiar. But when it came to business, he'd do almost anything to increase his sales. I decided to go back and talk to him as soon as Wormy finished his breakfast.

Wormy had slowed down his eating a little, but I could see he was going to finish everything. Finally, as he swallowed the last gulp of milk, a loud burp erupted from his mouth. He was laying back against the building, not looking any too well at all.

"I think I's gonna be sick, Johnnie."

"You shouldn't have eaten the whole mess of it at one time."

"Well, if I do git sick, it'll be worth it. Thas the best breakfast I ever had in my life. It was a humdinger! I should of saved some of that pie for my sisters, but it was so dern good, and I was 'bout starved. Yep, best breakfast ever, in my whole life."

"I wanna go to the Firestone store and talk to Mr. Arnold."

"Yeah, I know. I think I'll jist lay here fer awhile and

enjoy this feelin' my stomach has. It sorta hurts, but it's a good kinda hurt. You go and I'll see you later this afternoon. And thanks again, Johnnie."

Mr. Arnold was not from North Carolina. Firestone had transferred him to Scotland Neck from another state. Everybody knew he hoped to become the regional manager for Firestone someday. He was very progressive in selling and marketing and was always using some scheme to get people into the store.

Daddy was an avid hunter and the Firestone store was the only place in town to purchase guns, ammunition and hunting supplies. Every time Mr. Arnold got in any hunting equipment, he'd get Daddy in the store and somehow manage to sell him whatever it was that was new.

Daddy couldn't afford to buy anything, but Mr. Arnold would take one dollar and put the item on layaway. Daddy would pay a dollar now and again, until it was finally paid for. When he brought his purchase home, Momma would raise a big fuss about him throwing away his money on guns, as well as whiskey. She reminded him that the two didn't mix, and of his accident.

Some years ago, Daddy, Tazwell Judson and Shoofly were quail hunting across the river near Rich Square. In addition to ammunition, they always carried a goodly supply of whiskey.

That particular day, they didn't have a hunting dog with them (which was probably a good thing for the dog), so Shoofly was out in front of the other two trying to flush out the quail. When one was shot, he would fetch it, bring it back, and they would celebrate by taking another drink. They had gotten six or seven birds before the accident.

As the story went, one time when Shoofly did his flushing, none of them were seeing any too well. When

Daddy raised his shotgun, Taz knew he was going to hit Shoofly, so he yelled so loud that Daddy lowered the gun just as he was pulling the trigger. The gun went off and shot Daddy right in the foot. It was a fairly serious accident, but the more often the story was told, the funnier it became.

It seems they were so drunk that when Daddy looked down at his foot, he and Taz started laughing as Shoofly came running back. They couldn't wait to tell the boys at the barber shop how Taz had saved their "hunting dog," and in so doing, Daddy almost lost the big toe on his right foot. The truth was probably mingled somewhere between all the stories over the years. But Momma always reminded him of it whenever he bought any new hunting equipment.

That was also the first time they found out Daddy had diabetes, as it took nearly a year for his toe to heal. There was even a time when we feared he would lose his whole foot.

But that was history. It did, however, give me a slight edge in dealing with Mr. Arnold. I was counting on him to help me execute my fund-raising plan.

Except for Mr. Arnold, who was arranging a car tire display, the store was empty when I arrived.

"Johnnie, it's not 4 o'clock. You know I am not turning on that radio until then—unless, of course, you came back to buy it," he said with a sly grin on his face.

"Well, Mr. Arnold, maybe, indirectly. I have a business deal I want to talk over with you."

"I'll bet you want to put it on lay-away, like Gavin does."

"No, sir, but I gotta problem. I'm trying to solve it. We might help each other out. And it does involve Daddy."

As I unraveled my plan, he sat very attentive. Starting my discussion with "business deal" had gotten his attention.

When I concluded, he sat there almost a whole minute, stroking his chin and, from time to time, glancing over at the radio.

"You know, John, my boy, you may have come up with a big promotional idea. Harvest time is almost here. I need to do something to get the people in my store before they spend all that money somewhere else. I need a gimmick, a novel idea, an attention-getter. You know what I mean? You give me some time to think on this and drop back in this afternoon, and we'll talk some more. I heard about the Hudson. We can't let Scotland Neck go without taxi service, can we, John, my boy?"

Somehow, I didn't feel that the Hudson's salvation was his main concern. But I really didn't care so long as the venture netted me 83 dollars.

"Mr. Arnold, please don't say anything about this yet. I don't want to get Momma's hopes up and then have the plan fail."

"Oh, John, I think it will work out very well. Just let me do some figuring. I'll see you later on today."

I thought maybe I should get some kind of assurance from Columbus that if we got the 83 dollars, the car really could be fixed. Columbus was in the stall and Slim was pumping gas into Mr. Allsbrook's truck.

"Can I speak to you a minute, Mr. Columbus?

"Sure, Johnnie, whatcha got on your mind?"

"If we're able to raise the money, are you sure 83 dollars will fix the car and she'll be in running condition by the time Daddy gets home?"

"Johnnie, ain't many things for absolute sure in this life. But I'd bet a buck we could do it. Like I told your momma, the only thing that's wrong with it, far as I can tell, is the electrical system. Course, that radio is shot dead. But I believe we can get the car running, maybe not like new, but almost as good as she was before. If y'all get the money, we'll get the work done. We all want your daddy to have a job when he gits back home."

I sneaked a look around back to be sure the car was still there and then walked across the street to the Boston Store.

"Well," Momma said, "just in time to have some dinner with me."

I was really too excited to eat, but I waited for her and we walked home together.

"How was Wormy's breakfast?" she asked.

"Fine, I think. I left him looking like a stuffed pig laying up against the academy. I think he ate so much he'll probably be sick."

We had sandwiches for dinner. I had my very favorite: a banana sandwich with peanut butter on one piece of bread and mayonnaise on the other, and sliced banana in the middle. Nobody but Momma and Aunt Bessie could fix banana sandwiches just the way I liked them. Most people put on too much mayonnaise, which made the bread soggy, or too much peanut butter, which made it too dry. As usual, this one was just right.

I walked her back to work. I didn't want to get to the Firestone store too early, so I helped Momma unpack a few boxes and put the clothes on the tables. There was a 25 cent table, a 50 cent table, and a 75 cent table. Anything selling for one dollar or more was hung on racks to make them look as new as possible. The most expensive items in the Boston Store cost 5 dollars. To sell for that much, they had to be in very, very good condition.

There was one 5 dollar dress that Momma had talked about for a month, but instead of that purchase, she had some more school clothes set aside for me. She knew the manager, Duby White, would let her have them when school opened, even if they weren't all paid for.

Momma dressed real nice, but she always put me first. She was more concerned about my appearance than I was. I felt bad that she couldn't buy the clothes she wanted. When Daddy had the part-time with the W.P.A. and was still driving the taxi, we had more money than we'd ever had. Momma would go to Rocky Mount or Tarboro with her two sisters, Bessie and Marie, who lived in town. Of course, Aunt Bessie always came back with her colored rhinestones. Momma might get herself a new dress or sweater, but she always brought me something new, too. Two years before at Christmas, she'd bought me my first Bible. It had a red leather cover with my name in gold lettering, right on the front. I was real proud of that Bible and carried it with me to Sunday school each week.

I was getting so jittery thinking about Mr. Arnold, I told Momma I was going out to play for awhile.

"Just stop back here at quitting time, Johnnie. I've got to go to the grocery store on the way home, and I need you to help me carry some things. We about ran out of everything while I was away."

As I left the store, my pulse quickened. I scampered on down Main Street to the Firestone store.

Chapter 11

There were two customers in the Firestone store when I walked in—a farmer and a lady visiting town who was browsing around. I knew business came first, so I waited for Mr. Arnold to finish with the customers.

During my wait, I stood gazing at that little radio. I examined it more carefully and, for the first time, realized it was a Philco. I wondered if that was a good brand. With everybody in town wanting it, I imagined it must be okay.

The farmer finally left with a set of spark plugs for his tractor and the lady didn't buy anything.

"Come on back, Johnnie; we have some talking to do. You have a good idea, boy, a very good idea. If we can get folks excited about winning that Philco, they'll be flocking in here, looking at it again and again. And they usually buy something when they come in.

"John, my good fellow, we're going to make this a great campaign. By now, almost everyone in town knows about your daddy's illness and the Hudson. We're going to ply their sympathy, John. We'll call it the 'Save The Hudson' campaign. We'll appeal to anyone who ever took a ride in your daddy's taxicab. They'll know they're helping Gavin, your mother and even you, Johnnie. They'll also have the opportunity to help keep taxi service in their town and maybe even win this fine radio.

"This is our deal, Johnnie, yours and mine. We'll sell the raffle chances at 25 cents a ticket, just as you suggested. After we've sold enough tickets to pay for the radio, you, Johnnie, will pull the winning ticket out of the box and present the radio to the lucky winner. All the money we take in, over and above the cost of the radio, we'll split, 50-50.

The more he talked, the faster he talked, his voice reflecting excitement. I thought I also detected a touch of slyness, which worried me some.

"Wait a minute, Mr. Arnold. S'pose we don't sell enough tickets to get my 83 dollars? What am I gonna do then?"

"Johnnie, the business world is tough and sometimes even a little cruel. We take our chances in life. Suppose we don't sell even 25 dollars worth? I've still got to give the radio to the winner. Do you understand what I mean? I could lose money on this. But once we make a deal, John, a deal is a deal."

I couldn't imagine Mr. Arnold losing money on anything. Daddy called him the ultimate salesman, and I guessed that to be good. What choice did I have? He, or Firestone, owned the radio, and I needed a business partner.

"We gotta deal, Mr. Arnold. When do we start? What can I do?"

"The first thing I have to do is get a big sign to put in the window announcing the plan. Then I think I can get a couple rolls of tickets from Billy Joe Locke down at the Dixie. He should contribute at least that to a campaign this important. Then, when folks know what we're trying to do, you and Wormy are going all over town selling tickets. I'll sell them here too. That should attract a lot of customers. Then we'll have to set a date for the grand drawing."

He paused a moment, and then a happy little grin

jumped on his face and he said, "You know, Johnnie, the Crepe Myrtle Festival starts in two weeks. That may be just the time to hold the drawing. Say—maybe on the last day of the festival. I usually reserve an area and donate a prize or two, so the festival may very well benefit our campaign.

"You run along now, because I have lots of work to do. And yes, Johnnie, we do have a business deal. I hope we both make a lot of money. But, of course I hope you get that Hudson fixed, too."

I left the store feeling somewhat better about Mr. Arnold. I also had wonderful visions in my mind and thought, "Maybe we really can do it!"

I had to find Wormy and share the good news. I wouldn't mention it to Momma until the campaign was well under way. I didn't want her telling me not to do this or that. Besides, I had a feeling Mr. Arnold would carry out the plan, with or without me, even though it was my idea.

I didn't know where to find Wormy, but I was busting wide open to tell him. I felt he must have left the academy by then and probably gone home. I crossed my fingers, thinking about Momma, and headed for East Scotland Neck.

Scotland Neck was unofficially divided into four distinct sections. To me, it was all Scotland Neck. But over the years, each section had developed its own distinctive character. Often, folks were thought of in relation to the section of town in which they lived. There was downtown, which consisted of five blocks of stores and shops on each side of Main Street. Then there was Clarksville, a somewhat better section, located at the north end of Main Street in the direction of the Scout Pond. Clarksville was filled with fine, stately homes, all set well back from the road, with large front yards filled with oak, maple and dogwood trees. Every yard was a rhapsody of colors, with lovely flowering shrubs, well-maintained lawns and, of course, crepe myrtles. The third, located at the south end of Main Street, was Greenwood, a pleasant residential section of more modest homes.

And finally, there was East Scotland Neck. It was referred to as East, because it was on the east side of the railroad tracks. It housed most of the coloreds, and some of the less affluent white families.

As I walked through the motley streets of East Scotland Neck, I felt very comfortable. It lacked most of the amenities enjoyed by the rest of the town. But to me, it always seemed to be a very happy community. From every direction, I could hear the ambient noises of crying babies and laughing children. There was an occasional "Hey, Johnnie, where's Wormy?" or "How's yo daddy, Johnnie?" Some of the older coloreds would even say, "Howdy, Mr. Johnnie."

Daddy often commented that he had as many friends in East Scotland Neck as in the rest of town. I guessed that was one reason I was so readily accepted. Whenever there was any need for coloreds to travel by car, Daddy was always available. He rarely collected any cash fares, but would come home with a chicken, a cake or some collard greens. Momma might have fussed a little about no money, but was always happy to receive the food.

It's a little difficult to describe the homes in East Scotland Neck, for many of them were just the remnants of hundred-year-old houses. They reflected little maintenance and no improvements. Most of them were set several feet above the ground, with cement blocks supporting the four corners and the middle. Their front porches were crowded with rickety chairs, wood nail kegs or dilapidated benches. All the roofs were covered with rusty tin, dotted with splotches of tar, applied here and there, to seal out the rain. There were few window shades. Many of the window openings were covered with tattered towels or worn bed sheets. The small yards were the only play areas for the children, and most of them were cluttered with tire swings, old bicycles and hand-me-down toys.

As I walked through the area, I realized that Wormy was a product of this environment, and that his heritage was woven into the very fabric of his life in East Scotland Neck.

Walking up to his house, I marveled at how this tiny dwelling could accommodate such a very large family. It had much the same appearance as Mr. Allsbrook's shop, with weather-beaten clapboard siding showing signs of antiquity caused by a lack of upkeep. The front windows did have shades, but the left corner of the porch roof hung loosely, drooping almost off the supporting post. A couple of windows had shutters, angled off in different directions.

Three of his sisters were playing jump-rope in the front yard as I said, "Hey, girls, where's Wormy?"

Without missing a skip, Thelma Lou answered, "Hey, Johnnie. He's out back with his darn worms. Came home sick as a dog and been pukin' most of the time. Musta been somethin' he et."

"Is it okay if I go in?"

"Shore it is. Daddy ain't home and Momma's out deliverin' some ironin'."

I pulled open what was left of a screen door, with one rusty, curled-down piece of screen wire dangling from its frame.

Several things always intrigued me in the house. There was the color picture of a weeping Jesus hung carefully above a worn-down couch. The picture was in a bright brass frame with no glass. The frame was kept shiny-bright and the picture was dusted and clean.

Hanging from a sagging living room ceiling were

four or five pieces of gooey-brown fly paper. It had captured flies from today and many yesterdays past.

The impressive part of the house was the kitchen, which was Mrs. Wilson's pride and joy. Situated along the back wall was a large, cast-iron wood stove. It had metal handles attached to four removable lids. The stove was as immaculately clean as any you could see in the Firestone store. The oilcloth-covered table was spotless, adorned with a daily array of freshly-cut flowers. The floor was covered with clean, but worn linoleum, pitted here and there with burn spots. Next to the side window stood a handmade ironing board, also covered with oilcloth. One of the tools of her trade, a heavy black iron, rested on a metal stand on the board.

It seemed that Mrs. Wilson's only pleasures in life were her children and her kitchen. A tall, lanky, light-skinned Negro, she had the same thin face as Wormy, with high cheekbones. She resembled a mixture of a Negro and an American Indian. She was a pretty woman. She seemed to know well what she had, what she did not have—and what she would never have. She accepted this, except when it came to her children. I had heard her speak many words of self-improvement to Wormy, regarding his speech, appearance and personal habits.

"Woodrow," which was what she called him, "a person's only as good as his word. Giving—and keeping—your word is mighty important in this here life. Many people judge us on our appearance. If yo ever gonna become somebody important, you need to remember: always look yo best, try and talk right, and have a whole lotta religion. That religion will help give you an honesty. Jist look at yo daddy—him with not nary a drop of religion. And then look at that picture of our sweet savior. And then, Woodrow, you decide which one you wanna be like."

He would always reply, "Yes, ma'am, Momma. Someday I'm gonna be somebody important and do some good things in this world. Then I'll really be able to help you and the fambly. Don't ask me how, I jist know it, that's all."

Collectively, her children possessed a very limited selection of worn-out clothing. But they were always neat. The girls' hair was always platted in a delicate style, and shined of pomade, with a colorful ribbon or two attached to the plats.

Wormy was in the backyard, sitting in a tire swing with his head hung downward, staring at his collection of worms, most of which was shriveled up and dead.

As I walked out the back door, he looked up with a sickly expression on his face and asked, "Whatcha doin' over here?"

"I've got some news, but I hear you ain't feelin' too good."

"Yeah, reckon I jist had too good'a breakfast. I's feelin' some better now, but I done lost most of that good food I et. Weren't nearly as good comin' up as it was goin' down. Whatcha got to tell me?"

I sat down by the tree and brought him up-to-date on all the plans Mr. Arnold and I had made. He didn't seem the least bit excited with the news, but agreed to help me sell the tickets. He really thought the whole plan was doomed to a catastrophic failure.

"You know ole man Arnold is jist out to help ole man Arnold. He don't give a hoot 'bout you or that Hudson."

I hoped his attitude reflected his feeling so poorly right then, because I was really counting on his help.

To break his mood, I asked if he wanted to shoot some marbles. We spent many hours playing marbles, which always helped fill slow afternoons.

"Yeah," he said, "if I can git up and git movin'."

"I didn't bring mine, so you'll have to lend me a few of yours."

"Thas good, least you don't have any of them dern steelies."

Now, everybody knows marbles are made out of glass. But if you were fortunate enough to own some steel ball bearings from an old car wheel, they made the best shooters in the whole world. The several steelies I had were given to me by my daddy, who had used them himself as a child.

During the war, every conceivable piece of scrap iron, steel or metal went off to some distant factory, to be magically transformed into fighting equipment. I asked Daddy once if I should turn in my steelies to help win the war. He assured me that the government wouldn't miss three or four ball bearings. And anyway, according to him, they had helped make him the best marble shooter in Scotland Neck.

Wormy went in the house and returned carrying a small paper bag filled with multicolored marbles. They were one of his few toys and he treasured them, keeping them hidden in some very safe place. We took a stick, drew a circle in the dirt and whiled away the afternoon, taking turns saying "sicci-first," and each trying our best to out-shoot the other.

The afternoon passed quickly. Before I knew it, the sun had passed over the house, leaving us in the shade.

"Guess I better head on down to the store. Momma's gittin' off soon. I need to help her sweep the store and carry groceries home."

Walking around the side of the house, we met Mrs. Wilson returning with a basket of clothes in need of ironing.

"Hey, Johnnie, how's yo daddy gittin' along?"

"Pretty good, I hope, Mrs. Wilson. We're suppose to hear from the hospital Friday. We're hoping for good news."

"You tell your momma if she needs any help while

yo daddy is away, jist let me know. I cleans houses too."

"Yes, ma'am, and thank you. I'll let her know. See you in the morning, Wormy."

"Notice you ain't sayin' much 'bout who won in marbles," Wormy said, with satisfaction on his face.

"I reckon I did go a mite easy on you today, seeing as how you were feeling so poorly and all," I replied.

I got to the store too late to help clean up. Momma was just walking out the door, so we did our shopping. I was hoping to get some candy out of my efforts, but since she didn't mention it, neither did I. She seemed preoccupied all the way home.

I helped fix supper. Then we sat out on the front porch with Mrs. Whitehead, just swinging the evening away.

"If your daddy isn't coming home from the hospital early next week, I might take the bus down Saturday and come back Sunday," Momma said. "I hate him being alone and so far away. If he can come home, I'll ask Jimmie if I can use his car and drive us down and bring him back. Then I'll have to talk to him about him getting a bank loan to fix the car. He won't like it much, but we don't have any other choice."

I was dying to tell her about the campaign, but still afraid it might not work.

We went in shortly, took our baths and went to bed without any stories. I was beginning to think I was a little old for bedtime stories anyway.

Chapter 12

_T_hursday was rather uneventful. But Friday was to be a day to be remembered. I felt it was time to check in with Mr. Arnold to see how the campaign was progressing.

Walking up to the Firestone store, I paused and stared at the front window with amazement. He had painted a large cardboard sign that read, "**HELP SAVE SCOTLAND NECK'S ONLY TAXICAB AND WIN THE FINEST RADIO PHILCO EVER MADE.**" Sitting right in front of the sign was the small brown radio with its bright brass knobs sparkling in the sunlight. A smaller sign had been placed right on top of the radio. It stated, "**COME INSIDE FOR MORE DETAILS.**"

There were about a dozen multicolored balloons hanging in the window, and several colorful party streamers shooting off from the radio and splaying out to the sides of the window frame. Sitting to the left of the radio was a splendid picture of Uncle Sam pointing his finger towards the window and saying, "I want you!" On the right side was a captivating picture of the Statue of Liberty, with fireworks bursting gloriously all around the lovely lady.

Reflecting back on that moment, it was perhaps the gaudiest display I had ever seen. But that day, it looked like the 4th of July, and shivers of excitement rippled through my body. I was so proud, I felt like saluting.

Entering the store, there was a Victrola playing and Kate Smith's voice reverberated around the room with *God Bless America*.

There were about a half-dozen people gathered around Mr. Arnold, asking about the campaign and winning the radio. I'd never seen that many people in the store at one time. I just stood back, watching, listening and taking it all in.

I thought, "That was my idea, and all those people are excited about it." Now I felt I would be able to tell Momma.

Gradually the store cleared. As the people walked out, they smiled at me, patted me on the head, and one couple even said, "We're behind you all the way, Johnnie."

Mr. Arnold was beaming and rubbing his hands together as he said, "John, my boy, I think we've hit it big. After I finished that display last night, my phone started ringing off the hook. So far this morning, I must have had a dozen or more folks in here, and they all want to take a chance and pay their 25 cents. But I don't have the tickets yet. Billy Joe is supposed to get me two rolls of one hundred each sometime today. Then you and Wormy have to begin your work."

"Just tell me what you want us to do, Mr. Arnold."

I hadn't seen Wormy that morning, but I would round him up right away.

"First, I want you to run down to the Dixie and see if Billy Joe is back with the tickets. He had to go over to Rich Square to get them. Soon as you get them, I'll put you to work in the back of the store. When you two return, come around to the back entrance. I don't want anyone thinking Wormy's working here."

I didn't like that comment any too much, but right then, I would have done most anything he asked.

I rushed out of the store, hoping Wormy would be

at Mr. Allsbrook's. He was there, sitting under his favorite tree, plucking away on his mouth-harp, just making an awful noise.

"You know, Johnnie, I been thinkin'. I believe I got some musical talents here. Maybe I won't go to Washington, D.C., when I grow up. Maybe I'll go right to New York or Hollywood. Can'tcha jist see me now, sittin' up on some stage, pattin' my knee and playin' this here harp? I might jist join up with the Mills Brothers."

"Come on!" I exclaimed. "We got work to do!"

"Ain't we havin' no breakfast this morning? I done recovered from all my ailments."

On the way to the Dixie, I told him what was happening. "I don't rightly know what we're gonna do, but we gotta stop at the Dixie and get some tickets, then get back to the Firestone."

Billy Joe Locke was walking up the two concrete steps that led to the ticket office as we arrived.

"Mr. Locke, have you got some tickets for Mr. Arnold?"

"Right here, Johnnie. Lemme get the door unlocked."

As we walked past the popcorn machine, the delicious aroma of buttered popcorn wafted past my nose. Entering the lobby, Billy Joe turned on the lights, opened his leather case and handed me two large rolls of red theater tickets.

"You take these right to Arnold. I don't know what he's got up his sleeve, but he called me last night saying he had to have two hundred tickets right away. They don't have names or numbers on them. I don't want him giving them out to folks so they can get in the show for nothing."

"Yes, sir, and thank you, Mr. Locke." We each took a roll of tickets and scampered on down to the store.

Mr. Arnold was apparently waiting for us since it took just one tap on the back door for him to open it. This was a new experience for Wormy. He was never

The Dixie Theater

allowed in the store unless he was with one of his parents, who just might buy something.

The store room was very large with tall ceilings and shelves situated almost around the whole room. There were a couple of ladders for climbing up the shelves, which were filled with car tires and all sorts of interesting looking boxes. There were several desks with papers neatly stacked on each of them. He had cleaned off two of the desks and had chairs all set up for us.

"Okay, boys, here's the plan. I want each of you to take these black marking pencils and do as I say. John, you sit at this desk and Wormy, you take the other. Now pay attention because this is very important. Carefully unroll your tickets without tearing them off the rolls. Then, with the pencils, very neatly print the letters S.T.H."

"What's that stand for, Mr. Arnold?"

"Johnnie, those illustrious letters stand for Save the Hudson. Remember, that's the name of our campaign. Then, right below that, John, you will start with number one, numbering each ticket, right up to number one hundred.

"Wormy, old friend—incidentally, Wormy, can you write?"

"Shore I can write. What you think, I's dumb or somethin'? I can write words and numbers and everythin'. Now I ain't too good at spellin', but I shore can write."

"No need to worry about spelling, boy. All you've got to do is print the letters and numbers, just like John is doing. Only you start with number 101 and go through number two hundred.

"Look here, boy," he said as he walked over to the small blackboard that had a lot of writing and numbers on it. He erased a small area and gave us an example of how he wanted each ticket to look.

"All you young men have to do is get those two

hundred tickets ready as soon as possible. I've had people in here wanting to take a chance on that Philco. Even sold one of them an inner tube while they were here."

He stood there a good two or three minutes, lecturing us on the importance of our work and the campaign and what it would all mean to the town. Mr. Arnold talked a lot, and he talked real fast.

He concluded with, "Boys, we're going to do some kind of business here. We're going to save the Hudson, sell the Philco and, hopefully, each of us pocket a little change for ourselves."

When he finally left us to our chore and returned to the front of the store, Wormy said, "You know, Johnnie, that man shore talks a lot. Why, I'll bet when he dies, somebody's gonna have to take a stick and beat his tongue to death, jist to git it to stop flappin'."

As we started our work, Wormy showed some enthusiasm about the campaign for the first time. When he completed his first ticket, he called me over to his table and proudly displayed his penmanship. Fact was, he printed much better than I.

"I don't really care about how much he talks," I said. "What I do care about is raising that 83 dollars. I already talked to Mr. Columbus and all he needs is the money, and he'll send to Raleigh for parts. Then she'll be good as new—'cept for the radio, of course."

Mr. Arnold popped back in and said, "One more thing I forgot to tell you boys. You see the spot where you tear each ticket in half? Each half has got to have the same number on it. So when folks buy a ticket, we tear it in half, give them one half and deposit the other half in the big fish bowl. I thought a bowl would be better than a box so the folks can see how many tickets we've sold. On the day of the drawing, the half-ticket that's picked out of the bowl represents the winning number. The winner will have the other half. We match them up and somebody's got a new radio. Isn't that something, boys? It may be the best promotional idea I've ever had. If it's a success, and I'm sure it will be, I may just do it again for some other event."

Leaving us again, he did a little hop-and-skip and rubbed his hands together. It reminded me of something I'd seen Hitler do in one of the newsreels. Wormy and I sorta eyed each other, knowing full well it wasn't his idea at all. But all we cared about at that point was the money we were gonna make.

We had been working maybe an hour when Mr. Arnold rushed through the door shouting, "Johnnie, give me your first two tickets; Miriam and James Boyd want to be the first to buy." He could hardly contain his excitement, and I surely felt a little of it, too.

That was the only sale that morning. As dinner time approached, I told Mr. Arnold we would return after eating and try and finish our tickets that afternoon. He patted me on the head and told us to run along, but to get back as quickly as possible.

As we left through the rear door, I told Wormy to meet me out front at one o'clock. I headed down to the Boston Store, just bubbling over to tell Momma. I wanted to tell her before she heard it from somebody else.

But alas, I was too late. Entering the store, I received a rather stern look from Momma, who was waiting on a customer. I immediately knew she had already found out. I hung around the front of the store until she came out. She didn't say anything until we were a few yards from the store.

"Johnnie, what've you gotten us into now? What's this Buy the Hudson campaign?"

"Momma, it's the Save the Hudson campaign, and it's something I figured out to try and raise the 83 dollars we need to get the car fixed. Mr. Arnold really thinks it's a good idea, too. Wormy and me been working on it all morning. I wanted to surprise you with it."

"Oh, it's a good idea for Alvin Arnold all right. But I don't think I like it very much. Johnnie, it looks like we're asking everybody in town to give us money to get the car fixed."

"Momma, nobody's giving us anything. They're taking a chance on winning the Philco radio, just like the firemen's raffle last Christmas. And you sure didn't mind when they brought that food basket to our house."

"Yes, Johnnie, we did need and appreciate it, but we didn't ask for help. It was given voluntarily. And they did it for a lot of other folks, too."

We're not asking for anything here," I protested. "We're working for it. Somebody might just get that radio for 25 cents."

I proceeded to explain how Wormy and I were preparing the tickets that Billy Joe had donated, and how excited Mr. Arnold was about the whole idea.

"Momma, he's claiming it was a good idea and is even taking credit for thinking it up, right by himself. And besides, we already sold two tickets this morning."

I kept talking to her all the way home, trying to convince her it was good for everybody, and that we were not taking something for nothing.

"And anyway, what would Scotland Neck be like without a taxicab?" was my final plea.

By then, I knew she had stopped resisting, because she gave me a little hug as we walked into the house to prepare dinner.

"Just don't you forget to be at Bessie's this afternoon at 4 o'clock for that telephone call from the hospital."

I got back to the Firestone before Wormy. I was determined that *both* of us were going to walk in the front of the store together.

When he did arrive, he was in a rather somber mood,

but didn't say why. We were greeted with, "Welcome back, boys. I got a little chore for you before you start working on the tickets."

He had hand-lettered five small signs, telling the whole story of the raffle. He had added the words, "DROP INTO YOUR FRIENDLY FIRESTONE STORE TO PURCHASE YOUR TICKETS."

"I want you to run these signs out to the following places. All the owners are expecting you. And Johnnie, make sure you tell them to hang them right in the front of each window. They go to Hamilton's, the Dixie, the barber shop, the Sinclair and the Idle Hour. If they don't get us some customers, I don't know what will."

We took the signs in tow and headed out. Sure enough, we were greeted by each owner and they all wished us good luck. Melvin Smith even pulled out a dollar bill and said I was to bring him four tickets the next passing.

Our mission completed, we returned to the store. Mr. Arnold said, "Boys, we've already sold another one. Old Mae Booker bought it. Can you imagine that? She usually squeezes her nickels until the buffalo yells. People sure are interested in this radio."

The rest of the afternoon was spent numbering and lettering tickets, until it was time for me to meet Momma. We had both completed about three-quarters of our work.

"See you in the morning, Mr. Arnold. Hope you sell some more before you close today."

"Okay, boys, be here bright and early. Saturday is a busy day and I'd like to have all those tickets ready to sell. If I have time, I'll work on them myself."

As we walked out front, Wormy said, "Johnnie, I won't be here tomorrow, and I ain't shore about Monday. My daddy's got hisself into some kinda big trouble down in Raleigh, and Momma wants me to go along with her and see if we can help. I don't even wanna go, but Momma says I gotta. I hope they keep him in Raleigh forever. We is better off at home when he ain't there."

"Who's gonna take care of the girls and all?" I asked.

"Course my aunt's there, and Miz Helms next door is gonna help feed 'um. Soon as I git back I'll let you know. Don't you go and sell all them tickets while I'm gone," he said with a smirk on his face. He still wasn't sure our program would work, even in view of our modest success so far. "Hope yo daddy's okay," he said, walking away with drooped shoulders.

"Hope yours is too," I replied.

Momma and I left the store together and started towards Aunt Bessie's. I could tell she was a little nervous and anxious about the call. We got there right at 4 o'clock and had iced tea on the porch while we waited for the phone to ring.

"Bug," Bessie asked, "what are you gonna do if they're gonna keep Gavin on into next week? You going back down there again?"

"I'm really not sure, it all depends on—well, it just all depends. They really need me at the store on Saturday and I need the money. I just don't know."

Ruby and I got into a hopscotch game while we were waiting. It killed me that she always won, no matter how hard I tried or how careful I was. That day was no exception.

It must have been something after five when we heard the phone ring. Momma and Bessie went in the house, and I rushed up on the porch. I thought I should wait and get the results from Momma.

When they finally returned, I could tell all was not well.

"What is it, Momma? What did they find out?"

"It's his kidneys again, and they expect to keep him at least another week. The doctor said he has uremic poisoning because his kidneys just aren't working like they should. They're keeping him there to try and get it out of his system. Then, maybe he can come home."

"You want me to have Jimmie drive you down there tomorrow, Bug?" Bessie asked.

"No, Bess, thanks. I better stay here and work. We've got to have some kind of income; and who knows when Gavin will be able to go back to work again—and if he will, 'specially with the car broken down."

It was obvious Momma and Wormy shared the same lack of faith in our campaign.

We ate supper with Aunt Bessie and then went home for a quiet and worry-filled Friday evening.

Chapter 13

The Save the Hudson campaign was to become more successful than we ever imagined. By Wednesday of the following week, the first roll of tickets was completely sold out.

Wormy had returned on Monday and Mr. Arnold got another two hundred tickets from Billy Joe. We worked the better part of the week numbering and lettering and running around all over town delivering tickets and collecting money.

The Standard ran an inspiring article, right on page one, regarding the campaign. It included the usual promotional information on the festival, but highlighted the Philco and the fact that the grand drawing would be held on the last day of festival week at the high school grounds.

The historic crepe myrtle festival was a week-long affair, focusing on the lovely foliage along Main Street and flourishing in other cared-for areas throughout the town. It represented the remaining signs of summer's abundance and the beginning of harvest time. We knew that soon leaves would begin to yellow and the rich summer colors we had so enjoyed would give way to autumn's subtle plumage.

The festival was all to culminate on Saturday, August 30, with most of the final-day festivities taking place on

the school grounds. There would be horseshoe contests, potato-sack races, pony rides and lots of other
games and amusements for both children and adults. An
abundant array of local foods would entice everyone.
Many of the merchants had reserved areas on the grounds
and would be offering prizes and the opportunity to
make special purchases. The event would conclude with
the joyous Sadie Hawkins dance, just before sunset.

No one knew how or when the crepe myrtles had
been planted. But a headline in *The Standard* dated
March, 1925, indicated that Scotland Neck's Main Street
was to become an area of beauty with the planting of
over one hundred crepe myrtle shrubs, which would
adorn the center of the main thoroughfare. Everyone in
town enjoyed the blushing bushes. Even folks from
nearby towns would come to celebrate the festival. It
was always a busy week, with the last day being one filled
with fun for all.

By the middle of the week preceding festival day, we
had sold a total of 585 tickets—a number that astounded
even Mr. Arnold. We were setting our goal for six
hundred, which, as I had carefully figured, should cover
all the necessary expenses and yield us a tidy profit.

We had been back to Billy Joe so many times, he had
finally started charging us 50 cents for each additional
roll of tickets. Mr. Arnold gladly paid, smiling all the
while. He said he never had so much business in his
store since he had been in town. Wormy swore he could
see dollar signs flash in Mr. Arnold's eyes every time he
rang up a sale on his cash register.

Wormy's daddy had been charged with armed rob-
bery somewhere in the Raleigh area and was in jail
awaiting trial. I knew he cared little for his daddy, but,
like me, was worried about his Momma and all her
problems. When Wormy wasn't working with me, he was
home helping Mrs. Wilson. Some days he would go with

her and help clean houses. We had little time for play those last several weeks.

As festival day approached, the whole town was aflutter. Everyone was busy—some preparing their exhibits, some shaping up the bushes, and others generally cleaning up Main Street. We knew many out-of-towners would be attending, and we wanted Scotland Neck to look its best.

The school grounds were divided into sections that had been reserved by those who hoped to sell their wares. Mayor Dawson, who was in charge, was busy running hither and thither, tipping his hat and sweating up a storm. He had reserved an area for the preparation and sale of his Brunswick Stew.

The Moore farm had volunteered several of its ponies for the children to ride. Any proceeds from these community activities would go to the Fire Department.

Mr. Arnold had reserved the biggest space of all for the several items of merchandise he had carefully selected for display. We were to set up a large table right in the center of his section, draped with red, white and blue crepe paper. The fish bowl, with all the one-half tickets, was to be placed on the decorated table. Never again admitting the raffle was my idea, he had promised I would be the one to draw the winning ticket. In spite of that, I was beginning to like Mr. Arnold—just a little bit. Besides, I didn't care about the credit—just the results.

Both Wormy and I had wanted to buy tickets, but Mr. Arnold advised against it. He reasoned that if any of us connected with the raffle happened to win, it might look suspicious. I thought maybe if I won that radio, it would help Daddy get over the loss of the radio in the Hudson. I was disappointed, but agreed with Mr. Arnold's thinking.

The town's one big fear was that it might rain on

Saturday. But to our delight, the day dawned bright and beautiful. I lay in my bed a few moments, gazing dreamily out the window and thinking of all the day's events yet to come.

Most of the stores would be open only half the day, as everybody planned to be at the school grounds by noon. The Boston Store was closing at noon, and even Momma was looking forward to the festival. I was glad to see her happy about something. She and Aunt Bessie had reserved a small area to hold a rummage sale of clothes donated by the Boston Store. Aunt Bessie was going to sell some of her older costume jewelry, as she said it was outdated and beginning to look a little tacky.

After a quick breakfast, I headed for the blacksmith shop with a little added spring in my walk. I felt vibrant all over that day. Mr. Allsbrook was nowhere in sight, but Wormy was sitting on the large tool box, just outside the shop.

"Let's get going," I said. "Mr. Arnold wants us at the store by 10 o'clock to help him load up. We're in charge of setting up and decorating the table."

Mr. Arnold had his truck at the back door and was busy loading some car tires, a few tools and small appliance items.

"You boys know where your stuff is, so get her loaded."

"How we doing on ticket sales, Mr. Arnold?" Wormy asked.

"Boys, we need to sell just eight more to reach our goal of six hundred. I suspect we'll sell some during the day. This evening, when all the stands close, we'll come back here and settle up."

I had done some arithmetic the night before and knew we had already sold enough to pay for the radio and get me the 83 dollars. Mr. Arnold kept referring to "certain expenses" he had incurred, but I still felt pretty confident.

Once loaded, the two of us hopped in the back of the truck to hold everything steady as we set off for the school. The truck had to go over the curb and drive across the grounds to get to our space. Several areas were roped off, and there were already a few people milling around. As Mr. Arnold pulled up to our space, we jumped down from the truck, dropped the rope around our section, and all started unloading. We set all his items around the perimeter of the area and the table, with its patriotic colors, was set right in the middle, facing the tall flagpole by the school building.

As the morning wore on, more and more spaces were filled, and the crowd gradually grew larger. Most everybody walked past our area, pointing and casting admiring glances at the little radio.

Right out front on Main Street, the town's fire engine was on display, looking all shiny-red. Sheriff Calhoun's car was parked nearby. I noticed he had it all cleaned up. He stood at the main entrance, looking tall and handsome in his uniform. He was even wearing his sheriff's hat that day. He was supervising, directing traffic and generally shouting out orders here and there. Mayor Dawson stood right next to him, decked out in his usual white suit, but for the first time in my memory, wearing a different necktie. It was red, white and blue and must have had all 48 stars on it. He smiled and tipped his hat to every car and person entering the grounds.

Only a few Negroes ever attended. With most of the stores closing at noon, Billy Joe Locke had planned a double feature and five cartoons for them.

Pretty soon, the VFW, Post 25, of the North Carolina Regiment arrived. They were elderly men, all dressed in wool, World War I uniforms, with neatly-fitting canvas leggings and shoes shined to perfection. They wore their uniforms with pride and many had medals plas-

Crepe Myrtle Festival

tered all over their chests. I knew if Daddy were home, he would be right there with them. As he did, they also considered themselves our past champions of liberty. They carried their large American flag, which was to be run up the flagpole at noon, officially opening the day's festivities.

Harry Lee Smith walked by our area with a little tray hung around his neck. It was filled with comic books and various gadgets and trinkets that he expected to sell at a profit. Wormy was placing the radio in the middle of the table when Harry Lee remarked sarcastically, "Dumbest thing I ever heard of, trying to make money on some dern little radio that probably won't even work very long anyway."

As Wormy looked in his direction, I could see anger in his eyes. Wormy left the table and raised the rope as if to approach Harry Lee, who quickly hi-tailed it off to another part of the grounds.

"He prob'ly stole all them things he's selling," Wormy growled.

Once we had everything set in place, we walked over to find Momma and Aunt Bessie to see if we could help them. They were sorting out clothing and setting out cakes and pies Bessie had been preparing during the last week.

"Can we help y'all?" I asked.

"Maybe just run over and get us a cold Coke," Momma replied. "I swear, we're gonna die from this heat today. I hope we sell out soon so we can just sit in the shade and enjoy the events."

We hastily got the drinks and returned to our stand where Mr. Arnold happily said, "Well, we finally did it, boys. So far, we've sold 602 tickets, and we've still got a couple hours before the drawing."

Wormy and I clapped our hands, patted each other on the back and scampered off to get a look at everything else.

The school grounds extended from Main Street on the front all the way back to Church. The horseshoe area had been set up in the shade of the trees lining Church Street. There was a large group of men practicing, while others sat in the comfort of the shade, waiting their turns. It dawned on me where Mr. Allsbrook had been that morning. He was in charge of the contest and provided all the shoes. Some of them had been used in past festivals and others were brand new. They had all been painted red, white and blue, except for two gold painted shoes hung on the side of a tree. They were to be used in the final match of the day. The winner got to keep his set of gold shoes as a reminder of his monumental victory.

Perhaps the strangest sight of the day was at the Coca-Cola stand, which was operated by Tazwell Judson and Shoofly. The two of them were actually sipping on cold Cokes! I was sure they had a reservoir of their own making stashed away somewhere. It would be dipped into as the festival wore on and the crowd grew larger.

A group of men had gathered around the stand and were discussing the year that someone had run Shoofly's "cutoff" pants up the flagpole. The mayor had been fit-to-be-tied and quickly had the pants removed. He had said it was a sacrilege to our flagpole and a personal reflection on him as chairman of the event. But even Shoofly enjoyed the joke because it made him feel important to see his pants fluttering in the breeze next to the school house. The story was told each year and always got a big laugh.

Just at the stroke of noon, the entire crowd turned towards the flagpole as the men of the VFW proudly marched up bearing their flag. Colonel Earnest Javins, the oldest member of the regiment, clutched a shiny brass bugle in his hand. As the flag began making its way up the pole, there was a hushed silence throughout the grounds. Everyone stood and came to attention. Hats came off and hands went directly over hearts as Colonel Javins began playing, as best he could, The Star Spangled Banner.

Almost everybody in attendance had husbands, sons or other relatives scattered around the world, fighting in the war. That was a very meaningful moment to all of us. Tears were streaming down faces of men as well as women, and you could see feelings of anguish in their eyes. I think we were all thankful that we could enjoy such a day of freedom as that. But we knew it was at the expense of our fighting men.

We had to use a little imagination to recognize the National Anthem, but the old colonel did his very best. He was straining so hard his face was blood-red and his small, beady eyes were bulging. We all shared a sigh of relief for him when he pushed the final flat note out of his bugle.

Once the flag reached the top and the bugle went silent, Mayor Dawson mounted the school steps next to the flag. The solemn hush was broken only by the cry of a baby and the whimpering of the young children. The mayor delivered a very moving message about how lucky we were to live in a free country, enjoying such a glorious day, while many of our own brave boys were busy defending our rights to have such days. He offered thanks to them and said a word about what a great president we had, leading our country in such desperate times. Sheriff Calhoun, who was standing next to him, finally had to tug on his coat to get him to stop talking.

Then, each of the preachers from the four churches had a moment of prayer for our country, our fighting men and our wonderful town. I was very touched by the ceremony and silently thanked God for Scotland Neck and prayed that the war might end soon and that my daddy would be made well.

Following the prayers, the mayor took off his hat, bushy hair plastered down from perspiration, and waved it joyfully above his head, as he proclaimed that the festival day had officially begun.

The entire school grounds were filled to capacity. The games and contests were underway; and lovely red, white and blue balloons went soaring up in the clear blue sky. A small group of local musicians provided background music of mainly patriotic and traditional American tunes. It was indeed a fine festival and a grand day for our town.

Wormy and I were running from section to section, spending a nickel here and a dime there. Wormy won a toy soldier by tossing a penny in a small cup that was sitting in a tub of water.

Now and again, we would check with Mr. Arnold, who was busy selling and showing and talking a mile a minute. I really wanted to know the ticket count, but he was always in the middle of some big deal when we went by.

Finally, around 5 o'clock, when we went back to his area, he was entirely free of customers.

"Johnnie, it's almost time for the drawing. You boys stay nearby. I'm going to get everyone's attention soon, and, as promised, you, John my boy, will pick the lucky ticket." Mr. Arnold was aglow with enthusiasm at that moment.

"How many tickets have we sold?" I asked.

"At last count, John, a total of 613."

"Wow!" I shouted. "We sure done all right, didn't we, Mr. Arnold?"

As I said that, I was trying to do some mental arithmetic. But, for the life of me, I couldn't figure out how much 613 times 25 cents totaled. I just knew it was enough to get the 83 dollars.

Nervously, Mr. Arnold said, "Johnnie, I want you to

go get Colonel Javins and tell him to come on over here with his bugle."

I didn't know what Mr. Arnold had in mind, but I obediently scooted off in search of the colonel. I finally found him back by the horseshoe area, sound asleep in a rocking chair. His bugle lay at his feet and his head was flopped over to one side. Sporadically, gravelly snores erupted from his mouth, which was open wide enough to house a flock of horse flies. I was a little nervous about waking him, so I asked Luke Walker to please arouse him for me.

Luke gently tugged on the colonel's shoulder. One eye opened at a time and he attempted to focus on me. He shook his head back and forth a couple of times, and then, looking about a foot above my head, finally said, "I'm a comin', Johnnie, I'm a comin'. I know Arnold wants me to blow my horn and git everybody over to his area. Jist gimme a minute or so to git myself together. This here lumbago does me right bad sometimes. But, I'm a comin'."

He took his hat, put it on backwards and grasped the arms of the chair, but couldn't quite lift himself up. After he struggled for a moment, I suggested, "Mightn't it be better if a couple of the men gave you a hand, Colonel?"

It took Luke and Harry Willis to get him out of the chair. He was still partially dressed in his uniform, but his coat was unbuttoned down to his belt and one of his leggings hung loosely on the ground. He had stains all down the front of his shirt and generally looked a mess. Pulling his cap down, almost covering his eyes, he showed a great deal of determination to get over to our area and perform his duty.

Luke turned the colonel's hat around and buttoned his coat while I latched up the legging. Luke and Harry walked arm-in-arm with him. I followed carrying the bugle. I hoped he had enough wind left to play whatever it was he was supposed to play.

Mr. Arnold looked at him with distaste and said, "Look at you, Colonel. I told you to keep yourself straight until we get this event over with."

"Listen, Arnold, you jist git me up on that stand and everybody in Halifax County will know, Earnest Javins, Colonel, U.S.A., is here servin' his country, jist as I always done."

There was a small platform in front of the Philco display, which we somehow managed to get him on. Both Luke and Harry stood at his sides, steadying him. As I handed him his bugle, he came to attention and started on the National Anthem again, as out of tune as before.

"No! No! You old fool," Arnold shouted. "I told you to play Dixie, not the blamed National Anthem."

The colonel stopped in mid-note. Looking a little perplexed, he said, "Oh, yeah. Well, uh, I know that. I jist wanted to get their attention."

And then, sure enough, the familiar tune of Dixie began to rattle out of that old bugle.

Now, you have to understand that in those days, Dixie was almost as important to most folks in Scotland Neck as was The Star Spangled Banner. As soon as he got started, not only did it gain everybody's attention, but they all stood and began singing along to his irregular, quavering trill.

From somewhere over near the schoolhouse, the Stars and Bars suddenly appeared. Somebody was running through the crowd, frantically waving the flag back and forth on a hand-held pole. As the pole-bearer darted in and out of the crowd, loud cheers followed. When he finally ended his trip, right in front of our stand, I could see it was Fletcher Jenkins. He climbed up on the stand next to the colonel.

By then, all attention was riveted on the Firestone area. Mr. Arnold pulled out a megaphone and yelled for everybody to be quiet and give him their attention.

"Quiet, folks! Quiet, everyone! The big moment has finally arrived. And a proud moment, indeed, for Firestone, yours truly, Alvin Arnold and every citizen of Scotland Neck. You have all done a fine job for a worthy cause. Now, some very lucky person is going to walk away with the latest electrical innovation on the market—this very, very fine Philco radio, small enough to be held in one hand." As he said that, he took the radio and held it above his head, while an appreciative cheer went up from the crowd. "And remember, folks, while everyone of you can't win this particular radio, you can purchase another one from me in my very fine store, located on Main Street, right in the heart of our lovely town."

Another cheer from the crowd.

Placing one hand on my shoulder and using the other to hold the megaphone, he shouted, "Most of you folks know that Johnnie here had a small part in promoting this event, and it's his daddy's car, and your only taxicab, that will benefit. So let's all hush up now, so Johnnie can draw the lucky ticket."

By then, Colonel Javins had been mercifully relieved from duty, but Fletcher was still waving the flag back and forth.

"Get down now, Fletcher, and let Johnnie do his drawing," Mr. Arnold instructed.

My pulse quickened and I was both nervous and proud to be up there on the stand. The crowd had grown quiet again and people were shoving and pushing to get a closer look. I focused on Wormy's face and noticed a twinkle in his incredibly expressive eyes.

"Shazam, Johnnie! Go do yo thing."

While Mr. Arnold was retrieving the fish bowl, there were a few shouts of "Come on!" and "Pick the ticket!"

Mr. Arnold held the fish bowl up high so everybody could watch me reach in. I knew it held over six hundred

red half-tickets. I shoved my hand down into the bowl and smooched it around until my fingers locked on one ticket. I pulled it out, knowing Mr. Arnold wanted me to hand it to him. But my eyes shot down to the ticket and I shouted, "Number 211! Number 211 is the winner!"

Some of the folks in the back yelled that they couldn't hear the number. Instantly, Mr. Arnold grabbed his megaphone, jerked the ticket from my hand and shouted, "Number 211! Number 211!"

"Gracious sakes! Gracious sakes! I won it! I won it!" came from a woman in the back of the group.

All heads turned to see Mrs. Calhoun, the sheriff's wife, holding her ticket stub high above her head and trying to worm her way through the crowd. There were several cheers, but mostly sighs and moans. I instantly felt very good about the Calhouns winning the radio, with everything the sheriff had done for me recently.

When Mrs. Calhoun finally got to us, Wormy lifted the rope, and she bent under it and almost ran over to the table. After matching her ticket with the one I had pulled from the fish bowl, Mr. Arnold, who was beside himself with excitement, insisted that she mount the platform. He then said, "On behalf of the Firestone Company, and yours truly, Alvin Arnold, I am proud to present this fine radio to Eleanor Calhoun, wife of our distinguished sheriff."

A small cheer went up, but by then, most of the crowd was finding its way back to other activities.

Mrs. Calhoun said, "Johnnie, come here and let me give you a big hug for picking my ticket. I sure am pleased to be the winner. And Johnnie, we all hope your daddy's car gets fixed and that he comes home real soon."

After the drawing, the merchants began packing and disbanding their work areas. Sheriff Calhoun borrowed the megaphone, got out in the center of the field and directed everyone to clear the area so it could be set up for the dance.

We had packed everything in the truck, and Wormy and I climbed up on the back again. We would go back and help unload. Of course, my main thoughts regarded that financial settlement Mr. Arnold had mentioned earlier.

Back at the store, we quickly unpacked the truck, stored all the merchandise on the shelves and waited for Mr. Arnold to say something.

Somewhat to my relief, Mr. Arnold said, "Okay, boys, time to do some figuring out and settling up. I'm not exactly sure, but I believe we did right well."

Wormy and I sat down around one of the tables in the rear of the store as Mr. Arnold went over to a large safe. He brought out a small metal box, took a key from his pocket and unlocked it. My heart skipped a beat, as I looked down at all the money. There were one dollar bills, five dollar bills, a few tens and a lot of quarters.

"Johnnie, I turned in a lot of those quarters at the bank and had them give me dollars. Let's see what we've got here." He took a piece of paper and one of our marking pencils and said, "Well now, we've sold 613 tickets at 25 cents a ticket." He did some arithmetic and said, "That comes to a grand total of 153 dollars and 25 cents. First we've got to pay Firestone for the radio." So he counted out 25 dollars and set it aside in one pile. "Next, we've got to allocate 83 dollars for the Hudson." He slowly counted out a stack of money in front of me. The stack got so tall, I thought I had died and gone to heaven.

He said, "Here you go, son. Get that car fixed," as he shoved the stack of money to me. "Well now, that still leaves us with 45 dollars and 25 cents and we said we would split that 50-50. Johnnie, I'm going to give you 20 dollars and take 20 for myself. That leaves—let me see—

that leaves 5 dollars and 25 cents, which about covers the cost of the extra tickets, signs, balloons and crepe paper. So, I'll take that to pay me back for those certain expenses. Count your money, Johnnie. You should have 103 dollars."

My hands were sweating as I looked down at the money. I picked up the whole stack and Wormy and I walked over to the other table and started counting. Sure enough, I had 103 dollars in my hands! Wormy hadn't said a word, but just sat there, staring at the pile of money, as did I.

Finally, he said, "Garden peas, Johnnie! You really done all right. You gits yo daddy's car fixed, and you still got some money left over."

"Now, Wormy," I said, "it's time for you and me to settle up."

"Whatcha mean?"

"I shore couldn't have done this without your help. Since my share of the extra money is 20 dollars, I figure that half of this is yours."

To make it seem like a whole lot, I counted out 10 one dollar bills and pushed them over to him. For a moment, he was speechless.

Then, in a puzzled tone, he said, "What I'ma do first?"

He went silent again. And then, mimicking Mr. Arnold, in a very quiet tone, he said, "Well, John, my boy, I think I'm gonna keep one dollar fer myself and give my momma the rest of it to help her with the fambly. You think that's fair?"

"I shore do. And I know she needs it now more than ever," I happily agreed.

"I gotta git on home right now and surprise her. Why, that's mor'n she makes in—well—in a long time."

"You roll up that money and put it in your pocket and keep your hand on it all the way home. Don't stop for no Coca-Cola or nothing," I warned.

A broad smile spanned his face as he carefully rolled up the 10 one dollar bills, squeezed them tightly and shoved them down in his pocket. He looked me right in the eyes and said, "Thank you, Johnnie." And then all I heard as he raced out the door was "Shazam! Shazam!"

I felt almost as happy for Wormy as I did for me. I sat there another moment, enjoying the feeling of success and thinking about Wormy. He was and always would be my very best friend.

After one final count of my money, I knew what Zeb Kitchen felt like when he drove down Main Street in one of his new cars.

My trance-like state was broken when Mr. Arnold said, "Time to lock up and get back to the dance. Johnnie, what you had was a good idea. And sometimes—just sometimes, good ideas pay off. Also, what you did was a good thing. I know your momma and daddy will be proud of you. I'm right proud of you myself."

At that moment I decided that I really did like Mr. Arnold. I also realized the significance of a business deal and, like Mrs. Wilson had said, giving—and keeping—your word was very important in life. And Mr. Arnold had certainly done that.

"You get any more ideas like that, you just let Alvin Arnold know. You be careful with all that money and get on back to your momma."

"Yes, sir. And thank you for all you did, Mr. Arnold."

"All in a day's work, John. All in a day's work."

I felt like running back to the school grounds. But I walked with my money tight-fisted and pushed down in my pocket.

Approaching the school grounds, the sounds of music and laughing and fun-making brought happiness to me. The dance was then in full swing. I figured Momma would be sitting over on the school steps.

She and Aunt Bessie were sitting there, just resting and sipping Cokes, looking completely worn-out. They both smiled as I walked up and Momma asked, "Well, how did your business venture turn out?"

I told her to hold out her hand as I hastily withdrew my roll of bills and placed them in her palm. When she realized the quantity, she instantly asked, "Johnnie, you didn't do anything dishonest, did you?"

"No, ma'am, that's my share of the raffle. Count it, Momma! Please count it!"

As she counted it, bill by bill, she handed it to Bessie to keep it straight.

"Johnnie, I can't believe it! You have almost one hundred dollars here, 93, to be exact!"

"That's right. That should be enough to fix the Hudson, buy that dress you want and still have a little left over."

She had done so much crying lately, the tears were slow to appear, but her eyes were soon brimming over. For the first time in quite awhile, I knew those were not tears of sorrow, but of happiness—and maybe a little relief. She held out her arms, and I went and sat on her lap, enjoying another special moment in time with my momma.

Even Aunt Bessie had tears in her eyes.

I didn't know what else to say or do. We just sat there in the cool of the early evening, listening to the music and watching the gaiety of the dancers. The ever-familiar train whistle sounded from over in East Scotland Neck. The waning sunset seemed to linger, casting long shadows across the school grounds. A few of its beams stole their way through the trees along Church Street, lighting up the crepe myrtles in the center of Main Street, soaking them in fiery hues. Their beauty and the music drifting across the grounds were a serenade of joy for me. That day, I had passed from a mournful reverie to mighty revelry. I was filled with a satisfaction to be remembered forever. I knew that would be the grandest festival day of my life.

Chapter 14

School was to start in less than two weeks. Except for the fact that it separated me from Wormy, I rather enjoyed school.

It also ushered in one of the burdens of my life—piano lessons. Although Daddy played the guitar and he and Momma had beautiful voices, I had neither musical talent nor the desire for any. But Momma was determined that I learn to play the piano and always arranged for my lessons at school. Those lessons, along with Harry Lee Smith and a couple of other things, were on my most-hated list. Fortunately, because we didn't own a piano, my practice time was limited to one afternoon a week. That afternoon was always sheer torture, mainly because of Mrs. Wilhiminia Gretchem. She was the school's music teacher and a real disciplinarian. Most of her students referred to her as "Grouchy Gretchem." She would set a metronome up on the piano, while under her strict guidance, I practiced for 30 minutes. She kept a little wooden stick in her hand and kept time as if she were directing my every move. If I hit one wrong key, she gave a little tap on my knuckles and said something prissy like, "Mind your musical manners, Johnnie."

In addition to the beginning of school, I hoped that September would bring the repair of the Hudson, and my daddy coming home.

Monday morning, following the festival, Momma and I went to the Sinclair and gave Columbus Jones the 83 dollars. On Tuesday, Slim went to Raleigh to get the parts. They hoped to have the car running by the weekend.

Wormy and I had spent all Monday cleaning out the inside and washing the car. Considering its recent history, it looked pretty good. It still had a musty, damp smell inside, but we continued to air it out each day. I took some of Daddy's Old Spice and sprinkled it all over the inside. I sure hoped he didn't notice the smell too much. I knew he'd notice the radio and that still worried me.

The hospital was releasing Daddy, not because he was completely well, but because they had done everything they could for him. While his kidneys still weren't working just right, staying in the hospital wouldn't help them. He was to take several medications, rest a part of each day and abstain from alcohol. The last part was Momma's worst fear, because alcohol was his greatest weakness. Momma and Uncle Jimmie were to drive down on Saturday morning and bring them back that same afternoon. I couldn't wait for him to get home. We had managed to get along, but home wasn't the same without Daddy—especially with Poochie gone. I also realized that while we had a lot of family in town, Momma had been very lonely.

By late Friday afternoon, our first goal was achieved. The Hudson was running! I went by the Boston Store to walk Momma home when Columbus came bursting in shouting, "She's running! By God, Ethel, she's running! And believe it or not, she's purrin' jist like a baby kitten! I ain't felt so good about a thing since I got my new false teeth!" He was huffing and puffing and filled with excitement, and rightly proud of himself, too.

I felt a mite proud myself—and mighty relieved.

When Columbus handed Momma the keys, she gave him a big hug, and we both thanked him, over and over again. After we left the store, we went to Hamiltons where she bought a big box of Whitman's Samplers candy. We walked over to the station where she let me present the gift to Columbus and Slim. They beamed with pride and we all felt right good.

Momma and I took a short drive in the Hudson, just to check it out. We drove down to the cemetery and parked near the duck pond. The quiet and peace of the area, and the fact that Daddy was coming home the next day, had Momma in a good mood. We just sat there for awhile, watching the little ducks and talking about the festival, the car and all. Maybe our troubles were behind us. While there had been a lot of excitement, it had been a right worrisome summer. I hadn't felt that comfortable for a long time. Neither of us mentioned how, or what, we would tell Daddy about the car, especially the radio. I was hoping she would handle the whole situation, and I could be quiet as a mouse.

When we got home, Momma had a letter from Aunt Sadie. Her husband, Sam, had been taken to the hospital in Staunton, Virginia, with a liver ailment. Now Momma had to worry about Aunt Sadie. It seemed that when one problem ended, another began. Daddy always said that was what life was all about—getting one problem out of the way so you were ready for the next one. I was beginning to learn that it didn't take long for problems to pile up, one right after the other. "Maybe," I thought, "that's what growing up is all about."

The Whiteheads had invited us over for supper, since they knew Momma had to get ready to go to Fayetteville the next day. Later, at bedtime, Momma and I said a short prayer, asking that everything would be all right when Daddy got home. I added my personal note, thanking God for the Hudson.

Saturday morning, Jimmie came by early, dropped me off at Aunt Bessie's, and he and Momma headed for Fayetteville. Although I asked about going along, Momma said Daddy might have to lay down in the back seat, so I best stay home. I was excited that I would see him that night.

During dinner with Aunt Bessie, she reminded me to get my playing done and get home early. I needed to spend some time that afternoon preparing for Daddy's arrival.

About a half-block from Allsbrook's, I saw Wormy running towards me and shouting, "Johnnie, one of them dern Nazis has got away and is loose runnin' 'round somewhere. I jist seen the sheriff and a bunch of soldiers down by the sheriff's office. They got their guns with 'um, too! They think he's headed fer the river 'cause the farm he's workin' on is down that way. They even got bloodhounds, and the sheriff tole all the folks to be on the lookout if they seen anythin' suspicious. Think they'd let us go with 'um, 'specially since we knows somethin' 'bout them Nazis and jist how to handle 'um?"

I noticed he had his rubber gun tucked in his pants, but hadn't yet loaded it. He used to carry it loaded all the time, tucked right down in the front of his britches. One day it accidentally went off and caused him right much hurt. Since then, he kept his ammunition looped over his shoulder.

"You know they ain't gonna let no young boys go searching with them. I suspect they want us to stay away from them, as far as possible. Besides, I don't think they got any colored boys in Germany. Probably nothing would please that Nazi more'n having a skinny colored boy to drag along as a hostage."

Giving the matter some thought, he scratched his head and said, "I s'pose you's right. We jist might git in the way of the sheriff and all them soldiers with their guns and everythin'. We'll do our playin' somewhere else today. Les go over to the ole academy and 'tend like we is chasin' Germans. That might be a better idea."

I smiled and agreed, but said we'd have to go by my house so I could get my gun. No search party would be complete without the proper weapons.

As we went into the house, Mrs. Whitehead asked if we'd heard the news about the escaped Nazi. She said she had just heard it on the radio from a station in Raleigh, so it was statewide news. They had said he was the first P.O.W. to escape in North Carolina.

"Don't you boys think you'd better play around the yard, today? Nobody knows where he is, and you surely don't want to run into him."

"We don't plan to go in that direction, Mrs. Whitehead." I replied. "They say he's probably heading for the river. Maybe he'll try and hitch on a train going by there. We won't go anywhere near the river, I promise."

I gathered up my gun and leather holster Mr. Allsbrook had made for me. I had four rounds of ammunition left and I slid them through the belt that went with the holster. We felt like two musketeers setting off in search of high adventure.

Often, we would go in the woods behind the academy and set up rusty tin cans or old bottles and have target practice. Other times, we would sit in the shade of a tree, guns loaded, being as quiet as possible. Should any rabbit or squirrel pass by, we would take pot shots at them.

But whatever we chose to do, it was the pretending that was the most fun. We were Jessie James, Daniel Boone, the Lone Ranger, or any sort of villain or hero we could imagine. We would sit down and map out our strategy, deciding who would be the good guy and who would be the enemy. In executing our plan, we always escaped unscathed and saved someone from the ravages of a terrible foe. I was always saving Reba from some impossible dilemma. Wormy would keep Mary Beth from being scalped or some other fate worse than death. Whatever the pursuit, we considered ourselves the vanguards of American bravery. We would conclude by congratulating ourselves on being heroes.

Whenever we needed a fortress, the academy was the place. We knew every inch of it from past narrow escapes and adventures. The town had condemned the structure long ago. All the windows were boarded up and there were several "No Trespassing" signs posted. The front door had been nailed shut and a large "Condemned by the Town of Scotland Neck" sign hung loosely from the door. Inside, many of the floorboards were rotten, and two very unstable stairways took careful footing to reach the second floor. All these obstructions had only been slight hindrances to us. We had rigged the front door so it would open, and loosened boards covering most of the windows. Entry and exit had become no problem at all to Fort Academy, as we had come to call it. It was not the safest place to play, but heroes were afraid of nothing—the greater the challenge, the greater the conquest.

We walked down Sunset Avenue and crossed the canal at the same point where Wormy had enjoyed his banquet breakfast. Situating ourselves in the same shaded area, we plopped down and began discussing our plan for the day. After careful consideration, we decided that Wormy would be the army captain of the fort. I was to be leading a group of Nazis, trying to capture it, but killing as few Americans as possible.

"I'm goin' on in," Wormy said, "and when I git set up, I'll yell 'ready.' You don't tell me where you is comin' from, and then see if you can git in the fort without me shootin' you. Once you git inside, it's ev'ry man for hisself. Don't you do nothin' goofy now. You wait 'til you

The Old Academy

hear me yell 'ready' 'fore you starts," he said as he skipped on towards the dilapidated front door.

"Yes, sir, Cap'n!"

Sometimes he fooled me. But I usually knew where he would position himself. He would go up the back stairs and hide behind the railing that looked down into the once grand foyer. Then, if I entered from the front door, I was dead.

That day, I figured I wouldn't use the front door, but would go in the far side window. All I had to do was slide a couple of boards aside and I could quietly slip in.

I gave him a couple of minutes and began to creep around to the other end of the woods. From there, he wouldn't have a clear view of me. Once in place, I would wait for his "ready" command.

I took one of my rubber slings, stretched it over the barrel and securely latched it inside the clothespin. The other three I hung loosely over my shoulder. All the soldiers did that with their extra clips of bullets.

Suddenly, winning that battle became very important to me. Wormy usually turned out to be the victor, but this time would be different.

When I reached my window, I knelt quietly below it, rechecked my gun and felt totally prepared for my invasion.

I waited—and I waited—but no yell from Wormy.

Finally, waiting no longer, I swiftly darted around to the front of the building to yell, "Coming, ready or not," and pretended to enter the front door. Then I scurried back to my position and crouched beneath the window. Still, there was no reply. I wondered, "What kind of trick is he pulling today? He must have found a new hiding spot and doesn't want to let on where he is.

"Shucks," I finally thought, "I'm going on in. I already yelled 'Ready or not.'"

I quietly slid two of the window boards aside,

quickly climbed in and lowered myself to the floor. There was an ominous silence throughout the building. Visually scanning the area, I saw tiny dust particles flitting across the sun's rays as they filtered in through the profusion of cracks in the old walls surrounding me. I crawled across the floor and hid under one of the old desks, peering around the edge. Still, there was no sign of Wormy.

I was as sneaky as I thought he was being, until my knee hit upon one of the floor boards and shattered the silence with a mournful squeak. At that moment, I heard a noise and a scuffling sound on the upper landing.

As I looked up at the landing, my hair came to attention and I broke out in a cold sweat at the frightening sight. There, above me, was Wormy and the escaped Nazi. The prisoner's one huge hand covered Wormy's mouth and the other brandished an old piece of wood above his head, ready to strike a blow if either of us moved. I was petrified, and my sweaty hands seemed glued to the dusty floor.

∽ Chapter 15 ∽

1 didn't dare run. I couldn't. I was riveted to the floor and fear engulfed me. I thought I had felt fear on the glide ride. I knew I had felt it during our train ride. But this was the fear of my life. It caused me to forget everything but surviving. My knees began to shake like jello and I wondered if I'd see another minute, much less another day. We were face to face with a real live Nazi—with no U.S. guards to protect us.

In the next instant, and in very plain English, the Nazi said, "Come upstairs, boy!"

Germans couldn't speak English. "Was this really the escaped Nazi?" I wondered.

My thought was answered in the cruelest tones, as he said, *"ACHTUNG! I SAID TO COME UP HERE!"*

All doubts quickly slipped away. Hearing the German word and the slight hint of an accent, I knew our pretending had become real. My rubber gun stayed on the floor as I started walking helplessly up the stairs.

Wormy hadn't moved. His eyes stared out from above the large hand and seemed to yell to me for help. The weapon was still raised in a threatening position. Two things became apparent. The Nazi was an extremely large man with the face of a nervous young boy. The other thing—he was not blond. I believed that all of Hitler's youth had blond hair and blue eyes. This man's hair was dark and his eyes chocolate colored. Had it not been for the gray uniform and his accented speech, he may well have been some large farm boy from our area.

Again, in that same sharp, harsh voice: "You, boy, sit down on the floor." Releasing Wormy, he ordered, "You sit down right beside him. If you make a single sound, I will use this," he said, pointing the piece of wood directly at us. "I have been trained to kill, and two American boys mean nothing to me."

Hearing his words, I thought, "Surely and finally we've met our fateful end. I'm going to see Sweet Jesus much sooner than I had planned."

Wormy obediently followed his instructions and slid down the wall, resting next to me on the floor. A thousand thoughts were spinning through my mind. In all the movies I had ever seen, German soldiers were impeccably dressed, fully armed and afraid of nothing. This young man looked much like an American football player. His brown hair was tousled, and his eyes, which reflected both authority and anxiety, were deep-set and framed by firm cheeks which came to rest on a strong, slightly dimpled chin. He was, by any standards, a handsome young man.

I was surprised to read insecurity in his eyes. For that one moment, I didn't see him as a hated Nazi, but more as a lost, frightened man-child in the land of his enemies, a land that was as totally foreign to him as he was to us. I was sure that he harbored the same feelings for Americans that we did for Germans.

My mind was suddenly jerked from those thoughts as he demanded, "How did you know I was in this building? Are your soldiers coming here?"

Wormy finally spoke, saying, "Be right nice if they did."

"Hush up, Wormy," I said. I didn't quite know how to respond to this person. Something inside told me I'd better tell the truth. Finally, with fear and trepidation in my voice, I managed, "We didn't know you were in here. We play here all the time. As a matter of fact, everybody in town thinks you're heading in the other direction, down towards the river."

It instantly dawned on me that I'd said the wrong thing. I had given the enemy some vital information. The last thing I wanted to do was betray my country, even in a small way.

But words continued to pour nervously out of my mouth. "How did you get away? How did you find this building? You're a couple of miles from the farm where you were working. Didn't anyone follow you?"

"None of that is your concern. I am here, and now you are here. And you are my prisoners."

He had lowered his weapon, but still gripped it tightly by his side.

In an attempt to distract him from his "prisoner" comment, I asked, "How is it that you speak English so well?"

"That is also none of your concern. I must get away from here, and you will help me."

Sitting on the dusty floor, enduring the stagnant heat, and scared to death, I felt like a bombshell waiting to explode.

"Why do you want to get away? Where will you go?" I asked.

"I know that if I stay here I will be killed. Americans always kill prisoners after they have worked for them. Sometimes they even work them to death."

Wormy raised his eyebrows and began speaking with a courage I had seen in him when he was angry. "That ain't so. In the war, we shore killed a lotta Germans and Italians, and even them dern little Japs. But right here in Scotland Neck, ain't nobody gonna kill nobody, less course they hurts little boys. Then you can be shore they will ketch you and kill you fer good."

I wasn't at all sure of the wisdom of Wormy's words, but I did imagine a change in the German's expression.

I thought I should support Wormy, so I said, "I don't know what y'all been taught 'bout Americans, but we don't just kill people for nothing, 'specially for just trying to escape. We didn't even start the war. Everybody in our country wants it to end so's everybody in the world will stop killing everybody else and go back home and be happy. I've even heard the sheriff and the mayor talkin' 'bout how the government will get y'all back to Germany after the war is over."

He replied, "First, that assumes that Germany is defeated, and that will never happen. And what you have heard is through the ears of a young boy. It is just Yankee propaganda. I know if I am not killed right away, I will be sent to one of your concentration camps and be executed. I understand that your way of killing a man is to electrocute him."

"Sure," I said, "we've electrocuted some men. But they were always American criminals who'd been convicted in our courts for some terrible crime."

I thought the longer I talked, the longer Wormy and I would live. During the early moments of our encounter, I'd been sure we'd die. But now, I began to feel some gleam of hope. I didn't have the slightest notion how, but I felt that we might yet get out of this situation.

Changing the subject, he said, "I will wait until dark to travel again. Right now, I need food. And you, boy," pointing at me with the stick, "will get it for me. And if you have any doubts that I will not harm your friend here, you just dare and bring anyone back with you—or tell anyone where I am located."

"First," I said, "I don't have any money to buy food. And there's no place in town I can get any without somebody getting suspicious."

"That and your friend's life are your problems. I give you 30 minutes to bring back food or the boy dies."

"You better do what he says, Johnnie," Wormy said in a passionate voice. "I ain't right ready to die yet."

"How do I know you won't kill us anyway?" I asked.

"If you do exactly as I tell you, and I get away, I will have no reason to kill you. I do not like the idea of killing young boys, even Americans. But I must get free."

"You're in the most free country in the world. We don't have any concentration camps, only prisons for our own criminals. You'd be better off to stay right here in this country than return to a place run by anybody like Hitler."

As soon as I said that I feared I'd said the wrong thing again. I knew most every German had sworn his life and allegiance to Adolph Hitler and was ready to die for him. But I got no angry response. Instead, he said, "You have 30 minutes, beginning right now."

At that point, I felt I had no alternative but to go. It seemed that once again, both Wormy's and my life were at stake.

Then he added, "And water also; bring me cold water with the food. One last thing, boy, bring me some clothing. I must get out of these clothes."

"Yes, sir," I said. "I'll do my best. But 30 minutes sure ain't much time to get all that stuff." I stood and started walking towards the stairs.

"Boy, you take one look at your friend. If you fail, or trick me, it will be the last time you see him alive."

"Please git goin', Johnnie, and you better hurry it up."

The German grabbed Wormy by the arm and followed me down to the front door. I cracked the door and scanned the whole area. No one was around. Closing it behind me, my mind began racing again. I hoped I could find enough food at home to satisfy him. Then another thought: I would be helping the enemy. But what choice did I have? I dared not bring anybody back or Wormy would be a goner. His life was more valuable to me than betrayal. Yet, I had heard that traitors were shot.

Suddenly, the name Benedict Arnold went through my mind. I had learned about him in history class the year before. That man had betrayed his country over a hundred years ago, and people still remembered him. "Will I go down in history as another Benedict Arnold?" I wondered. I had always wanted to be an American hero, and I was about to become a traitor.

Regardless of the consequences, I had to save Wormy. So I blotted that thought from my mind and started for my house.

Fortunately, none of the other families were around as I walked in the house. The academy was less than 10 minutes away. But I still had to get the food, some kind of clothing and get back in around 20 minutes. My heart was vibrating.

I charged into the kitchen and found an old grocery bag. (Pound-thump-pound went my heart.) I opened the refrigerator and saw two biscuits left from the night before. I grabbed them and dropped them in the bottom of the bag. I also took the last apple and threw it in. There was half a cantaloupe covered with wax paper. That went in next. That wiped out the refrigerator.

Next I went over to the pantry where I found a half-box of saltines and a few cookies—in they went. There were several items of canned food, but how would he open them? "Better take them," I said, so I popped in some pork and beans and peaches. I raced over to the drawer next to the sink, found a small can opener and stuffed it right on top of everything else. I found an empty mason jar and struggled to get the lid off as sweat flooded my body. I filled it to its brim with cold water and carefully secured the top around the worn red washer, pulling the metal clamp down to keep it from spilling. I took one final look around the kitchen and knew there was nothing else to take. I peered down in the bag and none of it looked any too appetizing, but it was the best I could do.

I was in the front yard when I suddenly remembered the clothes. That could be a problem because Daddy was about half the size of that man. I scampered back into the bedroom, pulled the closet door open and sweated some more. Finally, I spied his hunting-coat hanging on a hook in the back. It allowed for plenty of ammunition and was large on Daddy. Maybe it would do—it would have to do. And then, pants? pants? pants? And just how much time did I have left? Then I remembered the overalls with suspenders attached. Daddy used them when he was working on the car. They made him look like Jumbo, the scarecrow. But where were they? Hanging on the back porch—I had just seen them recently. I rushed out the back door, grabbed the overalls and began my trek back towards the academy.

Again I wondered, "How much time do I have? Will the German think I have gone for the army? Has he harmed Wormy?" I was more nervous than when I was in the building with him.

All the way back I worried about the right and wrong of what I was doing. But all I could envision was Wormy's horrified expression when I left. And deep down, wherever your conscience stays, I felt I was doing the right thing. It must be the right thing—I hoped with all my tired heart.

The hurried trip back was uneventful. Entering the foyer, they weren't immediately in sight. Then I saw them upstairs by the window, watching my every movement. The German was checking the whole area out front to insure I hadn't brought anybody along with me.

"Up here, boy!" he hollered in that demanding tone.

My arms full, I carefully navigated the rickety stairway and met them at the top. He still held his weapon in his left hand, but immediately grabbed the bag from me.

"You two sit down where you were," he ordered.

He moved back over to the front window, ever alert to any trickery on my part. After another quick view of the outside, he sat down under the window and tore the bag open. He immediately went for the water, draining almost the entire jar without pausing for a breath. For the first time, he released his grip on the stick of wood and let it fall next to him on the floor. A rush of dust fluttered up in his face. He started eating everything without any comments, his piercing eyes glued on the two of us. When he reached the canned foods he asked, "What good are these?" He hadn't noticed the can opener amongst all the clutter. I pointed it out and he tore into the peaches. In just a few minutes he had consumed everything in the bag except the cantaloupe rind.

By then, he must have felt that I hadn't betrayed him as he leaned back against the wall, resting his head. He pulled his weapon over, lowered his eyes, and heaved a sigh. His eyes were red and seemed more weary than before. He sat quietly for a few minutes, as did we.

He slowly raised his eyes toward us and said, "I will wait until dark to travel. But what am I to do with you two?"

"Oh, I's ready to go home any ole time," Wormy replied.

"Ah, yes, I am sure of that. I am also sure you would go right to your soldiers and immediately bring them here to take me captive again. No, you must stay with me."

"Look," I said. "My daddy is coming home from the hospital this afternoon. Everybody in town knows that. They also know I'll be there to meet him and Momma. If

I don't show up, they'll surely start looking for me. They all know this building is one of our favorite playing places. Sooner or later, they'll end up here. If you're gonna leave, you better leave now."

Examining the clothing I had brought him, he said, "I cannot travel in daylight, even in these clothes. But you have now posed a new dilemma. If I leave here, someone will see me. If I stay, they will come here seeking you. So—what does that mean to me? I just dispose of you and take my chances on hiding, if and when they come here. Then, I leave at night."

He was not talking directly to us. It was as if he were thinking out loud, formulating his plan of escape in detail. But, *dispose of us*! Those were harsh words and the fear of death rushed through my mind again. I realized I had to do some fast thinking and talking to secure our safety.

"I don't rightly know what you mean by 'dispose of.' But right now, you're just an escaped prisoner of war, still wearing your prisoner's clothes. If you change into the clothes I brought, you might be considered a spy and then they could shoot you. [I remembered that from a movie.] And if you're thinking of killing us, you won't be a prisoner of war who was captured fighting for his country; you'll be a criminal here in America and probably be put in one of our jails. You might be executed yourself—not for being our enemy, but for the murder of two young boys. If they find you held us captive and released us, you'd be a prisoner who released two boys. Everybody'd certainly look on you more favorably. [I was afraid to stop talking.] Most Americans are fair-minded. Releasing two young boys would be good. And besides, even though you speak English very good, I can tell you there is no place to escape to around here. You're miles and miles away from any point where you could get out of the country. And another thing, just how do you expect to get out of the country? The whole state of North Carolina knows about you by now."

I had to pause and catch my breath. My mind was trying to stay ahead of my mouth. I was trying to sound as positive as possible. I truly believed our only chance of survival was to convince him he'd be better off by not harming us.

During my lull, he said, "Some of what you say, boy, makes sense. But I also know Americans cannot be trusted. You will say anything now to save your life."

Shifting gears and regrouping my thoughts, I asked again, "How come you speak English so good?"

He didn't answer immediately, but his face softened and he looked off into space. He seemed to drift back in time, mulling over my question. After all, he was in charge—he didn't have to say anything.

Finally, to my relief, he said, "My father was in foreign trade. I attended school in England for two years and had planned to return and enter the university in Heidelberg and study English, and perhaps even become a teacher. When the war started, we returned home and I was called into the naval service. I have continued the study of your language over the years and still hope to teach someday."

For the first time, the hint of a smile crept across his face. He loosened his grip on the weapon and said, "After hearing you two talk, I see that I still have much to learn about English."

Wormy erupted with, "Yeah, well, we'll be glad to give you a lesson or two. Me and Johnnie knows English real good."

"How and where were you captured?" I asked.

"I am in the submarine service. We were patrolling off the coast of your state of Florida when we were rammed by one of your navy destroyers. Most of my comrades were instantly killed. Only a few from my boat survived. We were picked up and taken to your naval base in Charleston, South Carolina. Then we were sent off to different work areas."

"Have you been mistreated while you've been a prisoner here in this country?"

He thought for a minute and responded: "I have not been mistreated, so far, but I have always done as I was ordered and have caused no problems—until now. It is the duty of every prisoner of war to attempt to escape."

The intense heat and his apparent exhaustion were beginning to slow his speech. I took that opportunity to pick up the conversation. "Maybe I can wear him down with words," I thought.

"You say our people haven't done you any harm. People are what a country is all about. My daddy always says people don't start wars—governments start wars. Here in America, the people really run the country. Course, we have a government and a lot of big officials who make big decisions. My daddy and me listen to President Roosevelt on the radio all the time. The president shore wants the war to end as soon as possible. We want to stop killing people and just have a peaceful world. My daddy was a soldier in the first war. He said he was fighting for peace. He saw lots of killing and he always says you can't beat peace with a stick."

"What is your name, boy?"

"Johnnie," I replied.

"So, Johnnie, how does one so young speak with wisdom?"

"I can rightly tell you it ain't wisdom. All you gotta do is ask my school teacher. Right now, I'm talking as much as I can 'cause I'm scared to death. Wormy and me are scared you're gonna kill us, and we shore don't want that to happen. So, I'm just talking, fast as I can, hoping you won't kill us."

The faint smile creased his tired face as he asked, "Wormy, what type of name is that?"

"Jist some old nickname my momma give me. Real name's Worthington Woodrow Wilson."

"So, Wormy, you are named after one of the presidents."

"You know about our presidents?" I asked.

"I know that one. He caused that false and weak treaty with my country after the first war. And, yes, I know something of your country. We were taught to know our enemies."

He lifted himself up, slid one of the boards aside and cast a glance out the front window. Then he said, "So, you feel that I will kill you two."

"You done threatened us 'bout a hundred times," Wormy said. "How you 'spect us to feel?"

I quickly added, "If I was you, I'd be more concerned about your life. Right now, you're only a sailor who will be returned to your country some day—and maybe become a teacher. Kill us and you probably won't never see your home again. Besides, what can you gain by killing us?"

"Time," he said. "Now someone knows where I am. Soon I will be gone, but only if no one knows where I am, or where I am going."

By then I was becoming weary and quite disheartened. But I continued: "Do you know where you're going? Do you have maps? Where will you get food and money? You can't get too far without money." I was grasping for ideas as he seemed intent on his escape plan. And where did that leave us?

"Truly, I do not know where I will go or what I will do. But I have had escape on my mind since I was pulled from the waters of the Atlantic."

"Think of your country. Think of your family, your hometown. I know if I was a prisoner in Germany, I'd shore do anything I could to get back to Scotland Neck. I'd shore never kill two German boys. Do you have a wife or other family at home?"

"I had both when I left. But now—who knows? All reports are bad. My country is being destroyed and families are being killed by your bombs and soldiers."

"Yeah, but you gotta realize that's being done to end the war. That'll also stop the killing."

Whether from exhaustion or reminiscing about home, his mood was changing. It was almost as if he were trying to look through the walls at what was in the past—and what would be in the future. I realized I had been bombasting him with questions. I thought maybe I should give him some time to think. During the pause, I looked very closely at his face and saw one small tear rolling down his cheek. It dropped on the floor and glistened in a sunspot that had stolen its way through the window.

When we made eye contact, he quickly rubbed his face and jumped up as if to conceal his moment of weakness. He left his weapon on the floor, walked to the railing and stared down at the foyer. For maybe the first time, he seemed more preoccupied with his predicament than with us. He folded his hands behind him and paced from the railings to the window.

Wormy bravely stood up and said, "I think I know a little 'bout how you feels. Johnnie and me was lost, and we was jist in Norfolk, Virginia, and we was plenty scared."

Hearing that, his strength seemed renewed and he abruptly replied, "Germans are not afraid. In the end, we will be victorious. It is Germany who will rule the world for a thousand years."

He made that statement with such bravado, I felt we'd lost some ground.

"You shore can't believe that anymore. You just told us your country is being destroyed. You must know the war will end soon—and Germany can't be the winner. It's too late for that. Just try and figure how you can safely get home to your family and help rebuild your country. In one way, you're sorta lucky to be here. At least you're still alive."

His hands still folded behind him and his head lowered, he murmured to himself, "What must I do?"

"Let us help," I quickly replied.

"How can you help me? And why would you want to?"

"Well, first, and to be honest, we wanna get ourselves outta this mess. And, just from talking to you, I don't think you're a bad man. I think you're worried and wanna get outta this, too, and now, just don't know how."

He didn't reply.

"Listen," I said, "the sheriff of Scotland Neck is a good friend of mine. Let me, by myself, go find him. I know he won't do you any harm. I promise I won't go to any soldiers. I'll just tell Sheriff Calhoun to come here and drive you back."

"You know, of course, I will be punished," he replied.

"Before I tell the sheriff, I'll get him to promise you won't be punished. I won't tell him where you are if he won't promise me. When I tell him you're gonna return, he'll just be relieved to git you back. You don't know how much you've scared our whole town."

"How can I trust you? And how do I know you can really do what you say? You are just a young boy."

"Well, rightly you don't. But like my daddy says, 'There's times when you gotta trust somebody.' You trusted me to leave before. And besides, you got Wormy here. If I come back here with anybody but the sheriff, you still got him as a hostage. And he's my best friend in the whole world."

"Hole on a minute, Johnnie. I ain't gonna be no hostage."

"Well, you're a hostage right now. And if the three of us don't work this out, you're more'n likely to be a dead hostage."

Wormy's eyes showed some pain as he slunk back down on the floor.

I said to the German, "You think about this as long as you need. But it's the best idea I got of gittin' all three of us outta here alive. And if I'm not home pretty soon, somebody's gonna come looking for me."

By then, I was pressed to the edge of my imagination. If that didn't work, well—we'd see.

Time seemed to stand still; but I could see he was thinking it over. Finally, he said, "All right, I will do as you suggest. But if you fail, or if the soldiers come back, I will kill this boy. That is a promise. Just go and do as you said. Bring only this one man back. I will return to the farm with him. But if you are not back by dark, I will be gone, and so will your friend."

The whole atmosphere seemed to change. I felt an insecure relief, and I believed the German did, too.

"Now, I don't know how long it's gonna take me. The sheriff is on the search party looking for you. I'll have to find him and convince him to do as I ask. This could take a while, so please, don't get impatient and do anything crazy. Give me time. If the sheriff won't promise me, I promise you on the Bible, I won't tell him where you are. But I'll tell him you have a hostage and just might hurt him if he don't do just as we've agreed."

"Go. Just be smart, boy, and remember your friend here. This had better work or you will never see him alive again."

Wormy added, "Johnnie, you jist do 'zacly what this here man says and git the sheriff back here as soon as you can."

"Okay, I promise you'll just see me and the sheriff come back here in his car."

I turned and started down the stairs, hoping beyond hope that I could do what I had said. An eerie feeling overwhelmed me. "Suppose my whole plan falls through and Wormy doesn't get out?" I wondered. That fear only accentuated the need for success and I was determined to give it my best effort.

The only place I knew to look was the sheriff's office. Once outside, I started running, waded through the canal, dodged my way through the woods and up to Main Street. Approaching his office, I saw a large group of soldiers and men gathered right out front. It seemed they had completed their search down by the river. They had come back for food and regrouping for the afternoon pursuit. Many of them were the town's men who had brought along their hunting dogs.

As I approached the sheriff's car, two heavily armed soldiers walked from the side of the building where the restrooms were located. My heart sank a little. If they got wind of the prisoner's location, my plan was doomed. They'd never believe my story.

Sheriff Calhoun was sitting in the car drinking a Coke. He had a puzzled expression on his face. The men were shuffling between his car and the building. He didn't seem to be paying them much attention, so I felt this would be my opportunity.

I stuck my head through the passenger's side window and said, "Sheriff, it's mighty important that I have a few words with you, in private."

"Johnnie, you know it ain't no time to be bothering me with some tomfool mess you and Wormy got yourselves into."

"No, sir, it ain't 'bout nothin' like that. Can I get in the car a minute? It's very important, and I know I can help you."

"No way you can help me, boy, 'less you know where that damn Nazi is hiding. These soldiers is giving me hell to lead them all over town. Why, the governor of the state jist called my office."

Before he had time to say no, I winked, slid in beside

him and rolled up the window. Nobody paid me much mind. Just as I began to speak, one of the soldiers walked right up to the sheriff's window and said, "Let's get this search started again. That German could be miles from here. You and these men know this area better than we do. This is rather an embarrassing situation for the army, and we're counting on your continued help."

"I realize that, Major. It's my damn town, and I wanna protect it, too. Jist lemme finish my dinner and we'll get organized again."

I knew I had to talk fast. The sheriff was mighty nervous as he was fidgeting with the patch over his eye. The only time he touched it was when he was worried about something.

Almost whispering, I said, "Sheriff Calhoun, if I can help you find the German, will you make a promise to me?"

"Whatcha talking 'bout, Johnnie? I already told you I ain't got time for no games today."

"Yes, sir, I know. But I also know I can help you; but you gotta make me a promise."

By then, I had his attention. He slowly rolled up his window and gave me a stern look. "Whatcha know, Johnnie?"

"How 'bout the promise?" I insisted.

"How can I make a promise if I don't know what the damn thing is?"

For a half-second I agonized as how best to approach it. As much as I respected and liked the sheriff, I didn't know whether to trust him with my secret. After all, Wormy's life hung in the balance of what happened in the car right then. But again, I didn't have much choice. I had already committed to telling him something. Remembering how fairly he had treated me in the past, I finally started. "Look, Sheriff, I know where the German is, 'cause I just left him."

"You 'spect me to believe that, Johnnie? I know he ain't dumb enough to let no young boy git away from him who knows where he's hiding."

In a choking voice, I said, "But he's got Wormy as a hostage." I had to fight back the tears as I began to unravel the past couple of hours' events, without giving away the location.

"Johnnie, you're telling me you know where the Nazi is, and if jist you and me git him, he'll release Wormy and return peacefully to the farm?"

"Yes, sir, that's the deal I made with him."

"Johnnie, you really believe you can trust a Nazi, 'specially one who escaped?"

"Yes, sir, I do, 'cause he wouldn't let me go if he planned to try and git away again. I talked to him a lot and I believe he knows he made a mistake, escaping and all. He seems right scared himself. He can't figure out how to get anywhere and now will just settle for returning to the farm."

I could tell he was giving this some deep thought, so I didn't interrupt his mood with anymore talk.

Grudgingly, he said, "You know, if we do this, Johnnie, you and me might be risking our lives without any of them soldiers with us."

"He don't have no weapons, Sheriff, except for a big ole piece of wood. I don't see how he can hurt anybody—except Wormy, 'specially if we don't git back there right soon."

"Where is he, Johnnie?"

"Sheriff, I can't tell you 'less you promise me we'll go there alone, and he won't be punished. I gave him my oath, on the Bible."

The car had become a chamber of heat, and the sheriff kept messing with his eye patch.

"Okay, Johnnie, we gotta deal. Jist keep on keeping on."

He rolled down his window and yelled to one of the soldiers, who immediately walked over to the car.

"Listen, this here boy's daddy is coming home from the U.S. Veterans Hospital in jist a little while. I'm gonna run him home. Soon as I git back, we'll git going again."

Before the soldier had time to protest, the sheriff started up the Ford, moved it through the crowd and pulled out on Main Street.

"Where we headed, Johnnie?"

"The old academy; that's where he's holding Wormy."

He made the next right down Eighth to Church and said, "I thought about him being there one time. I figured we'd stop and check it out this afternoon."

Passing my house, we turned left off Sunset Avenue and began bouncing down the dirt road that led to the academy. I noticed him reach down and place his hand on his gun.

"I don't think we should get outta the car with that gun out, Sheriff. We don't want to scare him into hurtin' Wormy."

"I don't plan to, Johnnie. I jist do that automatically. Other than practice shootin', I ain't fired this thing in over two years. And that was jist to kill Horace Buford's dog that went mad and was foaming at the mouth and chasin' Horace's chickens all over the yard."

As the building came into view, he slowed down, carefully looking over the entire area. He pulled up front and stopped.

"Maybe we outta just set here a coupla minutes so he can see we ain't got anybody else with us," I suggested.

A cooling breeze passed through the car and I felt a refreshing touch of relief from the heat.

Sheriff Calhoun patted his gun one more time and said, "Okay, son, you ready?"

"Yes, sir, let's get out and let him see us."

He inched the car to within 10 yards of the building

and shut off the engine. We climbed out, walked around and stood in front of the car for a short minute.

Spontaneously, I shouted, "Wormy, you still in there? You all right?"

A yell from the inside of the building answered, "Yeah, Johnnie, I's jist sittin' here feelin' like a roasted pig."

"Ask him if we can come in."

In just a second, one of the boards over the upstairs window slid aside and Wormy stuck his head out and said, "Yeah, but jist walk in kind'a slow like."

We walked up to the front door, entered the foyer and looked upstairs. The German had Wormy in his grasp again with the weapon poised above his head. Very calmly, the sheriff said, "Okay, son, you can put down your weapon. I ain't gonna do nothin' but take you right back to the farm, like Johnnie promised. Nobody else knows we're here and ain't nobody gonna do you no harm. Jist take it easy now."

Somewhat reluctantly, the German released Wormy and dropped the piece of wood. He kept Wormy in front of him as they came down the stairs. Finally, all four of us were face to face.

The sheriff said, "Johnnie tells me you speak right good English, so listen carefully. I gotta put these handcuffs on you, jist for the ride. We get to the farm, I'll take them off and turn you over to the guard and you can jist go on about your work."

The German never said a word, but came to attention and raised his hands to the sheriff.

While applying the cuffs and as if to reassure the German, Sheriff Calhoun said, "We jist gonna walk out to the car now so I can git you back to the Wilsons' farm. I'll take care of the soldiers. You jist relax and everything will be fine."

"Johnnie, you two git on outta here and go on home.

Don't you mention this to nobody, and I mean nobody.
I gotta deal with them soldiers and that damn crowd.
There's some mighty hot-headed folks back there. I
wanna git everything back to normal."

We followed them out the door. The sheriff had the
prisoner sit up front, next to him.

After he was seated, and just before the car door was
closed, the German said, "Wait a minute." These were
the first words he had spoken since our return. He
looked first at me and then Wormy, and in a serious tone
said, "Johnnie and Wormy, thank you. You may have
saved my life."

I really didn't know what to say, but Wormy managed, "Yes, sir. And thank you fer not killin' us."

The sheriff closed the door, winked at us and said,
"Good job, men." We stood there in the dust as the big
Ford rambled out of the parking area and on down the
dirt road to Sunset Avenue. We watched until it was out
of sight.

"Johnnie," Wormy said, "I weren't never really scared.
I knew we'd git outta that mess, jist like we always do."

"Naw, Wormy, I weren't too scared either," I lied as
I crossed my fingers, "but I was a little bit worried from
time to time."

We walked down the road, not really knowing where
we were headed, just so it was away from the old
academy.

Thinking back, I realized that we had both experienced our first real lesson in human relations, and a
frightful one it was!

Chapter 16

It was well past noon, and I knew Aunt Bessie would be worried, as usual. The thought of seeing Daddy that afternoon gave me new-found feelings of comfort and security—especially after the morning's quivering experience.

Wormy and I separated on Main Street, both agreeing not to mention the German until we were sure he was back in place and everybody felt safe again.

Walking on down to my aunt's, I had the queer sensation that the morning's events hadn't really happened. So much of my life had been spent watching German movies, hearing about them on the radio and even dreaming about them—and yet, we had actually dealt with one that day. It was almost like someone from outer space visiting Scotland Neck and finding out that they really existed and had feelings, just like we did. The German had looked like us, talked much like us and even expressed many of the same emotions that I had experienced. Before that day, Germans were emblematic of everything that I hated. But I was gradually realizing that most people all over the world were probably just like Americans, with the same wants and needs. One of those characteristics was certainly friendship. Strangely enough, I felt that I had made a new friend that day.

"Maybe," I thought, "that's what we need to straighten out our world—more friends."

I was greeted with, "Sugarpie, where you been? I was 'bout to send the girls out looking for you. You hurry and get your bath and dress up. I gotta serve you some dinner. You know they'll be here in a couple of hours."

"Yes, ma'am, I'll rush as fast as I can. But honest, Aunt Bessie, I ain't really hungry. It's been so hot I think I sorta lost my appetite, thinking about Daddy and everything."

"Well, whatever, you jist git yourself ready."

By 3 p.m., Bessie and the girls and I were on the front porch, just looking down the street and getting more and more impatient.

While we were waiting, we heard a noise up in the sky. It was a small airplane, probably from over in Rocky Mount. They had the only airport anywhere near Scotland Neck.

All of us rushed out in the yard to get a good look at it. In 1944, whenever an airplane flew over our town, it was an event. Everybody who heard it would go out in the streets and just watch in amazement. It was one thing to see the big army air force bombers on the newsreels, but to see a real airplane flying over Scotland Neck was quite exciting.

Daddy had always promised to take me to Rocky Mount where you could pay and take a short flight. But so far, we hadn't gotten around to it.

We returned to our vigil on the porch. Ruby said, "Wanna play some hopscotch, Johnnie?"

"Naw, I don't wanna get all hot and messed up. I'll just sit here and wait it out."

I really wouldn't have minded playing. But the thought of her beating me that particular day was more than I could handle. I always rationalized my hopscotch losses, knowing that it was a girls' game. I'd challenge her to marbles any day. But Jewel Star always said it wasn't very ladylike for a young woman to get down on her hands and knees and shoot marbles. So mostly Ruby and I just fussed when we were together, calling each other tattletales or sissies, until one or the other of us would run to Bessie, asking her to take our side. She always had a manner of settling our feuds, making us both feel like we'd won. I really loved my Aunt Bessie.

The long afternoon stretched into early evening before Jimmie pulled up in front of the house. I went charging off the porch and out to the car. Jimmie and Momma were sitting up front. Daddy was reclining in the back seat with a pillow under his head. I was not at all prepared for what I saw.

Daddy had lost considerable weight, and his coloring had changed from rosy-cheeked to an obscure paleness. His beautiful white hair was tinged with yellow. For a moment, his appearance really frightened me. But then he pulled himself up, smiled and said, "Come here, boy, and give your ole daddy a big hug."

Jumping in the car and hugging him, I felt somewhat better because he sounded just like he always did. Everybody gathered around the car. I sat in the back seat, asking him all sorts of questions.

"Slow down, son. When we get home, I'll tell you everything that happened at the hospital. Right now, I just want to get there and into my own bed again."

Bessie and the girls said their hellos and good-byes, and we headed on down Main Street towards Sunset Avenue.

We had to pass right by the barber shop, so Daddy said, "Pull over a minute, Jimmie. I want to say hello to Melvin and all the boys."

In a matter-of-fact tone, Momma said, "Gavin, you aren't getting out of this car until we get home."

"Well, Johnnie can run and tell 'um to walk out to the car and speak to me."

I could understand how he felt. Anytime we went away, even for a day, I wanted to see Wormy right away and tell him everything.

"Hell, Bug, won't hurt to stop for one minute," Jimmie agreed.

"All right, but just for a minute."

We pulled up to the curb and I ran in and happily announced that my daddy was out in the car. All the men walked out and warmly greeted him. Melvin seemed particularly glad to see him.

"I ain't had nobody to beat in checkers and pool while you been gone," Melvin chuckled.

"You ole fool, you can't beat me in anything and you know it. Just whose name is up there on the wall as one of the world's checker champions? I ain't seen Melvin Smith up there, and you own the damn place. I'll be down here soon enough and show you I still got it," Daddy said, his eyes crinkling.

Following the cheery welcome, we started home. In a couple of minutes we bounced over the log bridge and into our yard.

Spying the car parked up by the house, Daddy said, "Now that's a sight for sore eyes. The Hudson running all right?"

"Yes," Momma quickly replied. "Matter of fact, I just had it serviced at the Sinclair. Columbus said everything's fine, but something happened to the radio. They couldn't get it to work."

"Well, I'll be damned. That radio was my favorite thing about the car, that and that fancy step-down drive. I'll have Marmaduke look at it soon as I'm on my feet again. He can fix anything that's fixable."

During that particular conversation, I just sat in a hushed silence.

"Looks right clean, Bug. Did you have them wash it?"

"No, sir," I chimed in. "Wormy and me washed it, and cleaned out the inside, too. We wanted it looking good when you got back home."

That seemed to end the subject—for then, anyway.

Getting out of the car, Daddy wasn't too steady on his feet, so Jimmie helped him into the house.

"Mighty good to be home. I been starvin' for some of your cooking, Bug."

"Well, you'll get it tonight, 'cause Johnnie and I stocked up on all your favorites." (I wondered if I had taken any of those favorites that morning.)

Looking fatigued, Daddy said, "Right now, I think I'll just rest for awhile."

Daddy and Momma thanked Jimmie for all he and Bessie had done for us. When Jimmie left, I realized how good it felt, to have the three of us home again. I was looking forward to Daddy getting well, what with hunting season coming up, and maybe that airplane ride to look forward to. But right then, I settled for having him home.

It took only a couple of days to realize Daddy was a long way from being well. He stayed in bed for the better part of each day. In the evenings, he would usually sit on the porch for a short time with Momma.

Each night after supper, he would stretch out in his easy chair and have me turn on Gabriel Heater. Then he would almost beg Momma to fix him a little drink. She steadfastly refused.

"You know what they told you, Gavin. You have enough alcohol in your system to last a lifetime. That would be a crazy thing to do. I'll have no part of it, and neither will you. You already got diabetes and kidney problems. You fuel them with alcohol and you'll pay. You best do like the doctors say and get yourself well. Johnnie and I need you.

"I haven't talked to you about money. But with the expenses I've had traveling back and forth to the hospital, and with only my pay coming in, we're almost at the bottom of the barrel. You start drinking again, and we'll be put out of this apartment. It's only 'cause Mrs. Darden's so good that she lets us pay the rent whenever we can. You just listen to me now and help get you and your family straightened out."

Even though school was starting soon, I stayed close to home during the week, helping Daddy and trying to watch over him as best I could. Wormy had been busy helping Mrs. Wilson. He'd only been around a couple of times, and then we played mostly in the backyard. I was determined not to let us get ourselves into any more messes.

By Thursday of that week, Daddy was feeling some better and started getting restless. After Momma had gone to work, he said, "Johnnie, let's you and me crank up the Hudson and take a ride down to the barber shop. I need a haircut, and I'd like to visit with the fellows a spell."

"You sure you feel good enough to do that, Daddy?"

"Sure I do. Besides, the car needs a little workout. I know your momma don't drive it unless she has to. She's 'fraid of all the traffic in town," he snickered.

"S'pose Momma sees us? Won't she be mad with us?"

"I'm fine, son. You just get yourself ready."

I was a little worried concerning his first encounter with the car.

As we walked out, he said, "It sure is good to be home. I'm raring to go hunting, and you're old enough to go with me this year."

Much to my relief, the car started right away. We sat there a moment with the motor idling, and Daddy said, "Sure does smell funny in here. Sorta like down at the river."

"Yes, sir, I noticed it, too. I reckoned it was from

sittin' here closed up so long." He didn't say any more, and we drove on down Main Street. Everybody who saw the car waved and yelled how good it was to see him back. I wondered if people in big cities, like Washington, D.C., acted like that, being so friendly and all. I was just pleased that everybody thought so much of my daddy.

We walked into the barber shop together. The checker game stopped and all the men in the pool hall walked up front. Everybody seemed sincerely glad to see him.

Speaking to Melvin, Daddy asked, "You think your hands are steady enough to give me a haircut without cuttin' off my ear?" All the men laughed.

A few years before, Daddy had been getting a haircut and Melvin had had a few drinks. While Melvin was laboring away at his work, he'd snipped off a small piece of Daddy's ear lobe. The story went that when Daddy yelled, Melvin just handed him the tiny piece of flesh and said there wasn't any extra charge for "ear cutting."

I was sitting on one of the stools, enjoying Daddy enjoying himself, when Sheriff Calhoun walked in. He shook Daddy's hand and said he was happy to see him. Looking over at me, he said, "Well, there's one of the local heroes."

"Whatcha talking about, Orton?" Daddy asked, as I cringed at the question, wondering which story he was about to tell. So I just listened, quietly.

"Look, here," he said as he unfolded a copy of *The Standard*.

There, printed in bold headlines on page one, were the words, "LOCAL BOYS FLUSH OUT ESCAPED NAZI PRISONER." He then proceeded to read the story that only he could have told the newspaper people. It was all about how I had led him to the prisoner's hideout when the army and the whole town couldn't locate him. It even told of Wormy's bravery in dealing with the situation, and how he had volunteered to be the hostage while I sought out the sheriff. Of course, it referred to him as Worthington Woodrow Wilson.

"Lemme see that, Orton," Daddy demanded from the barber's chair. He re-read the whole story aloud. Then he looked down at me and asked, "Why didn't you tell me about this, Johnnie?"

"Well, Sheriff Calhoun told us not to mention it, and I sorta forgot about it until right now. You ain't mad with me, are you, Daddy?"

"Me, mad at you! Why, hell no, I ain't mad. I'm 'bout as proud as any daddy could be of his son."

By then, all the men were gathered around the chair, trying to get a glimpse of the story. They were all patting me on the back and saying how brave I was.

"Don't y'all forget how brave Wormy was, too," I said. "He showed a powerful lotta courage staying there with that Nazi, right by himself."

I certainly was excited about the whole thing and couldn't wait to show the article to Wormy. It seemed that our dreams of being heroes had finally been fulfilled. I couldn't believe our names were right on the front page of *The Standard*.

"There's some talk it might be run in *The News* and *Observer* in Raleigh, too," the sheriff added. "Why, Johnnie, you and Wormy might be famous all over North Carolina. Anything to do with them Nazis is big news, 'specially capturing one of 'um."

"He wasn't punished, was he?" I anxiously asked.

"Hell no, he wasn't punished," Sheriff Calhoun said. "The army was so glad to have him back, there weren't no thought of punishing him. Matter of fact, they was a little embarrassed that he got away, and then was captured by two little boys. You two boys done real good," he said as he walked out the door.

For the next half-hour, that was all the talk of the

barber shop. Daddy was even at the front door, stopping people on the street and saying, "Look at what my boy done. I fought them Germans in France in the Big War, and he captured one, right here in Scotland Neck. Ain't he something?"

By then, as much as I was enjoying the compliments, I was feeling right embarrassed with all Daddy's carrying on.

"Daddy," I asked, "when you finish your haircut, can we ride over to Wormy's house and show him the newspaper?"

"Sure we can, son. We're gonna show it to everybody in town."

With that said, I retired back to my stool, trying to be a little less conspicuous.

Leaving the barber shop, we headed over to East Scotland Neck, hoping to catch Wormy at home. When we stopped in front of his house, half the neighborhood gathered around the car.

"Hey, Johnnie. Hey, Mr. Taxi," many of the children said. Most of the coloreds in town called Daddy "Mr. Taxi." Many of the older men came out and said how good it was to see him, and how they hoped he was well now.

Naomi, Wormy's oldest sister, asked, "Whatcha doin' over here?"

"Just looking for Wormy," I said.

"He's helpin' Momma in the house. Y'all come on in."

About that time, Mrs. Wilson stepped out on the porch and yelled, "You two come on in. I jist finished a chocolate cake, hot from the oven. I was gonna have Woodrow bring it over to you, to welcome you home," she said to Daddy. "Lemme fix you a piece right now."

"Sure thing, Mrs. Wilson," Daddy replied. "Your cooking is mighty good to me anytime, 'specially after what I been eatin' at that hospital."

"Yes, suh, you do look like you needs to put some more skin on them bones of your'n."

She proudly ushered us into her kitchen. Wormy walked in the back door, his arms filled with clothes just removed from the clothes line and ready for ironing.

"Mr. Taxi!" he yelled. "I shore am glad to see you back home. Why, tryin' to take care of that whippersnapper boy of your'n has been right much of a handful fer me."

"You two boys ain't been in any mischief, have you?" Daddy asked, with a broad grin on his hollow face.

Wormy's eyes sort of sparkled, and he quickly replied, "No, sir, you know better'n that. Been right quiet fer us. Spent the whole blame summer playin' marbles and rubber guns." The sheepish expression on his face could only be read by me.

"Well, Johnnie and me have come over here with some right exciting news about you two."

"Oh, Lawd, Mr. Taxi," Wormy moaned, "whatcha done found out 'bout us?"

Daddy spread the paper out on the table and said, "Look here at this newspaper, boy. See for yourself what the whole town—and maybe the whole state—has found out about y'all."

The entire family gathered around the table, looking down at the paper. In a moment, Wormy shouted, "Looka there! There's my name, big as anythin', and Johnnie's, too! Golly days, we two is real heroes!"

Since most of the children were too young to read, Daddy handed the paper to Mrs. Wilson and said, "Here you go, ma'am. Why don't you read this story out loud, so everybody here can feel as proud of these two young men as you and me do?"

Mrs. Wilson slipped off her tattered calico apron and sat down. While Daddy and I were having cake, she proceeded to read every word, slowly and carefully, so all the children could take it in. She paused occasionally, looked up at Wormy and smiled.

"My goodness," she said, "these boys done right good for themselves. And to think, they never mentioned it to us, not one time."

"Shucks, Momma, won't hardly worth mentioning. Johnnie and me knowed that Nazi was on the loose, so's we jist set about to find him. After that, won't nothing to it. The sheriff did help some, but it was mostly me and Johnnie. I really done my part fer Cousin Elisha. Them Nazis got him, but we got even. Why—we prob'ly could'a handled a couple more, if we had to."

"Well, whatever," Mrs. Wilson said. "I'm jist so proud of you; and happy that nothin' bad happened to either one of you."

"Momma, we had our rubber guns with us; and don't nobody ever mess with us when we is armed."

Turning to me, he asked, "Johnnie, you think President Roosevelt will hear 'bout this, and maybe give us a medal or somethin'?"

Daddy answered, "It wouldn't surprise me one bit, Wormy. You might just get invited to the White House."

Wormy's face lit up like sunshine.

"We gotta be going, Mrs. Wilson. As always, the cake was delicious. Thank you, ma'am."

Her caramel-colored face showed the pride she felt, and she thanked us for coming around and sharing the news with them. She put the rest of the cake in a bag and handed it to Daddy and told him to fatten up some.

While they were talking, Wormy pulled me aside and said, "Johnnie, I gotta git a copy of that paper. I know when Mary Beth reads it, she will love me forever."

As we drove off, they all yelled, "Bye, Johnnie and Mr. Taxi."

"We gotta go by and show this to your momma," Daddy said.

When we pulled up in front of the store, Momma came out holding a copy of *The Standard*. Her face was beaming. She asked, "Have you two seen the newspaper?"

We sat in the car and Daddy said, "Sure we have. I s'pose by now, everybody in town's seen it. Ain't this boy of ours somethin'?"

"He is indeed," Momma answered. "Now, Gavin, you better get on home and get your afternoon rest. You shouldn't even be driving yet."

"I'm doin' fine, but maybe you're right. I do feel a mite tired after all the excitement. We'll go on home and rest up a bit."

I knew he was excited and had enjoyed his morning out. But his faced showed exhaustion, so I said, "Yeah, Daddy, let's go home and you lay down awhile."

When we got home, he had to sit in the car a few minutes before he was able to walk in.

I was worried as I asked, "You all right, Daddy?"

"Just tired out, Johnnie. We had ourselves a right excitin' morning. Guess I'll lay down for a spell."

While he rested, I sat in the porch swing. Summer vacation was almost over, and I had a birthday in September. Just like me, the year was growing older. Most folks hated to see fall begin, for that meant the end of summer. But I loved fall in North Carolina. It ushered in all my favorite holidays. While I liked summer, I was fully prepared to observe the signs of its decay. School would start and the Scout Pond would close, and everybody would be splitting wood for toasty winter fires. Fall was a glorious season for me. The autumn leaves would soon be flaring in fiery hues, and only the tall pines would keep their green needles as a reminder of the summer past. The fallen leaves would give way to bare trees, which would sigh and shiver in the winter's wind. But to me, autumn's quiet and beauty were more exciting than our most alarming summer escapades.

My mind wandered free through time. I reflected on all the events during the past three months. My thoughts were mixed. On the one hand, there was excitement and anticipation, since Daddy was home, the Hudson was running, and my favorite season was rushing towards me. On the other, I had an inexplicable feeling of dread for which I couldn't account. I tried to put it out of my mind and enjoy the day.

Swinging back and forth, the resonate sounds of a squeaky swing, the gentle breeze rustling the leaves and the chirping of some happy little birds caused me to feel a tad cozy. I think I dozed off.

Chapter 17

The last big event of summer was Skate Night. An annual affair, it was held on the last Friday night preceding the beginning of each school year. I anticipated it every year for as long as I could remember. Anyone in town, 10 years or older, could bring roller skates, assemble in front of the sheriff's office and enjoy a fun-filled evening of skating and good food. Since I was within a few days of my tenth birthday, the sheriff said I could join in.

As with most events in Scotland Neck, it was arranged and overseen by the sheriff and Mayor Dawson. They worked with the youth groups of the various churches in mapping out the route and ensuring there were refreshments along the way at the churches and homes to be visited.

I had my skates out several days in advance, oiling and polishing them in preparation for the big night. Once the skating began, Sheriff Calhoun would cruise along, at the tail end of the group, watching out for any accidents or mischief that might occur.

One year things had gotten out of hand. All the young skaters invaded the Dixie, skates and all. Billy Joe Locke raised such a fuss, they even discussed canceling the event should there be any recurrences.

Naturally, I planned for Wormy to be my skating

partner, but secretly hoped Reba would be around, too.

Because Wormy didn't own any roller skates, we built a scooter for him to use, just for that occasion. It was both an ordeal and quite a challenge for us.

First, we went to the sawmill out past the cemetery and begged enough scrap wood for our plan. We needed a bottom platform, an upright brace and a small handle for steering. We talked to Tatum Tatum, the mill foreman, and he gave us what we needed.

I always thought Tatum Tatum was a funny name, but Daddy had explained it to me. It seems that Elmer Tatum had married this third cousin, Claudia Tatum. When they had their first son, they both wanted their side of the family to be represented in the new baby's name. They almost got a divorce over what to name the baby, and finally just settled on Tatum Tatum. I never did know what Tatum's middle name was.

We thanked Tatum for the wood and headed to Mr. Allsbrook's shop. He allowed us to use some of his tools. We worked furiously for a day, determined to make all the parts fit properly. Once the frame was constructed, all we needed was some kind of wheels to attach to the bottom of the platform.

We trudged the two miles to the dump on a very hot day. I vividly recall the odor that erupted as we approached. It's still stored in my memory of smells. We even tried putting clothespins over our noses, but found the discomfort worse than the odor. It took us the better part of the day, but we finally managed to dig up some old skates. The foot holders were all bent over and the wheels were pitted with rust, but they were all we could find. At the Sinclair station, Slim spent about an hour working on them. He disassembled the skates, filed the rust off the wheels and put some lubricating grease on all the bearings. The wheels spun rather smoothly after Slim gave them a squirt of oil.

Wheels in hand, we finally completed the construction of the scooter and were pleased with our results.

As Skate Night approached, we decided to decorate the scooter. Since Wormy would be the only one without skates, we wanted his mode of transportation to be outstanding.

Now that we were friends with Mr. Arnold, we went to his store in hopes of finding some leftover decorations. To our delight, not only did he give us enough paint for the scooter, but crepe paper streamers as well. After we thanked him, he said, "Being as famous as you boys are, Wormy's scooter certainly should stand out on Skate Night." He smiled as he placed all our gifts in a paper bag and wished us good luck.

We spent a day and a half transforming his scooter into a vehicle of which he could be justly proud. The floor stand was blue, the frame white and the handle a brilliant red. As we stood back admiring our workmanship, I remembered the stickers I'd won at the last carnival.

I went in the house and brought out my treasure chest. It was an old Prince Albert cigar box, filled with my most secret and valued possessions. It held, among other things, two Indian head pennies given me by my grandfather, a few baseball trading cards, several rubber bands which were very scarce during the war and four stone arrow heads that I'd found at the old Indian burial grounds. An especially precious item was a medal that Daddy had received while in the army. I'd always imagined it was presented to him for some brave deed he'd performed. It was only when I learned to read that I noticed, inscribed on the bronze plate, "Good Conduct in Basic Training." I was still proud of it since his country had presented it to him.

My most treasured item in the box was a small school picture of Reba. Harry Lee had charged me five comic books for it.

Finally, sure enough, entangled in a small ball of string in the bottom of the box were three stickers. One had "U.S.A." on it; the other two had large, colored stars on them.

"Johnnie, git your dern head outta that dern secret box and let's finish this here decoratin'."

That box was probably the only thing in the world I didn't share with Wormy, or anybody else for that matter.

I closed the box, laid it on the porch and said to Wormy, "Okay, Scooter Wilson, these stickers will add the crowning touch to your vehicle."

Sure enough, after we applied the three stickers and the streamers Mr. Arnold had given us, we were prouder than ever of our accomplishment. It reminded me a lot of a bicycle I'd seen a clown riding during the carnival.

When Skate Night finally arrived, the town was filled with excitement. The sheriff stayed busy all day mapping out the route we were to follow. He didn't want any problems that year.

Wormy and I had been training all day to ensure that we could keep up with the more skilled skaters. I was pretty sure he'd be the only Negro taking part. But that didn't bother him any, as he proudly said, "I reckon I'll be 'bout the fastest and best lookin' thing on the road tonight. Don't you think so, Johnnie?"

"No question about it," I replied, feeling a small bit of pride in his courage.

After receiving last-minute instructions from Momma, the two of us set out for the sheriff's office. It had been a very comfortable day for that time of year. The sun was low on the horizon as we paced our way up Sunset Avenue towards Main.

Passing the Sinclair station, Columbus shouted, "Mighty fine looking piece of machinery, Wormy."

Between the sheriff's office and the post office was

a vacant lot. The town had converted it into a small park, decorated it with crepe myrtle bushes, a couple of trees and several benches set here and there. Sitting on one of the benches was Harry Lee and two of his friends. They had prepared a sign that read, "Oil Your Skates For A Better and Easier Ride, 5¢, Total." All three of them held oil cans with long spouts.

Harry Lee must have felt pretty brave with his friends there, as he said, "Hey, Johnnie, you know we don't allow no niggers to go on Skate Night. 'Specially them that likes to peek at white girls takin' a bath."

As I heard Momma say many times, hell flew in me!

"Ain't none of your business who goes on Skate Night," I angrily said. "You just mind your business and we'll mind ours."

Spying Wormy's scooter, one of his friends said, "Where'd that contraption come from, Mars?"

Hell apparently flew into Wormy, too, as he carefully leaned his scooter against one of the trees and started towards their bench, eyes flaming and fists clinched. As he got near, the two boys jumped up and dared Wormy to do anything.

"You still mad 'bout the whoopin' I already gave you, Harry Lee? Ain't nothin' to what I'm 'bout to lay on you now."

All the while, I was sliding around on my skates, trying to get between Wormy and the bench. By then, all three of the boys had sat down their oil cans and were in the midst of grabbing Wormy. I slipped and fell on the sidewalk, unable to help Wormy, as two of them held him, with Harry Lee aiming a punch to his stomach.

"Stop! Stop!" I shouted, as the first punch landed solidly, causing Wormy to bend over in pain.

I was in the midst of removing my skates so I could stand up when we all heard the booming voice of Sheriff Calhoun.

"All you boys want to be locked up for the night?" he shouted, as he began separating them.

They reluctantly turned Wormy loose. I knew he was hurting, as he rubbed his stomach and stepped back.

"We didn't do nothing, Sheriff," I yelled. "They just called Wormy a nigger and said he couldn't go on Skate Night."

The sheriff adjusted his eye patch and said, "Well, let me tell all of you a thing or two. I decide who can and can't go skating. And Wormy has as much right to be here as any of you. One more tiny bit of trouble and you'll either go home or spend the night in jail for disorderly conduct. That's the last warning—for all of you. Johnnie, you and Wormy come over here in front of my office and let's have a talk."

"Yes, sir," we both replied, as we followed him.

"We still gonna git you, Wormy," one of the boys yelled.

The sheriff took us off to the side and asked, "You two think it's a good idea for Wormy to come along? You know how some white folks feel about anybody from over in East Scotland Neck. 'Specially these boys who are still all riled up about a Negro boy getting his name in *The Standard* and all."

Still rubbing his stomach, Wormy stood straight and tall. Looking the sheriff right in his face, he said, "Yes, suh, Sheriff, I knows how lots of 'um feel. And it ain't jist the boys. Most of the grown-ups feels the same way. I lives here jist like they do. I got jist as much right to go skatin' as any of 'um. And I ain't scared of none of 'um. I gotta lot of other rights that I ain't really got, but I ain't botherin' none 'bout them right now. I jist wanna go skatin' with Johnnie."

"Well—okay, but just remember, while I'll be followin' behind y'all, I can't keep my eye on just the two

of y'all tonight. You be mighty careful, and yell if you
need any help."

"Yes, sir," I said, "we'll be most careful."

By the time we got back to the scooter, the three
boys, sign and all, had disappeared. Also missing were
the streamers we had nailed to each side of the handle.

"Them dadburn, nocount rascals," Wormy moaned.
"Now lookit what they done to my scooter."

"Don't worry none 'bout the streamers," I reassured
him. "You still got the best-looking scooter in town."

By the time we got ourselves back together, a fairly
large group of skaters had assembled and were standing
around chatting and waiting for starting time. Much to
my delight, Reba and Betts were among the latest arriv-
als. I still pined for the opportunity to skate with Reba,
but had about set that idea aside, feeling that I had to be
with Wormy the whole time. He was the only colored in
the group, and I knew that I was the only reason he was
there—that, and his obstinate pride.

As the first shades of darkness fell, Sheriff Calhoun
strode out of his office with a megaphone in hand. He
had his hat on again that night. His voice and air of
authority suggested that he would be a formidable
adversary, should anyone disobey his orders.

He proceeded to shout out his instructions, noting
that Charlie Milford, owner of the ESSO station, would
be our leader. We were all to follow him and not
meander off on any side ventures. He concluded that
any incidents, such as had occurred at the Dixie, would
result in a cancellation of future Skate Nights.

Most everybody knew the houses where we were to
stop for refreshments. They were to be further marked
by the presence of a lighted oil lamp on the front porch.
A feeling of excitement and enthusiasm was evident in
the group, which I supposed to be 60 to 70 skaters—and
one scooter!

Charlie Milford was wearing a white cowboy hat with a large yellow feather sticking out the top, so we could all see him. Finally, he shouted, "Everybody follow me, and stop when I stop!"

Charlie was an expert skater. He had actually won a skating contest over in Rocky Mount some years before. Some days, he even wore his skates at the ESSO station, and would skate out to the cars and pump gas, wash windows and check oil, just skating right around the car the whole time. Every now and then, he would back away, do a little twist, and return to the car. Sometimes folks even clapped for him.

Following his signal, the group gingerly started out, everybody trying to stay as close as possible to him. Wormy and I were some of the last to skate off from the station. I looked back to ensure the sheriff was behind us.

We headed south down Main Street in the direction of Greenwood. Some of the better skaters flared off to the side, doing tricks and different steps. The whole group seemed to be having a wonderful time.

As we passed the Dixie on our right, Billy Joe was standing up on the top step, arms folded and just glaring down at us. No doubt he was thinking about the incident and was probably a little upset that few in town were going to the show—and Friday was usually one of his best nights.

A lot of parents and older citizens were sitting on the curb and standing along the street, probably remembering when they had been participants in Skate Night. They smiled and waved and seemed real happy for us.

Our first stop was at the Graysons' house on our side of the street. They had set up two card tables out in the front yard. One was filled with pitchers of Kool-aid, lemonade and iced tea. The other had plates piled high with fried chicken and corn-on-the-cob. No one had really had time to get tired yet; but eating was an important part of the evening.

After spending about 15 minutes at the Graysons', we went on down Main Street until it forked, and Charlie had us make a U-turn, then head back on the other side of the street.

We continued those fun and food stops for almost two hours, with everyone enjoying themselves and experiencing no problems at all. It was indeed a wonderful evening. My mind paused again, thinking what a special hometown I had. "I'll bet the Moores up in Virginia don't have anything like Skate Night," I thought.

Wormy was wearing himself out pumping his scooter, but never complained once, mainly, I thought, due to the feast he was enjoying. I noticed his pockets bulging, and knew he must be packing them with food. Occasionally, someone would congratulate the two of us on the Nazi episode. It made me feel good that Wormy was included in those remarks.

As the evening wore on, the group grew smaller. Many of the skaters peeled off and headed for home, most of them with tired legs and stuffed stomachs.

Except for the earlier incident, the evening had been filled with enjoyment for Wormy and me. My only concern was that the evening and the summer were coming to an end. The events of the summer passed through my mind again. Some had been exciting and some very frightening. But its memories had become very precious and would always be included in my catalog of life, as they were infinitely worth saving. I knew that while they were mainly filled with childish frivolity, I had done a lot of growing up. Some had been good, and some not so good.

When the group returned to the sheriff's office, only a dozen or so skaters remained. The two of us rolled over to the bench previously occupied by Harry Lee and his friends and rested our weary legs. Finally, garnering up enough strength to remove my skates, Wormy and I said good-night and headed our separate ways. Knowing that only two days remained before the opening of school, we agreed to mark them by doing something special (and safe!). What that would be was yet to be determined.

In a few minutes, I was home. After reviewing the evening with Momma and Daddy, I begged off my nightly bath and wearily climbed in bed, immediately falling into a dreamless night's sleep.

❧ Chapter 18 ❧

1 woke up Saturday morning with an unaccustomed tiredness in my legs. I lay in bed awhile, reliving the events of the past evening and picturing Wormy enjoying a morning feast with all the food he'd tucked away. Daddy was still in bed, but I heard Momma rustling around in the dining room, getting ready for work. This was sure to be a busy day for her, it being the last shopping day before school opened. The rumbling sound of a car crossing the log bridge prodded me out of bed and towards the bathroom. From the bathroom, I heard a loud knock on the dining room door. Momma opened it and began talking to somebody. In just a moment she called me. Sheriff Calhoun was standing there with a concerned look on his face.

"Johnnie, when and where did you leave Wormy last night?"

Wondering what was going on, I explained that we had parted when we had left his office.

He tugged on his patch, looked down at me and said, "Wormy's been hurt, Johnnie, and right bad, too."

A sudden pang of fear shot through my body. I quickly asked, "What happened to him?"

Momma poured the sheriff a cup of coffee as we sat down around the dining room table, and the sheriff continued.

"After all the skaters left last night, I cruised back over the route we'd followed, just to check out everything. Then I took my nightly drive through East Scotland Neck. As I came up on the Community House, I noticed Wormy's scooter, or what was left of it, layin' in the gutter. When I got outta the car to look at the scooter, I heard a moaning noise comin' from the bushes over behind the building. What I found wasn't real pleasant. Somebody had beat him real bad. Then they'd made some kind of attempt to tar 'n feather him. Seems they couldn't find no tar, so they used some old car oil and poured it all over his body. They'd tore open a pillow and scattered feathers all over him. The pillowcase was layin' in the bushes next to him. He was jist barely conscious when I found him."

By then, Daddy had joined us in the dining room.

"Whoever done it had wrote on a piece of cardboard, 'We don't let niggers skate with white folk.'"

"Where is he now?" I asked.

"I took him to Dr. Thigpen's house last night. He proceeded to clean him up as best he could. The doctor determined that Wormy had at least a broken arm and needed some stitches in his forehead."

My fear instantly became anger as I yelled, "Harry Lee! Harry Lee Smith and those friends of his! I know it was them, Sheriff. They promised they'd git him and now they have." I began crying.

"Hold on now, Johnnie," Sheriff Calhoun said in a calming voice. "Don't jump to no conclusions. I saw what was goin' on with them last night. I'm gonna check out both the pillowcase and the sign, and see what I can determine. Looks to me like some grown-up men might of been in on this. Wormy's suffering an awful lotta hurt from jist some young boys."

"Men and boys and their soiled minds," Daddy added.

Community Building

"Dr. Thigpen's taking him over to Rich Square this morning. He didn't have all the necessary equipment to fix his arm. He did take care of the stitching last night and gave him a shot for pain. Said he thought Wormy'd sleep the night through and be mostly comfortable till he could get him over to the clinic this morning. He strapped that arm to Wormy's body so he wouldn't hurt it during the night. I stopped by here to tell you and see if you knew anything about it, Johnnie."

"All I know is who done it, Sheriff, and you gotta put them in jail, right away."

"I'm gonna handle all that. You jist take it easy and don't do or say anything till you hear from me."

He thanked Momma for the coffee and said, "Well, I best be about beginning my investigation. How you feelin', Gavin?"

"I'm doing pretty good, Orton. Hope to be running the taxi again next week. Taking me longer than I thought to get straight."

"See y'all later," he said, as he left the room.

I wiped my eyes and pleaded, "Daddy, I've got to get over to that clinic in Rich Square. I know he needs to see me."

"Okay, son. You get dressed and eat breakfast. We'll drop your momma off at work. Then we'll take a ride over there. That all right with you, Bug?"

"I still don't think you should be driving, but I know how important this is to Johnnie. You two get moving so I won't be late."

The 10-mile drive to Rich Square seemed an eternity. All the way, Daddy kept fiddling with the radio. He said, "Sure wish I knew how to fix this thing. I really miss it."

And then, in an attempt to cheer me up, he added, "Maybe all those little folks in those little tubes died while I was in the hospital. What'ya think, Johnnie?"

I made no comment, trying to forget the whole Scout Pond episode.

Since Rich Square was a main terminal for the railroad, it had its own clinic. It wasn't a real hospital, but since there were a fair amount of railroad-related injuries, it did have some of the better medical facilities.

I expected the worst as we entered the clinic. The first thing I saw in the waiting room was Mrs. Wilson sitting on a bench with Wormy at her side.

Before I could say a word, Wormy yelled, "Hey, Johnnie and Mr. Taxi! Lookit this! I got myself a brand new white cast on my arm! Ain't that somethin'? Ain't nobody in East Scotland Neck ever had no cast on any parts of their bodies that I knowed about. Now I'm a hero and got me a new cast to boot! And lookit this big bandage on my head! Ain't that somethin', too?"

Although his face was swollen, and the bandage came down to just above his eyes, he was beaming with pride. I felt an overwhelming sense of relief, and asked, "Ain't you hurting anywhere?"

"Yeah, I hurt 'bout everywhere a body can hurt. But this here cast helps a lot."

While Daddy was talking to Mrs. Wilson, Wormy took me aside and said, "Wish whilst we're here in Rich Square, ole Mary Beth could see me. Bet she'd be right proud, seein' how brave I am, being so hurt and all. She might jist think it's romantical. Course, she's jist my cousin," he concluded with a silly grin.

"Who did this to you, Wormy? Was it you-know-who?" I was careful not to mention any names after what the sheriff had said.

"I don't rightly know, Johnnie. Must of been three or four of 'um. I was scootin' on home last night when they jumped out from behind the ole Community House. They all had some kind of Halloween masks coverin' their faces. They run up behind me and throwed me down befo' I knowed what was happenin'. I think they all punched on me, and a coupla them kicked me. They was jist yellin' 'Nigger! Nigger!' Thas 'bout the last thing I remember, till I was at Dr. Thigpen's house and he was cleanin' all that mess offen me."

All the while, Mrs. Wilson sat quietly on the bench. I could tell she had been crying. Even at my age, I knew that the hurt she felt was much deeper than all of Wormy's wounds. She had a lot of pride in her family, and in trying to keep them fed and clothed and out of trouble, virtually by herself. Even then; Wormy was all bedecked in his best clothes and shoes. While she sent me a weak smile, I could read the pain she felt in her heart. It must have been a helpless feeling.

Dr. Thigpen walked out of one of the small rooms with a folder in his hand. When he saw us, he said, "Gavin, you know what I told you about driving till I said it was all right. But now that you're here, you gotta go back home. You can drive Mrs. Wilson and her brave son here back with you. I've done about all I can for him right now. I still have some work to do here at the clinic."

"How's he doing, Doctor? Is he hurt bad?" Daddy asked.

"Well, in addition to what you can see, I believe he's got a coupla cracked ribs, and might even have a slight concussion. But, he'll survive."

He handed Mrs. Wilson a piece of paper, which must have been a prescription, and told her to take it to the drugstore in Scotland Neck and have it filled. She was to give Wormy one pill every four hours for the next two days.

"You bring him to my office on Tuesday. I need to give him another shot. Don't want no infection setting in them head wounds. And, Mrs. Wilson, you keep a close eye on him. If he starts acting peculiar, or getting sick, you get in touch with me, right away."

"Yes, sir, Doctor. Is it all right if he starts school on Monday?"

Wormy interrupted and said, "Shore I'm gonna start school, Momma. I want everybody there to see my cast."

Dr. Thigpen said, "If he rests all day tomorrow and feels all right, I suppose he can go to school."

Reaching in her pocketbook, she said, "I shore want to thank you for everything you done, Dr. Thigpen. I also want to pay you this one dollar right now and the rest of what I owe you just as soon as I can."

"Mrs. Wilson, you keep that dollar to get the prescription filled. We'll settle up later. You know, it ain't every day I get to work on a war hero," he said, as he smiled and patted Wormy on his head. "Why don't you just make me one of your big chocolate cakes, and put lots of icing and some pecans on it."

I saw grateful tears in her eyes as her head dropped and she put the dollar back in her pocketbook. We all stood to leave. Getting in the car, I noticed how carefully Wormy was walking. When I opened the back door, he had difficulty getting in, and nearly fell back in my arms.

"You okay?" I asked.

"Yeah, jist a little dizzy. Feels like my head's big as one of Mr. Arnold's balloons."

During the ride back, I was filled with hate for somebody. I knew Wormy would recover, physically. For that, I was relieved. But it was the degradation that both he and his momma had experienced that really bothered me. I knew that he, being the stubborn individualist that he was, would be able to cope with it. He had been coping with despicable treatment all his life, due just to the color of his skin. I supposed that being around such treatment for so long—but not really seeing it for what it was—I was more surprised than I should have been at the cruelty towards Wormy. The color of one's skin seemed so insignificant to me. I wondered how God viewed it. After all, He made all of us. Daddy always said how surprised a lot of white folks were going to be when they got to heaven and found Negroes up there, too.

As we passed the cemetery, I noticed the morning had slipped into early afternoon. When we arrived at the Wilsons' house, all the family and neighbors rushed over to the car to welcome Wormy home.

I helped him out and he received a real hero's welcome. All the children wanted to touch the cast. Although a little shaky, he was wide-eyed and smiling, and was quick to point out the bandage on his head. He seemed to forget all his discomforts. I imagined he viewed the whole incident as just another glittering adventure of the summer.

The next day, after Sunday school, I asked Momma if I could go and visit Wormy. To my surprise, she agreed, and even gave me a candy bar to take to him.

He greeted me at the door and we sat out on his back porch discussing the whole event. I viewed it as a tragedy. For him, it was just another merciless trek down his already difficult life. We visited for awhile, until he finally said he felt like he needed to lay down.

"Them new pills make me right sick to my stomach. And, Johnnie, don't worry 'bout me none. I got me some plans, and someday, when my fambly grows up, and Momma don't need me so much, I'm gonna try my derndest to do somethin' 'bout this kinda stuff. But right now, I'm just a poor ole colored boy, doin' the best he can to survive."

While I was walking home, I realized that after Wormy's incident on Skate Night, my view of Scotland Neck had become slightly tarnished; and I didn't like that. I imagine I had an idealized view of reality, maybe just because of my age. Now I had learned that small town life, along with its joys and satisfaction, also had its share of bitterness and spite.

Momma, Daddy and I talked about it some that day. They told me disillusionments were just another part of growing up, and that I should expect many more. It seemed that the world that I thought I knew had both lived and died for me that summer. Perhaps the most meaningful things to come out of it were the lessons I had learned.

On Monday I started school, dressed in the finest the Boston Store had to offer. I looked at that day not just as the beginning of a new school year, but as the conclusion of a summer to be remembered forever.

Chapter 19

*I*n March, 1945, my daddy died at the veteran's hospital in Fayetteville, North Carolina. It was a mild sunny day for late winter. But sometimes in Scotland Neck, winter slipped right into spring with a hushed silence, punctuated by warm southerly breezes.

I was riding my bicycle down Main Street with Wormy pumping along beside me on his rejuvenated skate scooter. He was well healed from his injuries. The sheriff had never been able to prove guilt, so the Skate Night perpetrators had gone scot free.

Since "the incident," the ferocity with which Wormy had attacked life amazed me. He told me he was going to do "a lotta learnin'" in school that year.

"I'm gonna learn how to talk better, and I'm gonna learn how this here government works. I figure if I'm gonna change somethin', it's gotta start with the government. Ain't no white, black, yello' or whatever color folks gonna stop me," he had stated in our discussions. That incident, more than anything else, had brought out of him a determination to change things, beginning with himself.

We were headed for the Sinclair station to fill my bicycle tires with air when a car driven by my Aunt Marie pulled over beside us. Momma was seated in the passengers seat. From the expression on her face, I knew immediately something was wrong.

"Johnnie, leave your bicycle here and get in the car," she instructed.

Daddy had been in the hospital again, that time for over a month. I knew her concern must have been related to him. I dropped my bike and jumped in the back seat. Momma's emotions overflowed as she handed me a telegram from the hospital. It said that, regretfully, Daddy had died at 11:11 a.m. that morning. His body would be returned to Scotland Neck the next day. He would be accorded a military funeral by the VFW.

As the car pulled away, I vaguely heard Wormy shout that he would take care of getting my bicycle back home. I read the telegram over and over, and each reading became more difficult. In my mind, I compared it to Poochie's death, knowing full well I would never see my daddy alive again.

The funeral was held three days later in the Episcopal section of the cemetery. There was a very large crowd at the grave-side service. Momma had chosen Daddy's favorite people to be pallbearers. They were Sheriff Calhoun, Melvin Smith, Uncle Jimmie, Marmaduke Allsbrook, Tazwell Judson and Shoofly Smith.

There were almost as many Negroes in attendance as whites. All the whites huddled around the open grave. The coloreds stood some 20 yards away. I don't remember much about the service, except the preacher giving us assurances that Daddy was no longer suffering, and was, in fact, in the bosom of Jesus—with no further earthly worries.

In my heart, I knew Daddy was right where he wanted to be. Daddy and his friends had all agreed that whenever any of them died, the others were to go up to the cemetery and pour a "little drop" right on the grave, and then offer a toast to the deceased. Whenever this agreement was mentioned, during drinking bouts at the barber shop or our house, they all laughed, and even I thought it was funny at the time. But I had come to hate whiskey, because it had helped destroy my family and was doing the same to Wormy's.

From my seat, I stared blankly across the grave, past the group of whites. I saw Mrs. Wilson with Wormy standing by her side. I knew she must have bought him some new clothes just for the funeral, since I had never seen him dressed so nicely.

After the service, all the family and a large group of friends went back to Aunt Marie's for a meal that she had prepared. The Moores had come down from Virginia— all but Uncle Sam who was at home still too ill to travel.

That evening, when Momma and I were alone, the full impact of Daddy's death and our financial condition hung heavily over our small apartment.

During the past couple of years, we had experienced some difficult times financially because of Daddy's illness and very little income. At that time, Momma earned 15 dollars a week at the Boston Store. Daddy had left one insurance policy in the amount of 250 dollars. It barely covered the funeral expenses. Momma used all of it to purchase the casket and, what I considered to be, the grandest tombstone ever placed at the cemetery. Aunt Marie had taken us to Rocky Mount to choose it. Even though she couldn't really afford it, Momma had insisted that four corner markers also be installed. I was very proud of her choice.

We openly discussed our situation that evening. Momma concluded that she would sell the Hudson and use the money to pay some of our bills. I hated that idea, but it made sense. I just stared at her, wondering what I could do to help. I now realize that at some time or other, all of us would like to be taken back to the carefree days of our childhood. But maturity is thrust upon us, just when we least expect it. That evening, I reached down inside myself and pulled forth a sense of resolute responsibility that was to be with me the rest of my life.

The somber mood was broken by a slight knock on the dining room door. I opened it to find Wormy standing there, his arms filled with paper bags. He was still dressed up.

"Hey, Johnnie. My momma fixed y'all some food. I thought I better get it over here while it's still hot."

We walked into the kitchen and put everything on the table. Momma had laid down in the bedroom, not yet up to company.

After I thanked him, we went out on the porch and sat in the swing. For one of the few times in our lives, we didn't have much to say. We just swung and listened to the chant of a large flock of blackbirds as they made their annual trip through Scotland Neck.

He broke the silence. "You wanna meet at Mr. Allsbrook's after school tomorrow?" he asked, rather haltingly.

"No, I think I better come on home and do what I can to help Momma. She's taking the next couple of days off work."

As he stood to leave, he seemed to regard me with a little disappointment, like maybe I was letting him down. Then, as if sharing a little grief of his own, he turned back and said, "It don't look like we'll be seeing my daddy for some long time. He's got into more trouble in the jail in Raleigh, and they're sending him off to some bigger prison."

There was no sorrow in his voice, just a statement of fact. I had been around Mr. Wilson enough to know that he mistreated his family and possessed a thirst for alcohol and had a talent for profanity that was strong enough to melt some of Mr. Allsbrook's horseshoe nails. I imagined I heard a hint of relief in Wormy's voice.

I thanked him again for the food, as he walked off into the evening with drooping shoulders.

The next several weeks were not happy times. Momma, with the help of Columbus Jones, was able to sell the Hudson. But both of us had mixed emotions, feeling that the car was our last tangible link with Daddy. But those feelings were overcome by our need for money.

During that time, the people of Scotland Neck rekindled many of my previous good feelings for our town. They were constantly visiting, bringing food and offering to help in any way possible.

Wormy and I played whenever we could, but much of our time was taken up with household chores and school work. We would occasionally talk of summer vacation, which would soon be here, but the present was very demanding of our time. We both knew we had to deal with the major changes that had taken place in our lives since that last exciting summer.

Chapter 20

*I*n May 1945, my uncle, Sam Moore, died at his home in Alexandria, Virginia. His death was to have a profound impact on the rest of my life. Aunt Sadie was now left alone to raise her three boys.

Momma and I left for Alexandria the day after the news reached us. We took the train from Rocky Mount, passing through Richmond and arriving in the early evening. The burial was to take place in Scotland Neck, but Momma wanted to be with Sadie as soon as possible. Since she had buried Daddy only two months before, Momma felt she could be of help to her sister in handling things.

Even though the war was winding down, the train was a crush of congestion with service men. Our train was so full, we had to sit on our suitcases at the very back of the car. Several of the men offered Momma their seats, but she chose to stay seated by me. It was a bumpy and tiring 5-hour trip.

Pete, Sadie's oldest son, met us at the Alexandria train station and then drove us to their suburban, five-bedroom, rented house. It was not a happy reunion, but I knew Momma and Aunt Sadie felt comfort in being together at that time.

All the necessary arrangements were made. The Moore's Baptist preacher insisted on accompanying the family to Scotland Neck to conduct the services.

Sam's body was taken from Alexandria to Rocky Mount by train. It was then transported to Scotland Neck by the undertaker. Sam was buried in the Baptist section of the cemetery, approximately a hundred yards from my daddy's grave.

As we stood again, so soon, in front of an open grave, for the first time ever, I wanted to get away from the cemetery. I yearned for the happy, carefree feelings that Wormy and I had experienced on our train rides to Rich Square. Life, it seemed, was becoming more difficult. And recently, it had held more grief and sorrow than happiness.

During the burial, I looked across the train tracks and my eyes focused on Daddy's grave. I couldn't help wondering, "Why did God let so many bad things happen to us in such a short period of time?" We had lost Poochie and Daddy, and now Sam.

"Maybe I have sinned and I'm being punished for those sins," I thought. Yet nothing I had done seemed bad enough to cause all that grief.

I thought, too, of one of Wormy's expressions: "Life shore ain't no picnic for me and my fambly."

My current family problems were akin to Wormy's. But the one, overpowering difference was that my family was not also being subjected to hatred and racial prejudices. Again, I asked, "Why, God?"

Following the funeral service, we all returned to Aunt Bessie's house. While the rest of the mourners ate, Momma and Sadie sat alone on the porch in deep discussion for about an hour. At home that evening, Momma and I had one of the most significant conversations of my life. She and Aunt Sadie had decided that both our immediate families could do much better if Momma and I moved in with Sadie and the boys in Alexandria. She said that the two of them should join forces and funds, and raise their families together. She explained there was no way she could work and provide for the two of us on 15 dollars a week. Work and better pay, she said, were available up north. Additionally, Sadie's house could easily accommodate both families. The sisters both qualified for widows' pensions, since their husbands had served in the army. She concluded with, "Johnnie, it's the only way we can make it. We really don't have any choice. And I consider us lucky to have a place to go."

There was a bond between Momma and Sadie that went beyond sisterhood. They had both left home together at early ages. When Sadie and Sam had married, they were living in Scotland Neck. Momma was not married at the time, so they invited her to live with them. Shortly after that, Momma and Daddy were married. Now Sadie's and Momma's marriages had been shortened by the deaths of their husbands, coincidentally within two months of each other. Momma was only 39 and Sadie was 41. At my age, I didn't realize just what young widows they were.

All during Momma's comments, I'd been quiet. But a menacing feeling began in the pit of my stomach. It worked its way up my throat and I boldly stated, "Momma, I'm not gonna leave Scotland Neck. I'm not gonna leave Wormy. I shore don't want to go and live up in Washington. Those people are different from us." Tears began flowing and all the manhood I felt I'd recently gained rapidly dissipated as my whole body began to tremble. I was hurt, angry and afraid. I'd previously thought that the loss of Poochie and Daddy were the worst things that could happen to me. At that moment, they even paled in comparison to the thoughts of having my life so totally changed. I just couldn't fathom the idea of leaving Scotland Neck.

Momma, too, became very emotional, but did everything she could to calm me down. There was no anger in her voice, only a desperate tone in trying to help me understand her decision, and to accept it. I soon realized it was not a subject for discussion—no give and take—it was a foregone conclusion. Not only was it best for us, but really necessary for our livelihood. The more she talked, the more anger I felt—not with her, but with the situation. Now, on top of everything else, my entire life was going to be torn apart. All the splendid plans I had made for the future were now meaningless.

I wanted to take back all the bad thoughts I had about Scotland Neck and its people. I desperately wanted to seek another solution, but there was none, she assured me. As soon as school was out in June, we would be moving to Alexandria.

All I remember about the rest of the night was that a tremendous pain had been inflicted on me, and there was nothing I could do about it. That pain carried over to my sleep. I experienced a fitful night of dreams about Nazis, Ku Klux Klansmen, and Wormy on his skateboard, going over the side of the river bridge and helplessly falling into the rapids of the Roanoke River. I was standing on the bridge, reaching over to grab him, but he was swept away. I was left standing there, unable to do anything.

Momma woke me the next morning and said I would be going to school late. We had to go to Aunt Marie's to see the Moores off. She and Aunt Sadie had some more details to discuss, and she thought it would help me if I were there to hear them.

I didn't want to go to school at all. I didn't really want to deal with the day—or life. I just wanted what could not be, to continue my life in Scotland Neck.

We had breakfast at Marie's, followed by a lengthy discussion that included Momma, Sadie, Pete and me. I knew Momma must have told them of my unhappiness, as they spent a great deal of time telling me how nice Alexandria was and all the interesting things that would be available in the Washington area. It all sounded terrible to me.

I grudgingly got to school just before noon, but it was a wasted day. The new situation had drained me and I felt miserable. I even took my piano lesson book from under my desk, tore it in half and threw it in the trash can. I felt some small sense of satisfaction in that task. After school, I went home, changed into my play clothes and set out to find Wormy. He attended an all-Negro school in East Scotland Neck.

I was riding my bike towards his house when I met him and one of his sisters near the Community House. Their arms were filled with neatly-pressed clothes.

"Hey, Johnnie. You wanna go with Edna and me to take these clothes to Mrs. Lamb's house?"

"Yeah, I'll ride along with you. But I gotta talk to you in private when we're done."

"Okay," he smiled, probably supposing I'd devised some plan for the rest of the afternoon. We delivered the clothes and he collected the payment. Handing the money to Edna, he instructed her to be sure every cent of that money got back to their momma.

"Okay, man," he said, with that gleam in his eyes, "whatcha got on your mind today?"

He had picked up the term "man" from my cousin, Bobby, and it had become a new part of his vocabulary. He always seemed particularly happy when he was able to use it. I also knew he was trying to improve his speech. His manner of speaking had always sounded quite natural to me. But I was impressed with his efforts to improve himself, in any way.

I had given some thought as to how I would tell him the news, since I felt he would be as crushed as I was.

"Wormy," I said gloomily, "I've got some really bad news."

"Oh, man, not again. What kinda trouble you into now? Betcha skipped one of them fancy piano lessons and your momma's gonna switch you."

"I wish it was that dern simple. After school is out in June, Momma and I are moving to Alexandria to live with the Moores."

"Whatcha mean movin'? Jist for a summer vacation?"

"No. Moving up there, forever."

I expected much more than I got. A stunned expression briefly crossed his face. That was quickly followed by the comment, "Well, that jist means you can come back to Scotland Neck and visit and we can still play and stuff. Anyway, you bein' up there and all, maybe you can set up that meeting with President Roosevelt we always talked about. I still wonder if he heard 'bout our capturing that Nazi."

I was really overwhelmed by his lack of emotion. Surely he didn't feel as casual about the news as he acted. I thought for one moment I was going to cry. The one person I cared most about seemed quite unconcerned about my departure.

"Wormy, I don't want to leave Scotland Neck or you. I 'specially don't want to live up there with them cocky Yankees."

Many times, the things he said surprised me. What he said next was no exception, as he spoke philosophically.

"Johnnie, sometimes in this here life, a man's gotta do what a man's gotta do. Jist ain't no foolin' 'round 'bout it. I hate bein' the oldest one in my fambly. I always gotta do somethin' my momma wants me to do, and not what I wanna. The rest of the chillun jist run around playin', and not worryin' 'bout nothin' but playin'. But I know, next to Momma, I'm in charge of the fambly, and

I gotta act like it. Like ole Gene Autry says, 'You gotta bite the bullet.'"

He paused a moment and had a faraway look in his eyes. He continued with, "Besides, won't be too many years 'fore we're old enough to join the army or navy or whatever. We kin still do that together. Outside of catchin' that Nazi, ain't no other way we can be heroes anymore, is there? Anyway, it's jist May. We got almost a month. Maybe we better start workin' on your invisible medicine again."

We sat on the curb and talked about the future. Before I knew it, it was time for Momma to get off work. I peddled on home, feeling worse than before.

Chapter 21

Unfortunately, May faded into June much faster than I'd planned. Momma and I spent a lot of our time packing things and getting ready to move. Wormy would come by in the afternoon and help me with my after-school chores. That left little time for play.

As the days wore on, the pain of leaving became a little less intense. There were even brief moments when I felt little sparks of excitement thinking of living with my cousins. Giving myself little pep talks, I considered what Aunt Sadie and Pete had said. There would be much to do in the Washington area. And I would have something like brothers with which to enjoy those experiences.

I was constantly asking Momma how often we'd return to Scotland Neck, and if Wormy could ever visit us in Alexandria. Her answers were always the same. "We'll see, Johnnie, we'll see." Whenever I seemed to be adjusting to the idea of relocating, her indecisive answers would set me back a pace or two. I wanted to hear that we'd be returning for visits on a regular basis. But obviously, that remained to be seen.

I'd lay in bed at night and try to look ahead, wondering what the future really held for me. I came to the sad realization that I'd never own the pool hall or marry Reba. I feared that I would never experience anything as exciting as the glide ride, or see my name on the Checker Champion list.

Yet, a small part of me was awash with curiosity regarding the new sights and experiences that the move would surely bring. I was glancing at my past, and trying to compare it with my unknown future.

My disenchantment with Wormy's attitude continued. He seemed much more content in helping with the chores and enjoying what little playing time we had than in grieving our impending separation. Perhaps, I thought, it was because his life was filled with so many frustrations, he handled it better than me. Or, perhaps, I just imagined that to make me feel better.

Whenever I brought up the subject of our separation, he would pass it off as a temporary thing and assure me that something in the future would bring us together again. I only wished that I had the same confidence.

Although our furnishings were adequate at best, Momma treated each piece as some sacred relic, holding precious memories for her. Several of Daddy's friends helped Momma with the larger packing. Since only agricultural trains passed through Scotland Neck, our meager belongings had to be transported to Rocky Mount to be put on a freight train. Taz and Shoofly saw to that.

Many kindnesses were shown us by our friends during the whole process. Each of those caused an emotional upset for Momma. During those times, I realized that she, too, felt her life was being uprooted. I tried, as best I knew how, to be a source of strength for her during those sad moments. Suppressing my own feelings, and remembering what Wormy had said, I just "bit the bullet" and tried to cheer her up.

When the day to leave finally arrived, Pete was there to drive the two of us, along with a few personal items, to our new home.

Wormy and I had previously agreed to a farewell

meeting at Mr. Allsbrook's. I dreaded that meeting.

As we sat under the pecan tree outside the blacksmith shop, neither of us said anything of consequence. I spent my time assuring him—and maybe me—that we would make frequent return visits. The first thing I would ask Aunt Sadie was when Wormy could come and visit us. During those assurances, for one fleeting moment, I thought (or did I wish?), I caught a glimpse of one small tear in those large eyes.

However, when we finally parted, we shook hands and he gave me the most inconsequential nod, and he just walked away. He never looked back. And if he had, I probably couldn't have seen anything, for tears had surely filled my eyes.

In the past, I had generally been the leader of our relationship. But that day, I realized he was much stronger than I. I took one last glance at him crossing Main Street, wiped my face and headed for home.

Momma and Pete had been patiently waiting for me. Several members of the family, along with Mrs. Whitehead, were sitting on the front porch.

The good-byes were not easy.

As we started out of the yard, my mind wondered aimlessly between the past and the future. Hard as I tried, I couldn't force Wormy from my thoughts. Certainly our lives had had more twists than a corkscrew. But never before had I considered what my life would be like without him.

As the car bumped over the log bridge for the last time, I didn't wave good-bye, or even look back at the house. I just stared ahead with a dull expression on my face and a whole lot of confusion in my mind.

The future had finally arrived for me, and maybe buried my past forever. But I was determined it would not bury the memories of the most meaningful relationship of my young life.